10.

gitana

gitana

dominic martell

ORION

First published in Great Britain in 2001 by
Orion
An imprint of Orion Books Ltd
Orion House, 5 Upper St Martin's Lane, London WC2H 9EA

A CIP catalogue record for this book is available
from the British Library

ISBN 0 575 07061 7 (hardback)

ISBN 0 575 07062 5 (paperback)

Typeset in Great Britain at The Spartan Press Ltd,
Lymington, Hants

Printed and bound by
Clays Ltd, St Ives plc

This book is for Kim

The author wishes to thank the following people,
whose extraordinary generosity with their time and expertise
made this book possible:

Salvador Bosch
Marisa Collado
Manel Carmona
Pepe Vázquez
José J. Pérez Jiménez
Bruce Clorfene

I

The knives are out by the time Pascual gets there, and in two heartbeats there will be blood in the air.

Fernando has his back to a wall, good sound practice, but the stoutest wall at the back will never make up for three-to-one. The key figure is number of knives in sight, and even though one of the skins has only a chain, two blades to one is bad enough. Fernando smiles, his teeth flashing in the dark, and feints at the lead skin's groin.

Pascual's rapid footsteps have turned heads by this time, and as luck would have it it is the knifeless skin who is closest to him and turns with a snarl to warn him off. '*Camina, cabrón*. We've got business here.' This one is a skull with eyes, teeth missing and tattooed knuckles gripping the chain.

Pascual has been hiding the lead pipe at his side during his approach but brings it into sight now, raising it with both hands. He is operating on instinct rather than plan, and the instant the skin whirls, hands coming up, Pascual shifts and jumps hard for number two, the first knife in range. A short hard chop, straight down, cleaves through a tardy and inadequate defence and breaks a shoulder with a satisfying crack. Now Pascual ducks and spins, hearing the chain whistling through the air, and plants the pipe in the ribcage exposed by the futile swing. This time the sound of breaking bone is masked by the explosive cry of pain. Pascual leaps clear and looks for blades, but the remaining skin has Fernando to worry about. Fatally distracted by Pascual's arrival, he has let Fernando come off the wall low and fast and knife first, a skinhead's worst nightmare. By the time Pascual looks it is over;

he has missed the key moves and sees only the payoff, a flick of Fernando's blade that brings a ragged howl and a panicked lurch backwards. Perhaps five seconds have passed since Pascual turned the corner, and the three skins are absorbed in the choreography of defeat, stumbling, feeling for damage, sinking to knees.

Pascual would stand and gawk, but Fernando has him by the arm, pulling. 'Run. You want to spend your life explaining to the *pestañí*?' Pascual follows him down a dark passage, trotting with the length of pipe at port arms, dazed from the adrenaline shock. The streets are empty, all decent householders long since in bed. Fernando's black tresses shine under the streetlamps, tossing as he runs; the knife has disappeared. Ahead lie the Via Laietana and brighter lights. Another turn and the gypsy slows and pulls Pascual into shadow. They pant together for a moment, listening. Fernando's teeth flash in the dark pirate's face again; his hands grip Pascual's arms. 'I don't know where you came from, but you saved my hide.'

'Sara ran back to the bar and told me. You didn't kill him, did you?'

'Fuck, no. They'll sew his ear back on and he'll take it out on some other poor gypsy bastard, or maybe a *moro* next time. You know the drill.'

'What happened to the others?'

'They took off long ago. I stayed behind to talk to Sara. Where is she?'

'I don't know. I just grabbed this and came running.'

Fernando's grip tightens. 'There they are.' Pascual hears the mournful oscillation of the siren as a police car negotiates the narrow lanes somewhere not too far away, the *pestañí* arriving. 'Get rid of this,' says Fernando, tugging at the pipe.

'It belongs at the bar,' says Pascual stubbornly.

'So you hide it and pick it up tomorrow, *coño*.' Fernando pulls the pipe out of Pascual's hands and tosses it in a doorway. 'Lose yourself,' he says.

Pascual nods, starting to recover. 'You all right, then?'

Fernando puts his hands on Pascual's shoulders and for a moment Pascual thinks he is about to be kissed. Instead he gets a light affectionate slap on one cheek. 'Thanks to you. Now make yourself scarce.' Fernando vanishes in a quiet patter of footsteps.

Pascual chooses the long way back to the bar, down Laietana to the port before ducking into the narrow streets of the Old City, strolling with his hands in his pockets and a cigarette in the corner of his mouth, trying to feign drowsy unconcern. There are more sirens and an 091 car comes by on the Passeig, flashing blue lights. Nobody stops Pascual and he sneaks up the lanes to the bar, unmolested.

The place is dark and shuttered; Pascual stares stupidly. An aeon ago he ran out leaving the place wide open, glasses unwashed and floor unswept. At a brief hiss from behind him he turns to see a small bandy-legged figure beckoning from a doorway. He throws away his cigarette and moves towards it.

'Anybody hurt?' Joselito says.

Pascual can just make out the wizened face with its fringe of ragged grey beard. 'Only the bad guys,' he says.

'I told the girls to close the place up and get lost. The police will be combing the streets and why invite questions?' Joselito's right hand is buried in the pocket of his denim jacket.

'I didn't finish cleaning up.'

'It'll keep.' Seconds pass and nobody moves; only a few streets away a siren switches off, leaving absolute silence. Joselito removes his hand from his pocket and slips it inside the flap of the jacket, where he jams something into his waistband. 'Let's go.'

'What the hell was that?' says Pascual as they move.

Joselito's crooked teeth gleam in the dim light. 'What was what?'

'You weren't seriously thinking of firing that thing, were you?'

'Only if your pipe wasn't enough lead for them.'

'*Coño*, you don't want to get caught with that on you.'

'I don't know what you're talking about.'

'Maybe my eyes were playing tricks.'

They move quickly along the Passeig del Born away from the looming bulk of Santa Maria del Mar. The bars have closed and a few stragglers are drifting, looking for a place to watch the sun come up. At the far end of the plaza a cigarette glows in the shadows. Somebody whistles softly.

The three of them are there, huddled under an arch, Lola sitting

3

on the doorstep hugging her knees, Pilar leaning against the wall smoking, and Sara with her back to the door, nearly invisible in the shadows.

'What happened?' Pilar calls softly.

'Pascual scattered them like a dog going after pigeons. You should have seen the feathers fly.'

'And Fernando?' Pilar stubs out her cigarette.

'Fernando's fine,' says Pascual. 'They weren't ready for two of us. Those types do best with a single opponent, preferably on the ground.'

'Let's get off the streets,' says Joselito, glancing back.

Pilar helps Lola to her feet. Sara has not moved and Pascual steps into the doorway. In the darkness he reaches for her and she moves inside his embrace. A tremor goes through her. 'It's over,' he breathes.

'*Ojalá*,' she says. 'If only.'

They meet no one during the short walk home. Carrer Princesa cuts long and straight through the old warren of tenements to distant Laietana with its ceaseless traffic. 'Who's ready for bed, then?' says Joselito, already jingling keys.

'I could use a good stiff drink first,' says Pascual.

'What a coincidence,' says Joselito. 'I was thinking the same thing.'

'You'd better come up, the pair of you,' says Pilar. 'We'd hate to make you wait till the bars open again.'

At the table in the kitchen of the flat which the three women share, the light is not kind. Sara is pale and haggard; tension pinches Pilar's face as she places the bottle of Veterano on the table. 'Who's drinking then?'

'Not me,' says Sara.

'I'll have hers,' says Joselito, the bantam settling on to his roost. Even his eternal jauntiness is beginning to sound strained.

Pascual does not answer Pilar's enquiring look because he is watching Lola cry. She is sitting motionless on her chair with eyes wide open, staring at nothing with tears streaming down her plump cheeks. Pilar sees and moves to stand behind her. She bends to put her face next to Lola's, arms around her neck. She kisses her on the cheek, straightens up, runs a hand over the fuzz on her round skull. '*Vaya*. Nobody got hurt. Not this time.'

4

Lola's eyes close and her head lolls back against Pilar's breast. 'I'm tired of being scared,' she whispers.

'Aren't we all?' says Pilar, caressing her. Pilar is sleek and graceful and perhaps the most beautiful of the three, but there is a sadness in her eyes that never goes away.

'Listen, *hija*,' says Joselito gravely. 'As long as I'm around you don't have to be scared of the devil himself.'

'I'm not scared of the devil,' says Lola softly. 'It's people that terrify me.'

In the darkness in Sara's room, light just beginning to show around the edges of the shutters, bed springs squeak as Pascual gathers Sara in his arms. 'Hold me,' she whispers. 'Just hold me.' Pascual holds her, listening to distant noises in the early dawn and giving in to bone-deep fatigue. Sara stirs and murmurs, 'I was frightened for you.'

Pascual finds nothing to say to that, but he is aware of his great good fortune in having someone to be frightened for him. He parts his lips to tell her so, but before he can say it he is asleep.

'What the hell are you doing with that?' says Enric, looking up from his newspaper.

Pascual comes around the end of the bar and leans down to replace the lead pipe in its niche. 'We had a little fun at closing time last night,' he says. 'Fernando ran into some of our less tolerant compatriots outside. That's a handy tool, that is.'

'*Collons*. You don't mean to say you actually used it?' Enric is a Trotsky lookalike slouching towards fifty in a cloud of cigarette smoke.

'It makes a nice noise on a skinned head, I must say.'

'Good God.' Enric looks genuinely shocked, then recovers as his proprietary interests assert themselves. 'No police involved, I hope?'

'We didn't hang about. Sara locked up while I was exercising myself with Fernando and we stole away into the night.'

'Ah. That would explain why the place is a pigsty today.'

Pascual reaches for a broom. 'We assumed you would not care for this place to acquire a reputation as a den of gypsy trouble-makers.'

Enric concedes with a shrug. Scion of a minor property-owning family in the Ribera, this ancient and rapidly gentrifying quarter near the port, Enric was formerly Pascual's landlord in a squalid *pensión* in Princesa. Despite the pecuniary disagreement that led to Pascual's departure from the pension he was pleased to hire his former tenant to tend bar in this, his latest brainstorm, when he turned it from a somnolent neighbourhood *bodega* into the Tavern del Born, a poster-bedecked café with artistic pretensions.

Enric looks to the table in the window, where three men sit conversing in low tones. Antonio is tuning a guitar, interspersing melancholy chords with fine adjustments to the strings. Manolo and Diego smoke and watch. Their faces could be south Asian but they speak the rough Castilian of south Iberia, despite the fact that they have lived most of their lives in and around Barcelona. Wondering perhaps if his famous tolerance is not sometimes a mistake, Enric says quietly, 'Was Fernando in fact making trouble?'

'If walking around with a gypsy face is trouble, he's guilty as sin.'

Enric shrugs again and draws on his cigarette. 'I just don't want the boat rocked. I've got a big stake in this place.'

'You're not alone.' Pascual sweeps. In the months he has worked behind the bar at the Tavern del Born he has found the closest thing to a home he has had in twenty-five years. Whether due to Enric's promotional genius or to mere blind chance, the clientele of the little corner bar has coalesced into the perfect compound of regulars and random walk-ins, a balance of youth and age, modest wealth and modest poverty, inoffensive loners and generous extroverts. Even the ethnic chemistry works: Enric has never been the type of Catalan to make a point of it, and with the gypsies, the foreigners and those who simply prefer the language of Cervantes to that of Martorell, Castilian and Catalan float frictionless in the smoky air. Pascual's own ethnic identity is irredeemably hazy and he cherishes the fact that what language one chooses to speak over a drink has never been an issue here.

Pascual shoves chairs into place and stows the broom. Antonio has started to play, quietly, a slow mournful *siguiriya*. Behind the bar Pascual starts on the glasses. He loves the first moments of his shift, in the drowsy late afternoon when the streets are just beginning to fill again after the midday hiatus and the sun still just reaches the walls across the narrow street. Later in the evening Sara will appear; they alternate days on the early shift.

A shadow darkens the door and Pascual looks up from the sink. A tourist, Pascual estimates, a middle-aged man on a getaway, standing in the doorway of the bar transfixed by the music coming from the round table at the window. British or American, French at a stretch, too untidy with the greying beard and undisciplined hair to be a businessman slumming, too bemused to be a local. Recently divorced and always wanted to go to Europe, guesses Pascual. Throw a guidebook in the bag and away we go to chase ageing German secretaries on Costa Brava beaches.

The man wanders towards the bar, tearing his gaze away from the table where Antonio is coaxing the *siguiriya* towards conclusion, the aching dissonances begging to be resolved. The man has started to smile in the way a tourist does when he has stumbled over something he can market to his friends back in the prosaic north. Meandering in the narrow lanes behind Santa Maria del Mar, he must have heard the music and followed his ears. He surveys the dark wood panelling, the posters of long-dead theatrical productions and obscure films tacked to the walls. He fetches up at the bar, unslinging the shoulder bag and easing it to the floor. '*Cerveza,*' he essays uncertainly, *Sir Vaysa* in his execrable accent. '*Por favor,*' he adds as an afterthought. A Yank, thinks Pascual, betrayed by his r's.

Pascual tosses a beer mat on the bar and draws him a *caña*. Antonio polishes off the final *rasgueados* and surrenders the guitar to a chorus of *vales*. He calls for coffee all round and Pascual nods. He sets the glass of beer in front of the Yank.

'You must be Pascual,' says the Yank in English. Pascual freezes, the reaction of a man whose dog has reared up and begun to recite Shakespeare. The Yank is blinking at him, the idiot smile gone. Seconds pass, the gypsies in the window squabbling cheerfully over the guitar, and Pascual's mind is working at light speed. Strangers who know his name give Pascual cold sweats in the night. Everybody has a past; Pascual's is a nine-millimetre automatic levelled at his head. He opens his mouth and has the presence of mind to answer in Castilian. '*Lo siento. No hablo inglés.*'

7

The American has enough Spanish to understand that, anyway; his expression goes sceptical and sly and he says, 'And my Spanish isn't worth a damn. We'll just have to do our best. I was told to look for a man with two fingers missing, and unless I've counted wrong you've only got eight.' He nods at Pascual's left hand resting on the marble countertop.

Pascual's eyes flick to his maimed hand and then he shrugs and turns away. '*Ciento setenta y cinco*,' he says and goes to make the coffees. Manolo has won the guitar and is noodling his way up and down the neck, laughing. Pascual can feel the Yank watching him. New York Jew, he thinks. Pascual's own ancestry contains a generous measure of New York Jew and in one era of his life he spent a good deal of time around men who look and sound like this. He wonders he didn't spot it immediately.

When the coffees are served Pascual chances a look at the Yank, who is tapping a thumb on the bar less than perfectly in time to Manolo's stuttering *tanguillo*. The Yank beckons to him, flapping a hand. Pascual walks down the bar as slowly as a man can walk. He halts opposite the Yank, who squares around on his stool to lean towards him on his elbows and murmur under the beat of the music. 'I need your help.'

Pascual has decided on a strategy: total denial. He knows that he cannot fake broken English; once he opens that door the Brooklyn patois he learned in his youth will come spilling out. Carefully, in clear Castilian lightly accented with his native Catalan, he says, '*Escuche*. I don't speak your language and you've mistaken me for somebody else. One hundred and seventy-five pesetas.' He smiles to show no hard feelings and turns away.

The American stops him with a hand on his arm. 'Fair enough,' he says, meeting Pascual's icy stare. 'Just give me ten seconds of your time.' He fishes in pockets and comes up with a pen and a business card. He scribbles on the card and slides it across the bar to Pascual.

The card says *Morris Weiss* and gives a New York address, telephone and fax numbers and an e-mail address. At the bottom he has scrawled *Hotel Colon*, the accent missing of course, with a room number and a phone, presumably the hotel's. 'I understand your reluctance,' says Weiss, his look intent, 'but I mean you no

8

harm and I *will* respect your privacy here. You can help me turn over some rocks with some nasty things under them.'

Pascual exaggerates a good-natured shrug and tucks the card on the shelf behind him, next to the lost keys, abandoned books and love notes that wash up behind the bar. Weiss places two hundred-peseta coins on the bar and slides off his stool. 'I'm in town for a few days yet. If you change your mind, give me a call. Even a month from now. Call me collect in New York if you have to.' He takes a final token sip of his nearly full beer and stoops to retrieve his bag. Pascual gives him an ironic salute as he goes.

'What was that all about?' says Enric, looking up from his newspaper. Pascual has been aware of his employer carefully pretending not to eavesdrop, three stools down the bar.

'A case of mistaken identity,' Pascual says. 'Somebody told him there was a famous ex-bullfighter working here.'

Enric raises his eyebrows, and turns over a page of his newspaper with a shake of the head. He is perfectly aware that Pascual speaks English as well as he speaks Castilian. Enric has probed gently many times around the edges of Pascual's mysterious past and Pascual knows that curiosity plays a large part in Enric's apparent affection for him. 'What is he,' says Enric, 'a journalist?'

'Yes,' says Pascual, staring out into the sombre narrow street, 'I suppose that's what he must be.'

2

The first time Pascual saw Sara Muñoz, her eyes were closed and her mouth open, a light sheen of sweat just visible on her forehead, the expression on her face somewhere on the knife edge between distress and ecstasy. From deep in her throat came sounds that could have been cries of pain. When they resolved into release, Pascual and twenty-four other spectators felt it in their loins.

Still haunted by the image the next day, he was stunned when Enric brought her into the bar and announced she would be working beside him. Pascual had been asking for help on busy nights, but at the sight of Sara standing before him, looking at him with her cool, imperturbable expression, he was struck dumb for a long moment. 'I saw you sing last night,' he said stupidly.

Sara smiled and Pascual thinks that was the beginning; Sara's smile is a wonder of nature. 'Did you like it?'

'*Mucho.*' Sternly taking hold of himself, Pascual looked accusingly at Enric. 'What are you doing shoving an artist like her back here?'

'Artists have to eat,' said Sara. 'You saw how much I made last night. You counted out the bills yourself.'

'She knows the ropes,' Enric said. 'Her father had a bar in Badalona.'

'I could make a perfect coffee before I could read,' said Sara.

Pascual smiled. 'You may be just what this joint needs.'

And so it proved. Sara is competent behind the bar, ruthless with drunks and lechers and able to keep running tabs on a dozen tipplers at once; at the same time she can charm a miser into buying a round for the house. And every couple of weeks she can be persuaded to sing, electrifying the place.

'*La bulería es vals,*' says Joselito, thumping out the beat on the marble countertop. '*Un' dos tres, un' dos tres.* The *bulería* is a waltz, nothing more.'

Pascual, who six months ago did not know a *bulería* from a balalaika, frowns in concentration, absorbed in the frenetic sputter of guitar chords coming from the corner table. 'There may be a waltz in there somewhere, but they've disguised it pretty well.'

Joselito's grey beard spreads in a crooked smile. 'Of course. That's the art. In flamenco you can do anything, as long as you respect the *compás*. Like vines growing up a trellis – the trellis will be hard to see sometimes, but it's always there, holding up the vines.'

Pascual watches as the guitarists bring the *bulería* to a triumphant finish, ramming the final chords home. He shakes his head. 'Be patient with me, I'm a Catalan. I grew up with Bach and Vivaldi.'

'Me, I grew up with salt air in my face off the Bay of Cádiz,' says Joselito, raising his glass with a wistful shake of the head. 'Down there we get flamenco with our mother's milk.'

'They must put some in the beer as well. I don't think a drop of milk ever passed your lips.' Pascual reaches for a bottle to refill a glass being brandished down the bar. It is ten o'clock and the place is full; the air is thick with smoke and music. This is Enric's sole triumph as a promoter: a Saturday-night flamenco session which allows him to tack a surcharge on to the drinks. At a table by the door Pilar and Lola are sharing a laugh with a cluster of Pilar's colleagues from the travel agency in the Rambla de Canaletas where she earns her paycheque. Besides the regulars there is a contingent of strangers drawn by the music and the usual adolescent couple groping each other in the corner.

A rumba, thinks Pascual as the guitarists launch into another piece, the crowd catching the rhythm and starting to move. No, a tango, of course; listen to the *compás*. A black-haired girl has risen and is dancing in the tiny clear space in front of the door, hands tracing flowers in the air, less than classical perhaps in her form and dress, tight jeans being a shocking anomaly in flamenco, but

11

emitting satisfactory waves of eroticism, to judge by the slack male jaws. 'My heart,' says Joselito, feigning a swoon on his stool. '*Válgame Dios.*'

Enric tears himself away from the sight and looks to the far end of the bar, where Sara stands listening intently to a man dressed from head to toe in black. 'Who's the bloke with the keen colour sense distracting Sara from her work?'

Pascual casts a look over his shoulder. 'That's her new manager. Gabriel, he's called.'

'Her manager? What the hell does Sara want with a manager?'

'She's probably tired of being exploited by the likes of you. Watch out, he's going to demand half the gate if she opens her mouth tonight.'

'Good Christ, you're not serious?'

'I think he's here to check out Antonio, actually. He's got some flash guitarist of his own he wants her to work with. He wants her to move up the professional ladder.'

Enric stares gloomily down the bar. 'I suppose it was inevitable. You're right, next will come the shakedown. She'll be too bloody good to sing in a place like this, I suppose.'

'You're not going to begrudge her her success, are you?'

'Of course not. But it would be nice to get some credit for discovering her.'

'Oh, you discovered her, did you?'

'Well, gave her a place to sing. Her and all these fellows. How do you think they wound up here? They didn't just wander in off the street.'

Pascual draws a beer. 'Yes, how did that come about? A good Catalan bourgeois like you, rubbing elbows with gypsies.'

Enric shrugs, blowing smoke. 'Thank the old regime for that. I did my time in stir, you know.'

'You?'

'I was a revolutionary firebrand. Seriously, I spent some time in my idealistic youth trying to organize the poor benighted gypsies out in La Mina, raise their political consciousness and all that. All it got me was a few knocks on the head from the *grises* and some jail time. Well, a night or two here and there. Not to mention the fervent ingratitude of most of the people I was stubbornly trying to enlighten. But one of my old comrades from the barricades, who helped get me through my brief stay in Franco's dungeons, is now Tío José of the Amayas, head of his clan, and we've stayed fast friends.'

'Prison will do that, I imagine.'

'And I was one of the lucky ones. Listen, is Sara going to sing or not? She brushed me off when I asked her earlier.'

'How should I know?'

'You're the one who's got her ear these days.' Enric is giving him a sly look. 'It's no secret, you know. You think nobody's noticed?'

Pascual shrugs. 'We're good friends.'

'Fine, mum's the word. My lips are sealed. I won't even ask how it feels to have those great bloody legs wrapped around you.'

Pascual would be irked but for the transparent childlike envy in Enric's eyes; he shakes his head and shoves away from the bar. 'I'll see what I can do.'

'I have it in my blood,' she told him once when he asked her how she had come to the music. 'I'm a gypsy.'

'You?'

There must have been more surprise in his voice than he intended. 'Don't I look it?' she said, an eyebrow raised. 'Not dark enough perhaps, not ragged and filthy, begging in the street?'

'Heavens. Touched a nerve, have I? No, you don't particularly look it to me. But then I don't think much about that sort of thing.'

Her eyes softened just a touch. 'I'm only half, actually. My mother was a sort of gypsy Cinderella, ran away from a nasty stepfather in San Roque and into my father's arms. He was an orphan and a sailor and didn't give a damn about what people thought. He retired from the sea and married her and put his savings into the bar. My mother never talked to her family again. But there were always gypsies around and she taught me the music.'

He could see it now, the *gitana* in her: nothing he could have put his finger on but somehow not the classic Iberian look; something in the black eyes and the geometry of her face.

Pascual is hazy on the chronology, but it was a matter of weeks only before their easy companionship behind the bar began to

13

send tendrils of smoke into the air. Hours of proximity, long stretches of sociability in agreeable company, shared tedium and fatigue: everything moved them closer. Pascual had for months contrived to avoid adventures of the heart, his heart having been seared too often; at the Tavern del Born female beauty was always on offer but so far he had been content with flirtation and detachment.

He is not even sure Sara would have turned his head on the street. She has all the fundamentals, the mass of black hair, the eyes that one has to look into closely to distinguish iris from pupil, the skin that takes sun and goes a deep rich brown. But Barcelona is full of women with the same qualities. What first undermined Pascual's defences was the transformation of Sara's being when she sang. A dark passion powered her voice, animated her face and body; Pascual had never seen anything like it. After that, what beguiled him was her complete self-possession. Pascual began to sense that Sara, like him, had history. As the history emerged, it only increased his sense of kinship: dying parents, flight, dying illusions. 'First I tried to find my mother, and then I tried to find my father,' Sara said. 'She had relatives in France, but I found out that she'd done too good a job of cutting those ties. A woman without a father or brothers is a time bomb in a gypsy community. I wound up in Marseilles serving drinks to sailors and found out my father's world wasn't much nicer. Then I came home.'

If she is vague on the details Pascual has no right to press her; the corruption at the heart of his own odyssey remains a secret. Some day, he thinks, I will tell her.

When the tango finishes there is a lull; Pascual takes a bottle of Cardhu from the shelf and wanders up the bar. Sara is leaning over the countertop, bringing her face close to Gabriel's to hear him over the hubbub. The impression of intimacy gives Pascual a brief and very mild pang of jealousy. Gabriel is speaking to her with a faintly amused look on his heavy-jowled, thick-browed face, which ten years ago might have passed for ruggedly handsome. As he draws near Pascual can make out words. 'You have to raise your sights. You're working to higher standards now. If you want to be a professional you have to think like a professional.'

Sara straightens and gives Pascual a carefully blank look. He tips a healthy dollop of whisky into the nearly empty glass in front of Gabriel. '*Hombre, gracias.*' Gabriel puts a hand on Pascual's arm in appeal. 'Am I right?'

Pascual shrugs. He has never much cared for the affectation of dressing entirely in black, and he has never seen Gabriel Heredia in any other colour, from leather jacket to the tips of his boots. His abundant hair, Pascual suspects, would be grey if left to its own devices, but it has been made to conform to the scheme. Gabriel looks like a man trying to pass for twenty years younger and knocking off maybe five. 'She's loyal to her friends,' Pascual says.

'Of course. But she needs to understand what an opportunity this represents.'

'I understand that,' says Sara, eyes darting out across the room, 'I'm just not sure I'm ready.'

'*Mira*,' says Gabriel. Leaning across the bar, he thrusts a finger at her. 'You know how many heads you turned at the Feria de Abril? In the half-hour's exposure I got you there? You've got the voice, the presence. You can go as far as you want. Carmen Linares, Ginesa Ortega, Remedios Amaya. Now Sarita Muñoz. You'll be the next name on people's lips. But you have to be a professional now. And that means you move up from second-rate *guitarristas de barrio.*'

'Antonio's not second-rate.'

'In the circles you want to move in now, he is. Listen, Manolo Osuna will sit down with you tomorrow if you want. In three months you could be headlining at Tarantos. But you won't get there with Antonio. He's a good kid, but he's not a professional guitarist and never will be.'

'Tarantos? Busloads of German tourists go to Tarantos. I want to sing for people who know the music.'

'The German tourists are one reason Tarantos will pay you real money. It's time to move up to the first division. With Antonio you'll spend the rest of your life in some obscure *peña*, maybe get another guest shot at the Feria, and never make a single *duro*. You want to make some money, catch the ear of a recording company, you need to work the *tablao* circuit. If you're really serious, you shouldn't even be here. You should be in Madrid or Seville. But Osuna's good, the best you can do in Barcelona. And he wants to meet you.'

'You've got to understand, a singer and a guitarist are like brother and sister. The relationship is fundamental.'

'And singers never change guitarists? They shift all the time. This is a move up, Sarita.'

Pascual can see that her resistance is crumbling. 'I'd love to work with Manolo Osuna,' she says, 'but I hate to walk out on Antonio.' She gives Pascual a brief look, and he feels desperately for words of support. Before he can find any she moves abruptly away in response to a hand raised down the bar. Pascual and Gabriel watch her as she works.

Gabriel leans towards Pascual, in confidant mode. 'She's got a heart of gold, Sara, but she's as stubborn as a mule.'

'Yes.' Pascual feels he has let the side down. Because Gabriel seems to be waiting for a response, he says, 'How good is she, really?'

Gabriel gives him a calculating look. 'The truth? Sara's good. She's very, very good. She's got the voice, she's got the looks. She's a gypsy, she's got that passion. I'm going to make her an international star.'

Pascual nods slowly. He has known enough bitter failed artists in his life to discount pronouncements like this one. There is an electronic fluttering sound close at hand and Gabriel reaches inside his jacket and pulls out a mobile phone. He flashes Pascual a look and says, 'I'm a slave to this bloody thing. Excuse me.' He plugs one ear and answers.

Pascual watches as Gabriel shoves his way through the crowd towards the door, shouting into the phone. 'Where's he gone, then?' says Sara at his shoulder.

'Off to make deals for millions, I suppose.'

There is a small noise which might be a puff of laughter. '*Ojalá*,' says Sara. 'If only.'

They became friends in the sleepy afternoon hours, the bar cool and empty and nothing to do but talk and watch life go by outside in the street. Time was devoted to Pascual's musical education, Sara digging CDs out of the box and slapping them in, telling him this is a *petenera*, that is a *siguiriya*, listen to the *compás*.

Pascual smoked and listened. 'Fat ladies in polka-dot dresses dancing in tourist clip joints. That's what flamenco always was to me. And for a Catalan, it meant everything that was imposed on us. Bullfighting, flamenco, Franco. A Catalan wouldn't be caught dead listening to flamenco.'

Sara smiled. 'Try telling a gypsy he and Franco were on the same side. Listen to Camarón here, this will break your heart.'

Pascual listened as the fallen gypsy idol pushed his voice into far ranges of pain, winding his voice around the Phrygian cadences until it broke. The *cante* is an acquired taste, Sara told him; the ladies in their polka-dot dresses will always draw a crowd, and a blistering guitar *falseta* shouts virtuosity a mile away. But you have to listen with something more than the ear before the voice of a good *cantaor* in all its harshness will strike that note inside you.

'It's all I've ever had in the way of a vocation,' she said. 'When I realized that all I wanted to do was sing, it was like finding my way out of a dark room.'

For a time Pascual hears only with the ear, but then what he is hearing begins to converge with what is happening during the long shifts behind the bar. He begins furtively to borrow CDs from the box behind the bar, taking them home and listening into the wee hours through the headphones in his bleak room in the pension, puzzling out the words. And finally, he finds with a shock that this ravaged gypsy voice is his, for Sara's ears: *Por esta gìtanilla las horas de la noche me las paso sin dormir.*

The gypsies are taking a breather and there are glasses to fill, accounts to settle. There has been a certain level of clamour for Sara to step out from behind the bar and sing, but so far she has refused. When all the business has been taken care of, Sara stands frowning at a fingernail. When Sara frowns it is an impressive frown, dark and glowering. Pascual stands next to her, waiting. 'What should I do?' she says.

Pascual shrugs. 'I think you should do what Gabriel says. If you want to be a professional.'

'That's the question. Is that what I want?'

He can see the depth of her distress and it surprises him. 'Remember your vocation.'

She nods. 'I've lost that certainty.'

'You'll get it back.'

'Maybe.' She looks at the end of the bar where the gypsies have clustered, laughing, drinking. 'Antonio is a second-rate guitarist, isn't he?'

'Christ, you're asking me to judge?'

'Working with Manolo Osuna would be a privilege.' She reaches for her tonic water and looks at him over the rim of the glass. 'The thing is, I like second-rate guitarists. I like poor gypsy toughs from La Mina. I like singing in bars for a handful of banknotes, singing for friends. Just for myself maybe. Maybe *I'm* second-rate. Maybe a second-rate life is all I really want.'

Pascual lights a cigarette. 'You've got cold feet, that's all. It'll look different in the morning.'

'What if I can't do it? What if I'm not good enough?'

'You're asking if I'm going to be disappointed? Is that it?'

'I don't know what I'm asking.'

He can see confusion as she starts to drift away. He pulls her back with a hand on her arm. 'I didn't fall in love with some headliner at a big *tablao*. I fell in love with a poor gypsy barmaid.'

'Half-gypsy,' she says, pulling away, but her hand trails across his cheek, caressing.

'Where's my drink?' Gabriel shoulders his way to the bar.

'I thought you'd left,' says Sara. 'You've been gone for half an hour.'

'Just talking to some bloody idiots on the phone outside. Listen, to hell with the drink. Grab your jacket, I'm taking you to dinner at the Drolma.'

She gives him an incredulous look. 'I'm working.'

Gabriel levels his finger at her. 'Which is precisely the problem. You've got to stop thinking of yourself as a barmaid and start thinking of yourself as a *cantaora*. A flamenco *cantaora* on the verge of stardom does not wash glasses in a hole-in-the-wall *tasca*. And she most certainly does not sing for change out of the till.'

'She does if she needs the money. And she does not run out on her mates.'

Gabriel shakes his head, a man confounded by others' obtuseness. He looks at Pascual and says, 'What did I tell you? Like a mule.'

Sara puts a hand on Pascual's arm. 'Go and tell Antonio', she says, 'I could do a number or two if he's ready.'

★

Tendrils of smoke, and tinder approaching the point of combustion. Looks across the table, the bar shuttered for the night but the usual suspects, Pilar and Lola and Joselito and the gypsies, lingering at the round table in the corner, smoking, killing a bottle, passing the guitar. Walking her home in the wee hours, dawdling behind the others, parting with a squeeze of the fingers, a casual peck on the cheek.

Pascual listened, and watched her move, and tried not to think. For years his sentimental life had consisted of meaningless casual amours punctuated by sudden emotional holocausts. He did not dare allow himself to think beyond tonight, the next eight hours behind the bar.

Locking up, the final dousing of the lights, had become a ritual suffused with sweet tension. More and more it was a ritual carried out in silence. Finally one night in the dark there was an embrace that was pure magnetism, mere physics, beyond thought. And when at length it eased, Pascual knew that he was on the high wire again.

Pascual eases the shutter down to the pavement and padlocks it. A few metres away Sara and Gabriel stand close together, the murmur of Gabriel's voice just audible. The gypsies have gone more quietly than usual, clutching their guitar cases, eyes flicking this way and that, stealing away down the lanes. Tonight there is no sign of prowling skins, but the thought has been on everyone's mind. At Pascual's approach Gabriel blows smoke high in the air and says, 'I'll just see her home. You never know who's hanging about this time of night.' His tone is casual, but Pascual can see that he shares their tension.

'Don't bother,' says Sara. 'Pascual will get me there.' The glow that always suffuses her after she sings has faded and she stands with her arms folded, stiffly. Pascual feels an impulse to sweep her into an embrace, but first he would prefer to be off the streets.

Gabriel shrugs. 'My car's parked up by the market. I'll walk with you.'

Pascual has no objection to an extra hand in case of trouble. He walks with his arm resting lightly on Sara's shoulder. 'You were in fine voice tonight,' says Gabriel. 'The *tanguillo* was very nice, considering the quality of the guitarists.'

'I don't want to hear it,' snaps Sara. 'Not tonight.'

'As you like.' They have reached the end of the Passeig del Born and Gabriel glances back towards the massive church dominating the other end of the short avenue. His eyes narrow and Pascual follows his look. He sees nothing at first, then a match flares in the shadows and Pascual can see a man, just visible, taking a long time over lighting a cigarette. 'Has he been with us long?' says Gabriel.

'I don't know. At least this one's got hair,' says Pascual, but he is uneasy none the less and their pace quickens a little.

At Sara's door Gabriel takes his leave, kissing Sara on both cheeks and shaking Pascual's hand. 'She could make a lot of money,' he tells Pascual. 'See if you can talk some sense into her.'

'I believe that was an appeal to your self-interest,' Sara says, pushing open the heavy outer door and watching Gabriel stride away.

'I've already told you what I think.'

The closing door shuts out the light from the street. Sara is feeling for the switch when Pascual reaches for her, turns her gently and pulls her close and seeks her lips in the dark. He kisses her, waiting for a response, waiting for her lips to come alive, her embrace to strengthen. '*Te quiero*,' he breathes against her cheek. Sara says nothing and he pulls back just far enough to make out her face. '*Estoy por decí*,' he says, stealing the line complete with dialect, '*no quiero a naide más qu' a ti.*' Like clear water coming down the mountain, he thinks, *de día y de noche.*

'You can't love me,' she whispers.

Pascual's spirits sink. 'Don't say that.'

'I'm a bad risk.'

'That's my line. I'm the stray dog in this street, remember?'

Sara places her hand over his mouth. 'Do me a great favour.'

Pascual knows what it is and he knows there is no fighting it. 'Anything,' he says for form's sake.

'Let me be by myself tonight. I'd be bad company anyway.'

Pascual holds her and waits for his turbulent feelings to subside. Over the months he has tried to resign himself to Sara's sudden bouts of black depression; he tells himself they are a small price to pay for her incendiary charms. Weeks of joy punctuated by brief episodes of Arctic desolation: loving Sara is a harsh vocation. 'I don't know what to do except love you,' Pascual says.

'Nothing is your fault,' she says, pushing away already. 'It's me. I don't know who I am.' This is an old theme, Sara's cultural dislocation: Pascual thought he was the expert, but nothing in his rootless upbringing burdened him with anything like the sexual guilt that lies coiled in Sara's psyche. 'Forgive me,' she says.

'Always, everything.'

Straggling home alone, Pascual has less cheerful tunes running through his head. '*Pobre corazón mío*,' he thinks, for all the blows it takes, it never gives up.

3

'The Raval isn't what it once was,' says Puig. He spits into the gutter. 'They've ruined it. It was better when the whores could make an honest living here. I'd rather have a whore for a neighbour than a *moro*.'

Pascual, who has considerable experience rubbing elbows with both whores and *moros*, gives a casual shrug. 'It is nice to see the sun now and again.'

Puig gestures menacingly but vaguely with his cane. 'Ah, fine, yes, they knocked down a lot of houses, threw people out in the street, so they could put up their museums and their fine plazas and things. But the spirit's gone. Even the *traficantes* used to stand and pass the time of day with you like a Christian should. They've ruined our Raval.'

Pascual pulls Puig gently out of the path of a creeping automobile and takes his leave; he is in no mood today to listen to the old man's regrets. The truth is Pascual finds plenty of the old Raval left in these crowded lanes; despite twenty years of ruthless urban renewal this warren of tenements hanging over crooked streets will never be mistaken for Sarrià or Gràcia. If the whores who made this quarter famous as the Barrio Chino have moved out to Camp Nou to ply their trade, they can still be encountered here late of a morning, blowsy and cheerful, in the queue at the baker's or the greengrocer's.

Pascual turns into the Carrer Nou de la Rambla and makes for his *pensión*. At the end of the street he can see a glimpse of plane trees on the Ramblas, the great river of life that slices down to the port through the Old City, separating the Raval from the Gothic

22

Quarter. After nearly a decade in a succession of lodgings in the Gothic Quarter, Pascual has shocked his friends by crossing the Ramblas to take up residence in the Raval; the closer the quarters and the smaller the scale, the more bitter are the territorial rivalries. 'People over there are different,' the morose Ibáñez warned him, shaking his head. 'You'll see.' What Pascual has seen is the same patient struggle with poverty and the same half-hearted tribal conflicts that have marked all his home grounds in Barcelona.

In front of the Pensión Alhambra a blue Renault is parked with two wheels up on the pavement, obstructing both foot and automobile traffic in the narrow street. Two men are leaning on it, smoking, and Pascual's step slows because he knows one of them. He pulls out his key as he approaches the door but has little hope he will get to use it. 'Somebody ought to call the police,' he says as the older of the two men straightens up and throws away his cigarette. 'Can't you see you're blocking the street?'

The older man has hair cut close to his skull and well down the road from merely grey to an impressive white. His jaw is square and could light a match. His eyes could frighten children. 'Don't worry,' he says. 'We're leaving. Hop in.' He opens the rear door for Pascual.

'I've got fresh milk in here,' says Pascual, hoisting his plastic bag. 'Can I just run it upstairs?'

'It'll keep.' Serrano has his moods, and Pascual can see that today there will be no banter, no pleasantries.

'Am I going to need a lawyer?'

'Have you done anything illegal?'

Pascual considers. 'No.'

'Then you won't need a lawyer.' Serrano cocks his head at the car. Pascual shrugs and ducks into the back of the car. Serrano closes the door on him and gets into the passenger seat in front. His partner, a thin bearded man no older than thirty, slides behind the wheel. 'This is Delgado,' says the older policeman. 'He wasn't even born when I joined the police, but he's a lot smarter than I am, so we make a fabulous team.'

Pascual is remembering the vicious upward slash of Fernando's knife and the shocked look on the skinhead's face: the look of a man with a severed jugular? Has Fernando vanished into gypsy byways to leave Pascual to make the explanations? Or worse: Pascual remembers the thwack of the lead pipe into unprotected ribs. A punctured lung, a slow death, a description gasped into a policeman's ear? Pascual's stomach has gone queasy. 'What's the occasion?' he says, trying to sound a light note. 'Got a card game going, up in the office? I have to tell you, I'm a little short this week and can't throw much in the pot.'

'I have fond memories of this neighbourhood,' growls Serrano by way of reply. 'You see the bar here, on the corner? When I worked in this district the old bastard who ran the place used to take in stolen goods by the truckload. His wife finally shopped him because he took up with a fresh young thing in a miniskirt. As I recall he lasted about a week in the Modelo before he took some *cacique*'s chair by mistake and got beaten to death for it.'

'Charming anecdote.'

'The Raval's not what it was, they say. Fond memories, I assure you.'

They fight through traffic along the seafront and up the Via Laietana to the Jefatura in silence. Serrano does not tell stories just to pass the time and Pascual has taken his point. Soberly he follows the two policemen in the side entrance and up the stairs. In the lift from second to third the silence becomes uncomfortable. 'If I'm going to be here a while, I hope you've got a fridge to store the milk in,' Pascual says.

Serrano just looks at him. 'Give it to me,' says the younger man, amusement in his eyes. 'We'll stick it in with the *jefe*'s carrot juice.'

'Your chief drinks carrot juice?'

'State secret. You spill it to the papers, we'll have your arse.'

'Mum's the word,' says Pascual, handing over the milk. Serrano remains unmoved.

Pascual has visited the Sección de Homicidios before and it has unpleasant associations for him. It is a modest office, as befits a section consisting of only ten full-time inspectors, with a main room six metres square, which contains a few desks haphazardly disposed, a smaller interrogation room visible through a large window to the right and the office of the section chief to the left with a broad desk visible through the open door. When Serrano ushers Pascual in, there is one man typing at a desk opposite the door and nobody else. 'In there,' says Serrano, pointing to the interrogation room.

Settled in a tolerably comfortable chair, Pascual watches Serrano through the glass as he murmurs to the man at the typewriter, grins sourly at a joke, shakes his head. In his leather jacket and black jeans Serrano could be a lorry driver or a CGT organizer. He is as sere and weathered as the Castilian *meseta* where Pascual judges from his accent he was born. Under Franco he no doubt did his share of knocking heads, clad in the historic grey, but in Pascual's experience he has been an impeccably modern, democratic and European policeman, if hard as granite. He has been posted in Barcelona for thirty years and Pascual has heard him answer enquiries in creditable Catalan. Since Pascual first crossed his path in connection with a triple homicide in which Pascual was very nearly the fourth victim, Serrano has taken an interest in him which Pascual feels he ought to find flattering.

Serrano goes to a desk drawer and pulls out an accordion folder, which he tucks under his arm. His partner returns *sans* milk and the two policemen join Pascual in the small room. Serrano hoists his flanks up on to a desk, his partner taking up station behind Pascual.

'What have I done?' Pascual has decided that Fernando can take his chances; jumping into the fight was enough and he will not lie for him. None the less there is no reason to volunteer.

'You tell me. Anything on your conscience today?'

'A hell of a lot. But it all happened years ago.'

'Then I don't have to care, thank Christ. I'm a little more interested in last night.'

'Last night?' Pascual gapes. The fight was four nights ago. 'What happened last night?'

Serrano has noted the surprise. 'I'll say it again – you tell me. How did you spend the evening?'

'I was at work.'

'Work. Ah. You still teaching German girls how to order *sangría* and calling it work?'

'I'm a barman. In the Tavern del Born, down behind Santa Maria del Mar.'

'A barman? My God, you've landed on your feet. They've put the rat in charge of the granary. Nice work?'

'It is, in fact.'

'What time did you work last night?'

'I came in about four and closed the place up eleven hours later.'

'You were there the whole time?'

'Of course. It gets rather busy.'

'Anybody working with you?'

'Yes.'

Serrano waits. 'Well?'

Pascual's anxiety has eased and he chances a smile. 'You're looking for an alibi? The owner's name is Enric Bonell. I can give you a phone number.'

'We'll take it.' Serrano listens while Pascual recites the number for his partner. 'He was there the whole evening? At your side?'

'No, he was in and out.'

'So he doesn't help us much, does he?'

Pascual blinks. 'I worked with a girl called Sara. She'll be there again tonight, with me.'

'Sara what?'

'Muñoz.'

'And she was with you the whole time?'

'Right up until we closed at three. Until closer to four, actually. We cleaned the place up and I walked her home.'

'And she didn't invite you upstairs?'

'No.'

'Ah, your technique is slipping. Where would we find her now?'

Pascual glares at Serrano for three seconds. 'Calle Princesa.' He gives the address.

Serrano's eyes flick up over Pascual's shoulder and his partner stands and makes for the door. When he has left the office, Serrano slides off the desk and pulls up a chair, face to face with Pascual. 'Tell me about . . . *coño*, you tell me how it's pronounced. Tell me about this bloke.' Serrano reaches into the folder and pulls out a dark blue American passport, the fearsome eagle embossed in gold on the cover. He tosses it into Pascual's

26

lap. Pascual opens it and sees the photo of a middle-aged man with a beard staring glumly into the camera. He reads the name as a Yanqui would: 'Morris Weiss.'

Serrano the linguist squints at him. '*Gwice?* I'd have thought more like *Bayce.*'

'Whatever.'

'So tell me about him.'

Pascual closes the passport and hands it back to Serrano. 'What happened to him? Nothing good, I assume.'

Serrano's smile is not a pleasant one. 'Good things are not our department, I'm afraid.'

Pascual nods slowly. 'Is he dead?'

Serrano is losing patience. 'Why don't you just tell me all about him?'

'That I can't do. I only met the man once.'

'When?'

'Two or three days ago. Wednesday or Thursday, I think it was. Let me think. Thursday.'

'And what did you talk about?'

'I didn't talk to him. I refused even to admit I spoke English.'

'Why?'

'He knew who I used to be. People who know that mean nothing but trouble.'

'So he got that much across despite the language barrier. Anything else?'

'He said he needed my help.'

'For what?'

'We didn't get any further than that. He left me a card and he went away.'

'And you never saw him again.'

'No.'

'And you'd never heard of him before.'

'Never.'

'Was anybody else there who can back you up on this?'

'Enric was there. He'll tell you.'

Serrano grunts softly. 'Weren't you curious?'

'No.' Pascual wants a cigarette badly.

Serrano's eyes narrow, a look he does exceptionally well. 'A man comes all the way from America to find you and tells you he needs your help, and you're not curious?'

'I can guess how the story goes.'

'Ah, bravo, good for you. I wish I could.' Serrano stands, throws up his hands, paces, whirls. 'Me, I'm curious as hell. An American journalist turns up dead with your name in his notebook, that makes me curious.'

'What happened to him?'

'Somebody shot him. Him and two other men, actually. Three dead men in a stolen Fiat. Quite a little party.'

'Who were the other men?'

Serrano appears to be studying him. 'Domestic rabble. Thieves and addicts. Not good company for a visitor to our fair city.'

Pascual shakes his head. 'Where did it happen?'

'You know where Avillar Chavorro is?'

'Not really. Heard of it. That's where the junkies go.'

'That's right, at the foot of Montjuïc. The other side, away from the port. A squalid housing estate next to the cemetery, lots of brush, nooks and crannies on the hillside. It's a fucking supermarket. Fifteen hundred pesetas gets you a syringe full. Nasty place to die. My guess would have been he went out there to have a look, the journalist at work, and got himself into the middle of a deal gone bad. Except he had your name in his notebook. That gets my attention fast.'

Pascual nods. 'How did you know he was a journalist?'

'A brilliant feat of deduction. It was written in his passport. Getting interested now, are you?'

Pascual stares at the floor, unease settling deep in his bones. 'Scared. I'm getting scared. You've seen what can happen when my old friends turn up. That'll cure curiosity fast.'

'Yes. But I have to be curious. It's my job. So I want you to guess some more. Because I'd really like to know how the story goes.'

Pascual sighs. 'You know who I am, who I used to be. At this point your guess is probably as good as mine.'

'Don't give me that.'

Pascual has had enough suddenly. 'Why do you think I refused to talk to him? *I didn't fucking want to know!*'

The man in the other room has stopped typing and is staring

28

through the glass at Pascual. Serrano is staring too, absolutely impassive. After a few seconds he says, 'How do you think he found you?'

Recovering, Pascual says, 'I don't know. The last time somebody found me, you told them where to look.'

'That was professional courtesy. This time I had nothing to do with it. He gave no indication?'

'I've told you everything he said, as closely as I can remember.'

Serrano goes on staring at him for a while, then shrugs. 'Let's give it some time. Maybe something else will come back to you.' He slides off the desk and leaves the room, closing the door behind him.

Pascual watches through the window as Serrano chats with the typist, shuffles papers on a desk, smokes a cigarette. He closes his eyes and tries to knead away a headache that is just beginning to ferment behind his eyes. Out in the office a telephone purrs. The man at the typewriter answers, motions to Serrano. The call is brief. In ten seconds Serrano is back in the smaller room, a grim smile on his lips.

'Bad news, friend. She's not going to cover for you.'

Pascual laughs, a quick contemptuous huff. 'You have to do better than that.'

Serrano shrugs, closing the door. 'So you paid someone to do it.'

Pascual stifles another surge of anger. 'Are we going to go the full seventy-two hours on this? You know I didn't do it.'

'We'll go as long as we have to. You're going to sit there until I've got five or six people, not just one, who will swear you were behind that bar when Weiss was getting killed. And if you stop being a suspect you'll still be my number one witness. Just because he was here to talk to you. That makes you the star.'

'I never heard of the man.'

'He'd heard of you. That's the important thing. You know what that means?'

Wearily Pascual says, 'What?'

'That means you've got the answer.' He leans forward and taps Pascual gently on the forehead. 'Up there. Even if you don't think you do. You've got the answer.'

Pascual stares him down for long ticks of the clock. 'God help us then,' he says.

Pascual pauses at the side exit of the Jefatura to light a cigarette, and that is his undoing. He is shaking out the match when a hand is clapped on his shoulder. 'Got a moment?' a voice says.

Pascual turns, draws on the cigarette, blows smoke discourteously close to his assailant's face. 'For you, never.'

Campos grins. 'Now, now. Manners, my boy. *Vamos*, I'll buy you lunch.' Eyes that never met a man who couldn't be mocked twinkle behind glasses perched above a neatly trimmed beard and below a round gleaming pate.

'A journalist chiding me about manners? Remarkable.' Pascual strides off into the Gothic Quarter, wild notions of escape in the narrow streets dancing in his head.

Campos is keeping up stride for stride, almost trotting. 'And a journalist offering to pick up the tab is even more remarkable. I'd say yes if I were you.'

'I've got nothing to tell you.'

'Funny, that's what Serrano said, too. I suppose he won't mind when I come out with the usual wild speculations.'

'Write what you want,' says Pascual with a sinking feeling.

'You mean that? *Dios mío*, at last. Permission to tell the world about Pascual March and his curious relationship with the Policía Nacional. That's very kind of you.'

'You're a cold-hearted, unscrupulous bastard.'

Campos is grinning again as they swing around a corner. 'No doubt. But I'm still willing to buy you lunch. There's a tolerable little place up ahead in Canuda.'

Pascual knows he has few cards to play. 'You're going to get me killed,' he says.

'And lose a good source?' says Campos. 'Never. I'll handle with care, believe me.'

With a bottle of *tinto* on the table between them and a cheerful bustle of waiters in motion around them, Pascual has mellowed enough to look the reporter in the eye. 'You have an unhealthy obsession, you know. I'm really not worth your time.'

Campos raises his glass. 'I beg to differ. You hacked a man to death once and walked out of that building back there a free man. That fascinates me.'

'Justifiable self–defence. That's in the records.'

'Certainly. But what fascinates me is the way the real identity of the victim was suppressed. You'd think the death of an internationally sought Palestinian terrorist would be cause for official celebration. But I had to move heaven and earth to find out who he was, and it was made clear to me, subtly of course, that I'd never get in the door of the Jefatura again if I published it. And then you were held for a while as a suspect when those two *etarras* turned up shot, only to be released suddenly with the word that no, it wasn't you after all. And the killing is still officially unsolved. And now, *hostia puta*, one fine morning an American journalist turns up dead in a stolen car with a local ne'er-do-well and who does our friend Serrano haul in for a talk? You again. That enthrals me, I have to say.'

Pascual scowls at him. 'Serrano said there were three victims.'

Campos looks blank for an instant and then smiles. 'Oh, the wicked man. Testing your reaction, of course. He says three, and if you had anything to do with it, you protest it was only the two and by God somebody's setting you up. No, there were two of them, the driver in front and the American in the back, I got it direct from the officers who found him.'

'The bastard.' Pascual reaches for his glass.

Campos is grinning, evidently enjoying himself. 'Well, you must have passed the test. Anyway, I think you're the most interesting man in Barcelona and I have a feeling that if I ever put the whole story together I might finally make it off the police beat and up a couple of rungs on the journalistic ladder.'

'So I am at the mercy of your ambition.'

'I wouldn't put it that way. I'd say we have a nicely balanced symbiotic relationship.'

Pascual vents a quiet whiff of disgust. 'What's in it for me?'

'Maybe some money. Books do sell. A first-person account, as told to Ernesto Campos, formerly of *El Mundo*.'

'First-person account of what? Who the hell do you think I am?'

Campos lowers his voice, leaning closer over the table. 'I think you're Pascual Rose. I think you're the man who defected to the

31

CIA and sold out half the terror networks in Europe back in '89, just before the Wall fell. Not many people know about you. The story's never been told. But it's a great story. I think I'm the one to tell it, and I think your best option is to co-operate with me. Look, it's not in my interest to expose you. I'd protect your identity, your whereabouts. But I could make us both some money. Try and see it that way.'

Pascual is chilled to hear his former name on Campos's lips. He pours more wine, concentrating on keeping his hand steady. 'Somebody's been telling you fairy tales.'

'The pieces of the story are out there. There are references to you in various places. Know where I found one of them?'

'Where?'

'In a book by an American called Weiss.'

In the silence that follows the soup arrives. Pascual pokes half-heartedly at his with a spoon. He has no appetite. 'If you know anything about Weiss, take it to Serrano.'

Campos dabs at his beard with a napkin. 'I ran across the book a couple of years ago when I first got interested in you. Weiss didn't mention your name, but he knew you existed. He knew someone had gone over to the CIA and blown an extraordinary number of terror operatives. It was just a passing reference to the way the Soviet world collapsed in the late eighties. The main topic of the book was scandals involving the CIA and other intelligence agencies. That seemed to be Weiss's speciality. So you can imagine what effect the name of the dead American had on me this morning, and how my heart leapt when I saw you walk down the stairs back at the Jefatura. This, I said to myself, cannot possibly be coincidence. This is another chapter in the book. All I have to do is persuade my old friend Pascual, with the mutating surname, to unburden himself to me.'

'I don't know anything about Weiss.'

'But I do, a little. And if we put together what we both know, we can do two things, maybe. We can help Serrano solve this killing and after that we can write a book that will really turn some heads and make some money. And I don't know, but just from what I've seen of your lifestyle, I'm assuming you could use a little more money.' Campos sucks soup out of his spoon and smiles.

'I don't need money. I don't need anything. Except complete anonymity.'

With a shake of the head Campos says, 'I'm afraid that's always been precarious. How many more of these little incidents can you survive? You're better off co-operating with me and using the proceeds to buy yourself some real privacy. Money can do that, you know.'

Pascual shoves his plate away. He fixes Campos with a glare and says, 'You enjoy what you do? You like what you see when you look in the mirror?'

Campos stares back, spoon halted half-way to his mouth. 'I'd be very interested to hear you answer the same question. First a terrorist and then an informer. My, my. No wonder you drink.'

4

Joselito is mopping the stairs, clad in his blue *conserje*'s coat. At Pascual's approach the little man straightens and leans on the mop. '*Hombre,*' he says, 'you missed the excitement. We've had an inspector of police around this morning looking for Sara.'

'I didn't miss a thing. I've had a bellyful of cops today.'

Joselito's voice drops to a murmur as Pascual passes him on the steps. 'About the other night?'

'No. About a man who got himself killed last night.'

'*Válgame Dios.* Anyone we know?'

'No.'

'So how do you come into it?' Joselito calls after him.

Pascual shakes his head. 'I don't come into it at all. There was a misunderstanding.'

Upstairs a pleasant breeze is making the gauze curtains billow gently in the window overlooking the street. Pascual is apprehensive about his reception, but Sara greets him with a kiss and ushers him into the dining room, where the remains of a lunch litter the table: scraps of bread, a half-empty bottle of wine. Pilar is lingering at the table, smoking. From the kitchen come clattering noises. Pascual pulls out a chair and sits down heavily. 'Want some coffee?' says Sara.

'Something stronger would be nice if you have anything.'

Sara sets the bottle of brandy and a glass in front of him and sits, chin on her hand, watching him pour. 'I'm sorry about the policeman,' Pascual says.

'He was polite,' says Sara. 'He could have been the man from Telefónica come to see about the wires.'

34

'He gave Lola a fright,' says Pilar. 'She thought he'd come to tell her somebody had escaped.' Pilar's protectiveness of Lola is fearsome.

Sara waits a beat while Pascual winces and then she says, 'So what mischief have you been getting up to?' If there is no warmth in her gaze there is at least no hostility either.

'Nothing. You were with me the whole night, weren't you?'

'And what did they think you had done?'

Pascual downs a healing draught and sighs. 'Two men were killed last night, out on Montjuïc. One of them had been looking for me.'

Sara stares at him for a long moment. 'Are you in danger?' she says, going straight to the heart of the matter.

'I don't know. It appears the man was a journalist.'

'And what did he want from you?'

'I don't know that either.'

This meets with some scepticism, judging from the several seconds of silence that follow it. 'You must have some idea what a journalist might want from you.'

'Some idea, yes.'

Sara is looking at him with no particular expression, mere curiosity perhaps. 'Anything you can share?'

This is treacherous ground for Pascual. He has told Sara a factual but carefully edited tale of his wanderings, geographical and otherwise. The overtly homicidal dimensions of his career and its sequels he has concealed. Pascual looks across the table at her and thinks about diverse things: the corrosive effects of secrecy, the possibility that she will despise him. 'Now might be a good time for you to hear the unabridged version of my autobiography,' he says.

Pilar and Sara exchange a glance. 'Walk with me,' says Sara, rising. 'I've got early shift at the bar.'

In the street there is noise and anonymity. The shops are just reopening and the foot traffic in Princesa jostles in benign post-prandial humour. 'Fifteen years ago every police department in Europe wanted me,' Pascual begins. By the time he finishes, they are standing on the Moll de la Fusta looking across the harbour. The sun is declining and a chill is rising off the black water. Pascual shrugs to show he has nothing more to say and smokes,

35

not daring to look at her. He waits for a long time, wondering if he has just tipped everything he has won in the last six months on to the rubbish heap. When he finally turns to look at Sara, she is giving him a look he cannot read. He is not sure what he wants but he wants something – pity, horror, a derisive laugh even. 'So now you know who I am,' he says.

Sara stands with her arms folded, eyes locked with his. 'I guessed some of it,' she says. 'The things you won't talk about betray a lot.'

'I should have told you long ago. Shame is a powerful thing.'

'I know,' Sara says simply. She gazes into his face and he thinks what he is seeing may be shock. 'I don't know what to tell you,' she says.

Pascual wants to gather her in his arms but her body language is not encouraging. She has made the right noises so far, but there is no sign she is ready to come back to his arms and Pascual feels a faint stirring of despair. After a time Sara says, 'So what happens next?'

Pascual flings the cigarette into the water and turns away. 'With any luck, nothing. With any luck, the whole thing has nothing to do with me.'

'And what are the odds against that?'

'Steep,' says Pascual after a moment. 'I'd say the odds against that are fairly steep.'

At the Tavern del Born Enric is presiding over a catatonic crowd of five early drinkers. He has jazz on the CD player, something moody and aimless for saxophone. He hands the reins to Sara and comes out from behind the bar to sit with Pascual at the table in the window. 'If you're the secret nexus of a vast international criminal conspiracy, it would be common courtesy to notify me,' he says, pouring himself a stiff one from the best Scotch off the high shelf. 'It's my bar, after all, and if you're running the white slave trade for the whole western Mediterranean out of here, I should think I have a right to know.'

'If I told you, I'd have to kill you,' says Pascual.

Enric does not appreciate the witticism, such as it is. 'I don't like talking to cops. Hangover from my days on the barricades, no doubt. They can be as polite as they want and they still leave you with the impression they'd have you down in the cellars for a good thrashing in an instant if all this democratic nonsense didn't hamper them.'

'I can't say I had much fun myself.'

'Well, if they let you go, they must have decided you didn't do it.' Enric peers at Pascual. 'You are a mysterious fellow. Some day I'd like to hear the story.'

'There is no story. This fellow came looking for me but I wouldn't talk to him. Then he died. It probably had nothing to do with me.'

'I don't mean that story. I mean the whole story. Who you are, why things seem to happen to you. I've known you for years and I know fuck all about you. You have the damnedest way of revealing nothing in a pleasant and interesting fashion.'

Pascual, who took great pains to develop that particular survival skill, shrugs. 'My life is an open book.'

'Why do I get the impression you've torn out a few pages here and there?' Enric shakes his head and looks to the bar, where Sara appears to be fending off advances from a solitary drinker in a fleece-lined jacket who has been roused from his stupor by her appearance. 'They asked me about Sara as well. If you've got her involved in something shady I'll ram your teeth down your throat.'

Pascual watches her as she listens gravely to whatever line the alcoholic Lothario is feeding her. 'If I get her involved in anything shady,' he says, 'I'll save you the trouble.'

Pascual leaves Enric and Sara presiding and trudges to the Metro station on Laietana. There are times when the narrow alleys of the Old City oppress him. He descends to the station and slumps in the first train heading away from the port. The Barcelona part of his fragmented childhood was spent up in the Eixample, the grid of perfectly square blocks with chamfered corners that sprawls between the sombre medieval *ciutat* and the tonier hillside precincts. Emerging into a different city, Pascual wanders. He loves these long straight streets with their apartment blocks looming above, balconies stacked elegantly one atop another with flowers in boxes, spindly arthritic plane trees meeting to form a canopy overhead. These streets hold what pass for fond memories for Pascual: a bar here or there where he and his mates played pinball, the *xocolateria* where his mother indulged him. He gazes wistfully into shops where women like the one his mother might have become queue for hams or a bottle of *tinto* for tonight's supper, string bags dangling from their fingers. His mother's family still lives hereabouts, and cousins and whatnot collar him on the Ramblas once a year or so: *Hola*, Pascual, still here I see, you reprobate, how are you keeping body and soul together, you must come to aunt Eulàlia's party next month, she's ninety now, *sorda com una tapia* but still sharp as a tack. Pascual has come as close as a finger on the doorbell at times but never found the courage to face what family is left him.

The Clinical Hospital occupies two blocks in the middle of the Eixample, below the Diagonal; it is a massive pile of brownish stone with an impressive main entrance and a narrow, dusty park stretching the length of the façade. Pascual ascends the front steps and becomes lost, wandering along interior passages before he locates the room he is looking for.

Father Costa is supine and visibly enfeebled, but his eyes flash and he musters the strength for a firm grip on Pascual's hand. 'My boy. What a pleasant surprise.' The voice no longer booms, but there is breath behind it yet; this is a man who will not go gently.

'I should have come when I first heard.' Pascual has known of the old priest's illness for a week but been unable to stir his limbs in the right direction or even to dwell on the implications. 'I'm sorry.' Pascual draws up a chair; low murmurs come from the bedside in the other half of the room, where a family are clustered around a wasted figure under a sheet. 'You'll be out of here before too long, I imagine,' Pascual says, just to say something.

'That would surprise me,' says Father Costa. 'I'd need more entrails than I have left, they inform me.'

Pascual nods. He has already heard the prognosis. 'Does it hurt you much?'

'Not until the drugs wear off. But then they give me more drugs. The hard part is not eating. I'd give a lot to be able to enjoy a decent meal again.'

'You've treated me to quite a few.'

'My pleasure. I haven't seen you in a while. Been staying out of trouble?'

Pascual hesitates and then says, 'I am in love with a woman.' He wonders why of all things he has blurted this out.

The death mask on the pillow softens for a moment. 'That can be trouble. Or am I misunderstanding you?'

'Today, I'm not sure. I am devoted to her.'

'I congratulate you.'

'But she has found out what I used to be. I am afraid that I have disgusted her.'

'If she does not forgive you, there is one who will.'

'So you say. I wish I could believe it. But when one faith has proved so hollow it's hard to take up another.'

A faint smile stretches the old priest's lips. 'Listen, He will find a way to give you faith without violating the rational faculties you prize so much.'

'That *would* be a miracle.'

'He's pulled off a lot of those, my boy.'

Then let's see Him heal you, Pascual thinks bitterly. 'I'll let you rest now,' he says.

In a bar in Rosselló a few metres from the hospital, jostled by white-coated medical students busily discharging smoke into the air, Pascual downs a *coñac* to steady himself. Loss is something he is accustomed to, but each one seems to cut deeper. He shoves his way out of the bar, suddenly aware of the kilometres that separate him from Sara.

Shutters are clanging shut on shops in the Passeig del Born as night falls. Pascual's spirits rise; this is the beginning of his working day. Those who have no one waiting supper on them will be drifting into the Tavern del Born, and until long after midnight there will be companionship and escape. Mostly, there will be Sara.

Pascual can see her through the window as he approaches the bar, pouring a drink. The place is nearly empty. Inside, smooth guitar work is coming from the CD player. Enric is poring over the *Vanguardia* at the bar. At the corner table Antonio and Diego wave him a lazy greeting. Sara gives him a lingering look as he doffs his jacket and moves behind the bar. He is finding it increasingly hard to conceal his feelings; tonight he wants to grab her and rattle bottles on the shelf. '*Hola jefe*,' he says to Enric, who is glaring at him over the top of his spectacles. Pascual shrugs off the look, a relic, he supposes, of his brush with the law. Pascual tidies, fiddles with glasses, shakes out a towel and hangs it up, moving inexorably towards the end of the bar where Sara is leaning with her arms folded.

'¿Qué tal?' he says quietly.

Sara makes no answer. Her eyes flee his. Pascual frowns at her and moves closer. 'What's wrong with you?'

Sara tosses her hair. 'Nothing.'

Seconds pass. Pascual says, 'Don't give me that. What's wrong?'

She looks up at him and he is startled by what he sees in her deep black eyes: a flash of pure pain. 'Will you do me a great favour?' she says quietly.

Pascual wants to reach for her but cannot move, looking into those eyes. 'What?'

'Leave me alone. I have a lot to think about.'

Pascual's mood crumbles with a loud psychic crash. 'I'm supposed to be working with you, remember?'

'Look, I've talked to Enric. He'll cover for you. It'll be a slow night, you won't be needed.'

Until now the conversation has been held in an urgent undertone. Now Pascual looks at Enric and says, cutting through the music, 'You're in on this, are you?'

Enric glowers. 'She doesn't want you around tonight. Hasn't she made herself clear?'

Pascual puts a hand on the bar to steady himself. Moods and spells on Sara's part have never before interfered with their working relationship. 'Are you kicking me out?'

'Not at all. I'm giving you the night off, that's all.'

Pascual slips into Catalan for the most robust oath he can find. 'Cago en Déu. Tell her to take a holiday. This is my job.'

Enric sighs. 'Quite frankly, given the choice, I'd rather have her behind the bar. She's better for business.'

Staggered, Pascual spins to look at Sara. She holds her hands out, palms together, and now she is pleading. 'Pascual, I swear to you, tomorrow we'll talk. Just please go.'

Desperately he says, 'I haven't changed since this morning. I'm the same man.'

'So maybe I'm not the same woman. Please, just give me a little time.'

40

Pascual feels panic rising. 'You can't just close up on me. You can't do that.'

'Tomorrow. Tomorrow we'll talk.'

This is what a knife in the back feels like, Pascual thinks. For a long moment he is simply frozen, looking at Sara and groping for words. He shakes his head. 'Don't give up on me. It's not right.'

'I'll talk to you tomorrow,' says Sara. There is pain in her eyes, but her voice is cold.

Enric is deeply absorbed in the newspaper again. Pascual grabs his jacket off the hook and goes. As he passes, Diego and Antonio watch him, inscrutable, thankfully remote from *payo* domestic dramas. Outside in the street Pascual makes ten paces and has to stop, reeling. Two minutes ago he was happy and now he cannot think what hit him. Passers-by eye him. He begins to move again, leadenly. A drink, he thinks. I could use a drink.

Two hours later he has had a number of them, and he feels they have helped him regain his composure. He has worked his way clear across the Gothic Quarter to the lower reaches of the Ramblas, revisiting old haunts long neglected, plying casual acquaintances with drink, leaving a trail of abandoned change. His money is gone but his head is clear; he is able to take the philosophical view. He has frightened Sara with his confession; only to be expected. What woman would enjoy finding out that her lover plotted murder in the service of tyranny? This is the weight of his sins which he will carry until he dies. But he will not lose Sara; a night's rest, a little perspective, contrition and quiet reason on his part, and she will love him again.

Numbly he suppresses the black fear that she will not, and steers for the harbour. He wants sea air in his face to clear his head. He crosses the Passeig de Colom against the light, dodging cars, and shambles along the Moll de la Fusta, veering perilously close to the water's edge. The night is benign, with more of the coming summer than the departed winter in the air. Couples pass, arm in arm; across the water lights blaze at the Maremagnum. Pascual has smoked his last cigarette.

He knows where he is going but will not admit it; he has always detested drunken scenes and piteous spurned lovers. He wants only a sight of her through the glass. Just a sight to carry him over until the morrow, or maybe even closing time. With the bar closed, the shutter half-way down, he will slip in, sober and penitent, and they will talk. Tempers will have cooled; he will take her home. Pascual stumbles on the cobbles and nearly pitches into the water.

Again he risks death crossing multiple lanes of traffic, cars speeding at him from unimaginable angles, klaxons blaring. He rounds the corner of the Llotja into the Plaça del Palau and turns up a narrow lane towards Santa Maria del Mar. He is going home; the Tavern del Born is his home and nobody can throw him out. He wheels round a corner and sees the lighted windows ahead.

He slows, breathes deep, feels for his dignity. No drunken scenes for him; a sight of Sara through the window and he will go home to bed, walk off the last two hours' excesses and throw himself on her mercy tomorrow. Of course, if any acquaintances should spot him passing by and beckon, he will stay a moment. Pascual halts; he can see her through the window, behind the bar, talking to a man whose face he cannot see. The crowd has grown and the music is loud enough to be heard in the street, a thumping *bulería*. Pascual feels in his pocket for cigarettes and finds only the empty pack. He crumples it in his hand and stands there holding it, watching Sara talk, watching her move, watching her through glass. Strollers brush by him. Despair has taken hold of him again.

He is surprised to find himself pushing the door open and plunging headlong into the smoke and music. A head or two turns but the most important one has only to look straight ahead to see him; Sara is watching him like a woman seeing a ghost. There is a vacant stool and Pascual claws at it, managing to clamber on to it without toppling it. He surveys the crowd. Enric is nowhere to be seen; at the far end of the bar Pilar and Lola are observing him. He stares at them, looking for a sign. Pilar gives him a cool nod; Lola is blinking rapidly, looking from him to Sara and back again. Sara has spun away from him, black hair flouncing. Pascual looks desperately at her back, at the curves of her waist, her hips in the tight jeans. Talk to me, he wants to scream at her. He passes a hand over his face, grimacing. There will be no scenes; quite apart from his ingrained habits of discretion there is his dignity to consider. When he opens his eyes, Lola is sliding off her stool. He watches her come around the bar towards him, looking formidable.

'She doesn't want to talk to you now,' says Lola, with a gentleness that does not match the look in her eyes.

'I love her,' says Pascual. 'Tell her that.' Articulation is suddenly difficult; what has happened to his tongue?

'She knows. She needs a day or two to think, that's all.'

'Think about what?' Pascual tamps down another rush of panic. 'It's simple. I'll tear out my heart and hand it to her. What's complicated?'

'*Todo*,' says Lola ruthlessly. 'Everything. You're drunk, and that's not going to make things any simpler. Talk to her tomorrow.'

Teeth clenched, Pascual fights manfully against the personality-eroding effects of his alcohol intake. To his left he hears a timorous request for drink in poor Castilian. The words seem to have come from a Nordic type who has just wandered up to the bar in a *boina* that looks absurd on him. Pascual wants to knock it off his head. Instead he places a hand on Lola's arm. 'Tell her I want a coffee. I'm going to sit here and drink it and then I'll go. I'm not going to bother her. But I'm going to have a coffee.'

Lola stares, gives a faint sigh and returns to her place at the end of the bar. Sara has been hit with a rush of orders and Pascual watches as she fills them. She moves with her customary grace, her black eyes occasionally meeting Pascual's and lingering for a moment, a message he cannot read. Pausing finally at the far end of the bar, she listens as Lola's lips move. In a couple of minutes she is setting Pascual's coffee in front of him.

'You're killing me,' he says to her over the music.

Sara pauses just long enough, leans just close enough, to say, 'I don't talk to drunks.'

Pascual downs the coffee in one gulp and frowns into the empty cup. He replaces the cup on the saucer and rests his chin on his fist, the picture of a man ruminating on deep matters. Soon it will be time for an exit, but first he must show her he is sober. He twists on the stool to look out of the big window into the street. He can feel people looking at him. These are his friends, but he can sense them lining up behind Sara. The door swings open.

Gabriel is the type of man who cannot enter a toilet stall without making a production of it; when his dramatic pause on the threshold goes unnoticed by all except Pascual, he picks his

43

way to the bar with a peevish frown. Sara detaches herself from Lola and Pilar and comes down the bar to meet him. Gabriel leans over the bar for a perfunctory kiss, and this time Pascual's jealous pang goes all the way to his guts. Gabriel murmurs, looking up and down the bar. Sara shrugs and says something in return as Gabriel hoists his rump on to a barstool.

'*Cuidado al vaso.*' It takes Pascual a moment to figure out who has spoken; more than directional clues it is the distinct foreign accent in the Castilian that fingers the tourist at his elbow. Pascual turns and peers at him, the wanker in the beret, the typical German or Swedish or British wastrel who brings a pocketful of dole money south looking for sun and easy women and buys a funny hat to show he gets the joke. He is giving Pascual a faintly amused look and shifting his glass away from Pascual's elbow, which has strayed out and nearly knocked it off the bar.

'You be careful where you put it,' says Pascual, putting as much contempt into his look as he can muster.

He sees the face slowly lose its humour and turn into the hard mask of a football hooligan, sizing up a crotch for a kick. '*Fuck you, mate,*' the wanker says in English. He jostles Pascual as he pushes away from the bar, harder than could be accident. Pascual glares at his back. He wants Sara to notice him, but not with blood pouring from his nose. He is dimly aware that he is making a poor job of customer relations tonight.

Sara and Gabriel are in consultation, heads close together over the bar. Gabriel reaches out and places a hand on Sara's arm. He is murmuring to her, a look on his face that is almost tender. Jealousy is eating Pascual alive. Gabriel looks to his left and his eyes meet Pascual's. He nods. Pascual blows him a kiss. Gabriel freezes and then looks amused. 'Not working tonight?' he calls down the bar.

'Quality control,' Pascual answers. He has missed his chance for a cutting remark, he realizes. Pascual catches Sara's eye, but she is not having any; already she is heading back to her coven at the end of the bar. Pascual sways on his stool. The door opens and he sees Fernando and Diego coming in from the street. Pascual raises a hand in greeting. 'The champion returns,' he proclaims, rather loudly.

44

Fernando has sussed out the alcohol situation and is grinning. '*Coño*. Been getting at the stock again, have you?'

Pascual shrugs as best he can, clutching the bar for support. 'Rough day.' He frowns in concentration. 'I didn't expect to see you back in this end of the woods so soon.'

'Can't let them scare you off your turf.' Fernando's hair is tied back in a ponytail revealing the gold ring in his earlobe. He is dapper in a sport jacket over a collarless cotton shirt and his wicked grin pulls at the long scar that creases his cheek. 'As long as they've got ears to spare, I'm happy to take them on. No trouble with the *pestañí*?'

'Nothing to do with you,' says Pascual. 'It's me they're interested in now.' He wants desperately to tell somebody the whole story, despite the voice in his head that is screaming at him to shut it.

Fernando grins at him. 'And what have you been up to?'

'Nothing. They got the wrong end of the stick.'

'Ah, they're good at that. What were they trying to hang on you?'

'Acquaintance with a dead man. In the first degree.'

'*Joder*. If that was a crime I'd have the longest sheet in history. Sara! Give us three brandies, will you?'

Pascual does not hear Sara's answer, but Fernando laughs and says, 'I can see that. Give the poor boy a glass of water, then.'

'I want a fucking *coñac*,' says Pascual.

'No, Sara's got your best interests at heart,' says Fernando, pulling something from his pocket. 'Look here. This is for you.' He offers Pascual a small box.

'What's this?' The question is more than rhetorical, for Pascual has to muster all his faculties to read the inscribed word *Rolex*. He takes the box.

'A present. For a friend who helped a poor *gitanillo* the other night.'

When the penny drops Pascual shakes his head. 'Forget it. *La shukra ala wajib*.'

'What?'

'The Arabs say that.' With furrowed brow Pascual gropes for the translation. 'No thanks required for a duty.' He tries to return the box, but Fernando gently pushes his hand away.

'Take it. You saved my arse, and I don't forget things like that. Go ahead, try it on.'

With only minor difficulty Pascual opens the box. The watch is massive and elaborate, and unless it is a clever knock–off it is worth more than what Pascual makes in a good month. Pascual knows he will only fumble it if he tries to put it on now, and he closes the box. '*Hombre*, you shouldn't have.'

'Don't worry, I paid for this one,' says Fernando. Diego laughs.

Pascual reaches out and clasps the gypsy's hand. He is not so drunk after all, he finds, focusing on the gypsy's face. 'If that's the way you want it. I'd do it again, for free.'

'The next time you may have to,' says Diego through a cloud of smoke. 'Fernando's money always runs out before his enemies do.'

Suddenly Sara is there at Pascual's elbow, beckoning to Fernando, who leans across the bar to listen to her. Pascual affects to ignore her, trying to make out what she is saying while scowling over Diego's shoulder at the wanker, who has taken up a new station by the door, glass in hand, looking vacuous.

'*De acuerdo*,' says Fernando, straightening up. To Diego he says, 'Let's go. We're taking Pascual for a walk.'

'Like hell you are,' says Pascual, turning to see Sara move away down the bar. 'I want my drink.'

'We'll get you a drink somewhere else. *Vamos*, some fresh air will do you good.' He takes Pascual by the arm.

The phone behind the bar bleats and Sara reaches to answer it. 'One drink,' says Pascual.

'All the drinks you want, *primo*. But first we go for a walk.'

'Look at her,' says Pascual. 'The flowers weep when they see her.'

'*Coño*, it's getting serious. He's about to break into song.'

Sara reaches across the bar and hands the phone to Gabriel, who takes it with a puzzled look. '*Me quisiste, me olvidaste*,' says Pascual, allowing himself to be pulled away from the bar.

'*Joder*, let's get him out of here before he starts blubbering,' says Fernando.

'Pascual.' The name hangs in the air, not loud but distinct, just audible under the music, but when Pascual looks past Fernando to see who is calling, nobody is looking at him. He has time to wonder if he imagined it, searching for a face fixed on his and finding none, and then motion catches his eye and he sees the arm come up with the pistol at the end of it. Gabriel is still talking on the phone, the cord stretched across the bar, but he has seen it too and he turns, phone to his ear, eyes going wide, wide open. The first shot knocks the phone receiver out of his hand despite having passed clean through his head beforehand, testimony to the power of a nine-millimetre cartridge. The second and third are gratuitous and serve only to increase the scope of the clean up that will be needed some time tomorrow when the police have finally abandoned the premises.

All this passes through Pascual's addled mind before he even thinks to look at the shooter, who is stepping calmly, magisterially towards the door while sweeping the room with his automatic, a totally unnecessary precaution. The astounding noise of the three shots has silenced all talk and nobody has thought yet to scream; it is only when Gabriel's body hits the floor, precipitated by a panicked shove from his neighbour on the next stool over, that a woman at a table along the wall begins to exercise her lungs. Pascual is watching the shooter with a sense of wonder. The wanker in the *boina* wheels towards the door, stuffing the automatic in his waistband, and now Pascual wishes he had decked him when he had the chance.

5

The august personage of the *juez de primera instancia y de instrucción* has taken possession of the premises. He is a morose-looking man with untidy grey hair and heavy black eyebrows, who is making it clear from stance and facial expression that this particular aspect of the jurist's trade is one he would be happy to leave to others. Hands in trouser pockets, he is watching the forensic team at work: measuring, jockeying for camera angles, conferring in quiet tones. At his back lurks the uniformed officer who convoyed him in, while at his elbow Serrano stands placidly with the air of a man awaiting orders.

The shutter has been pulled half-way down over the door, disappointing the meagre shuffling crowd in the street outside. Enric is slumped on a stool at the end of the bar furthest from the mess, head in his hands, staring into a whisky. Pascual sits hunched over the table where in normal times the musicians play. He is trying to decide if it was mere drunkenness or a befuddled sense of responsibility that prevented him from joining the gypsy-led rush for the door in the minute after the shooting. He has come a long way towards sobriety, but there is a fair distance to cover yet. Midnight has come and gone.

Apparently satisfied with the work of his minions, the magistrate turns and murmurs a few words to Serrano before shaking hands and departing with his escort in tow. Serrano drags out a chair and sits across from Pascual. 'I must remember not to stand too close to you,' he says, a faint ironic light in his eyes. 'Imagine. Two in two nights with you cropping up in the middle of things. You're having an interesting week, aren't you?'

He waits for a response, but Pascual has none to give. He is staring at the worn soles of Gabriel's boots, which will never tread pavement again.

'So what do you think?' says Serrano. 'You have a theory? You have an idea why people who know your name are suddenly a high-risk category? Care to take a guess why association with you seems to work faster than radiation sickness or Ebola?'

Pascual nods at the body on the floor. 'I think that should have been me.'

'Is that a moral judgement?'

'He said my name.' Pascual can hear it still, cutting through the ambient noise. 'The shooter called my name, but he wasn't looking at me. He was looking at Gabriel.'

Serrano drums fingers on the tabletop. 'You're sure?'

'Ninety per cent. That's where the voice came from. I think he took Gabriel for me. I think he called my name to make sure and Gabriel looked just because he heard a voice at his side. But that sealed his fate.'

Serrano thinks about it for a while, fingers drumming, and then slaps the table. 'And how did that happen? Why would he mistake somebody else for you?'

Pascual's stomach is threatening unpleasant reactions. 'I don't know.'

'Did he look anything like you? It's a bit hard to tell now.'

'Not much. Same general type maybe, dark hair and all. He was a little older but trying to look young.'

'How long had he been talking to the young lady?'

'Not long. He'd just come in.'

The young lady in question has been grilled along with the handful of other witnesses too dumbfounded or curious to flee and then released to the custody of her friends, still pale and unsteady on her feet. Pascual is haunted by the look he saw on Sara's face in the moments after the shooting, eyes wide with horror, hands pressed to her mouth, backing into a row of bottles and toppling them as Gabriel himself toppled.

Serrano nods. 'Now I want you to tell me about the shooter again. Everything you can remember.'

Pascual passes a hand over his face. 'Not young. Mid-thirties to early forties. Blond hair, but muddy, darkish, not a bright type of blond. Long at the back, lying on his collar. He wasn't Spanish. Nordic, maybe English. He spoke English, anyway, and I don't think he was a Yanqui. Fair, but I got the impression he might have spent a lot of time in the sun. He was wearing a *boina*, but it looked all wrong on him. I got the impression at first he was trying stupidly to go native, something he'd bought at a souvenir shop that just made him stand out more. Now I think it was a purposeful disguise. He knew people would notice the hat and not him. I'd bet the *boina* came off right outside the door.'

'Well, it worked, judging from the accounts we got from your clientele. What we got in the way of a description narrows it approximately to the male population of Europe. You're our best bet, I'm afraid.'

'He was a professional,' says Pascual. 'He knew what he was doing.'

'You'd know, would you?'

'I recognize competence when I see it. He wasn't nervous. He could have been turning out a light, from the look on his face. That much I saw.'

Serrano looks at him for a long time, just a patient professional look that gives away nothing at all. Finally he says, 'And he spoke your name.'

'I think so.'

'Then you would seem to have had a lucky escape.'

'Yes.'

Serrano pushes away from the table and stands over Pascual, hands in his pockets. 'A man comes to Barcelona to find you and is killed. The next night another man who seems to have been mistaken for you has the same thing happen to him. You tell me what's going on.'

Pascual cannot take any more of Serrano's stares and has to look down at the smooth marble of the tabletop. Everything upon which his happiness rested has been obliterated in a couple of hours. 'I think somebody's got a secret,' he says.

'Yes,' says Serrano. 'And what are you going to do for me?'

Pascual looks up into Serrano's pitiless black eyes. 'I'm going to tell you what it is,' he says. 'Just as soon as I know.'

'Smart boy,' says Serrano.

★

50

Pascual finds them outside the bar, dazed and shuffling while Enric pulls down the shutter and locks it. The last ghouls have gone home and the street is empty. Pilar gives him a piercing look, her devastating eyes narrowed. Lola with her shaven head is shivering and forlorn. Joselito glowers to one side, a pug in denim. Sara looks as if someone has sandbagged her at the base of the skull. 'I'm sick,' she says. 'I saw it happening and I couldn't stop it.'

Pilar puts her arms around Sara. '*Pobrecita*, you can hardly stand.'

'And you,' Lola says to Pascual. 'You don't look so fucking cheerful yourself. They put you through the wringer, didn't they?' She pulls him into the communal embrace. He sways slightly. Somebody to hold him when he can hardly stand; this is all he has ever wanted.

'What a fucking disaster,' mutters Enric. 'Better move it along or those reporters will be back.' He stalks away.

Sara raises her head. Pascual is looking at a stranger suddenly. 'It was you he wanted to kill, wasn't it?' Sara says.

Pascual nods. 'I think so.'

'Do you know why?'

He can see her slipping away from him; he can feel it. 'No.'

Her hands are on his chest now, pushing. 'I'm sorry,' Sara whispers, wide-eyed. Abruptly she turns, thrashes free of them all and runs. Lola shoots Pascual a quick frightened look and follows. Pilar and Joselito trade a look and Pascual can see that in the space of a few seconds he has been cast out of this family. Pilar has the grace to squeeze his hand in farewell, but he can see in her eyes where her sympathies lie. She picks up speed as she goes.

'*Ven*,' says Joselito, taking him by the arm. 'Let's go lose ourselves.'

The sun creeps over the horizon shamefacedly, dreading what it will find. The sea has caught fire, but overhead Pascual can still see stars, shining in deepest indigo. Here towards the end of the long breakwater the wind in their faces is cold. Neither of them has spoken for a long time and neither has turned to look at the city behind them, a welter of corruption and horror sprawling away from the sea. They are perched on the bonnet of Joselito's ancient

SEAT, taking occasional swigs from the bottle Joselito has pulled from his jacket pocket. Sleep is hours and maybe days away and Pascual is hoping simply to pass out from fatigue and alcohol before too long.

'Don't crowd her,' says Joselito in his rasping voice. 'Give her some time.' There are lights far out on the water and in the air; a freighter is riding at anchor two kilometres offshore and above it an early jet is wheeling into its approach to Llobregat, slow and stately.

'Who can blame her?' Pascual manages to say. 'I'm a bad bet. In her place I'd run the other way as fast as I could.'

Joselito shrugs. '*Mira*. If I thought you were such a bad bet I wouldn't have let you near Sara in the first place.'

The remark penetrates through the haze and Pascual turns to look at the old bantam, staring grimly out to sea. 'They're my daughters,' Joselito says. 'They're all I have.'

Pascual knows he cannot mean it literally. 'Tell me about them,' he says.

'Tell you what? That the world hasn't been very kind to them? You know the story.'

'Not really. Sara's dropped a few hints. I can see they're as close as sisters.'

Joselito takes the bottle from him and drinks. 'Closer.' Pascual waits; he knows the story will come. 'Pilar I've known her whole life,' Joselito says. 'I've worked in that building since her grand–father was alive. She was a pretty child.'

'I can believe it.'

'Everyone knew it wasn't the happiest family, but until five years ago Pilar was always pure sunshine. That only made it worse. That was a pity to make God Himself weep.'

'What happened?'

'She found her mother dead. She'd cut her wrists in the bath. A tub full of blood, *coño*. I heard Pilar screaming. I covered her eyes and hauled her out of there, but it was too late.' Joselito drinks again. His eyes are watering, whether from the liquor or the things he can see far out over the water, it is not clear. 'And that was the end of the family. The father, the bastard who drove the poor woman to kill herself, he's long gone. And the brother too, another villain. When Pilar got out of the *sanatorio* she was a hundred years older inside and the sunshine was gone, but she was more beautiful than ever, *válgame Dios*. And she had Lola in tow.'

Joselito pauses, shaking his head, and after a time Pascual prompts him softly. 'What's her story?'

'Ah, they raped her, *la pobrecita*. Three villains in the back of a van. They drove her around and kept her back there. For days.'

Pascual's head droops. '*Hostia puta*.'

'She was nearly dead when the police finally pulled her out. The villains got a few years in jail and Lola got a lifetime of nightmares. She was a beautiful girl too, I've seen pictures. That's why she cut her hair off, see? She's scared to death of being beautiful again.'

'And yet she's got spirit. I've seen Lola laugh till the tears come.'

'Well, she's got Pilar. They'd become fast friends inside there, in the hospital, and Pilar wanted her home back but she wasn't going to live up there alone. So she took in Lola, and by God I think they're happy. And I'll knock down anyone who says anything smutty about them. I don't know and I don't care if they're, you know, more than friends. All I know is they're happy.'

Pascual reaches for the bottle. 'And Sara? Where does she come in?'

'Sara, *Dios mío*, what a creature. Sara's the one who keeps them all going sometimes. If there's a catastrophe in her life I haven't heard about it, other than the fact that she's always had to make her own way in life, and God knows that wasn't easy. She's steady as a rock, Sara is. She and Lola grew up together, in Badalona. Had their First Communion together. But Sara was away for a long time, in France, God knows where else. When she came back she found Lola somehow, and there was an extra room in the flat and now Sara's up there too. The three of them together, and they're my daughters and I'll die before I let anything happen to them.'

Time passes and the sky lightens. Pascual's spirits have hit bottom. He has a feeling that this whole session has been a gentle warning off by Joselito. At this moment he would not give a *duro* for his prospects of regaining Sara's esteem, and the notion of clambering down over the rocks in front of him and swimming out into the cold sea until he sinks is beginning to appeal to him. He passes the bottle back to Joselito. 'I love her,' he says.

Joselito drains the bottle and then winds up and flings it as far as he can towards the sea. It glints in the light, tumbling, and shatters on the rocks just shy of the gently breaking waves. 'You'd better, *chico*,' he says.

6

Pascual has long since learned to sleep through morning street noises; his life in the lower quarters of Barcelona has been spent in a succession of *pensiones* in narrow echoing streets, and the reverberation of passing motos and cries of street urchins no longer suffice to awaken him. This pounding on his door, however, is problematic.

When he has managed to separate dream from reality and identify the noise, he snarls for silence and rolls from the narrow bed to forage for clothing. Clad in jeans and imperfectly reconciled to consciousness, he jerks open the door to find Enrique Campos leaning on the frame, smiling. 'Did I wake you?' coos Campos.

Pascual slams the door in his face. He has sunk on to the bed and is poking ineffectually at a packet of Ducados, wondering if he can possibly survive this feeling of complete constitutional devastation, when Campos eases the door open. 'I'm taking advantage, I know. But I have a feeling you've got interesting things to tell me.' He tosses a cigarette lighter on to the bed.

Pascual shoots him a glare, but uses the lighter and tosses it back. 'Get the fuck out of my room.'

'You might as well talk to me. The longer you put it off, the wilder the things other people are going to write will be. And that could hurt you worse.'

Pascual draws in life-giving smoke and blows it back at Campos. 'There's a bar on the corner. Wait for me there.'

Campos beams. 'Shall I order you a coffee?'

'Two. With milk.'

Dressed and drained if unshaven and still unsteady on his pins, Pascual descends the narrow stairs and emerges into a sublime early May morning, with a band of glorious blue visible high above the street. The bar on the corner is little more than a counter open to the street, and morning custom is already thick. Campos, however, has reserved him a place at the end, where he can spit on cars as they creep past his toes. Two *cafés con leche* in tall glasses stand waiting for him. Pascual drains one in three gulps and turns to Campos, who stands patiently watching him. 'What do you want?'

'The story, as usual. Things are happening to you again.'

Pascual reaches for the second coffee. 'I barely knew the man who got shot.'

'Don't try and sell me that. Mayhem follows you like an odour. You've left a trail of bodies across the Old City in the past few years and this is one more. I don't care if you didn't know him. We don't get that many killings in this town, and when two happen in two days and you're connected to both of them, you don't have to have the journalistic instincts of Oriana Fallaci to suspect that you could say something interesting about them. Am I wrong?' Campos's intensity is showing through the amiable veneer like brick through a bad paint job.

Pascual busies himself with lumps of sugar. His blood is beginning to move sluggishly through his veins and he has begun to think. Stirring his coffee, he says, 'I'll make a deal with you.'

'I'm listening.'

Pascual drinks and looks at things from different angles and decides he has little to lose. 'I'll tell you something about last night if you'll tell me a few things.'

Campos nods after the briefest of hesitations. 'All right, that's fair. What happened last night?'

'Oh, I have to go first, do I?'

Campos gestures impatiently, slopping coffee out of his cup. 'For Christ's sake. Fine, what can I tell you?'

Pascual jabs a finger into his chest. 'I want to know who else knows about me. How many people have you told?'

Campos stiffens. 'A handful. My editor, a couple of mates maybe. Not many.'

'A couple of mates. Wonderful. And how many have they passed it on to in their turn?'

A look of caution has settled on Campos's face. 'I never told anybody any particulars, like your name. I just commented on the peculiarities of your case, that's all.'

'And your editor? Has he been bandying my name at cocktail parties? Am I a good topic of discussion for half the city because of you?'

'No. He wouldn't spread it around. He barely paid attention when I told him, actually. I'm telling you, I'm the only one who's interested.'

'No, you're not. There's a man out there with a gun who's very interested.'

Campos's eyes narrow. 'In you?'

'That's right. The killing in the Tavern del Born was a case of mistaken identity. It was supposed to be me who got shot.'

Campos peers at him as traffic brushes by and laughter breaks out along the bar. '*Hostia puta*. How did he mistake Heredia for you?'

'I don't know. Ask Serrano. He's wondering the same thing. The point is, it was me he was looking for. And somebody told him where to find me.'

Campos sees where Pascual is taking him and digs in his heels. 'Now listen, there could be dozens of people in this city who know who you are and how to find you. You're not going to blame me for this.'

'I believe there are dozens of people who know little parts of the story, who have wondered about me, maybe. I don't think there are more than a handful who have put it all together, and you're at the head of the list. So I'm very interested in who you might have passed it on to.'

'Nobody.' Campos himself does not sound as if he believes it; his focus has gone soft and there is not a great deal of conviction behind the word. 'It's a potential scoop, you understand? I'm not going to go trumpeting it about, am I?'

'You had to talk to somebody to piece my sordid history together. Who knows?'

The journalist has no ready answer this time. He scratches at his beard, scowls, drains his coffee. 'I'll have to think about that.'

'You do that. While you're polishing up my life story for public consumption.'

'I told you, I'll protect you as much as I can.'

Pascual drains his coffee. 'I'd be very grateful.'

The work ethic has never been Pascual's strong point, but this is one job he will take great pains with. The great splotches of dried blood are gruesome enough, but there are bits of things clinging to the bar that do not bear much scrutiny. Pascual clenches his teeth and wrings out the rag over the pail. On the other side of the bar Enric is shoving a broom randomly to and fro, his heart clearly not in it. 'When it rains it pours, *collons*. Twenty years I get by without talking to policemen and now all of a sudden I've got brigades of them loitering on my doorstep. So much for keeping my nose clean.' He jabs a broom savagely into a corner.

'What a harrowing existence you lead.'

Enric appears to have missed the acid note in Pascual's voice. 'Where did I go wrong? You, I might have known better: you've got a history. Don't think it's a secret — everyone knows you were some kind of gangster, it's all over the neighbourhood. But Sara, who'd have thought she'd be involved with the type of character who gets himself shot by roving *sicarios*? It's the gypsy element, *collons*. I should have known better.'

'If it wasn't for the gypsy element you'd still be drawing crowds of three to your Friday night poetry readings.'

'I'm starting to pine for the days of the Friday night poetry readings, believe me. You know what kind of rumours are running about the neighbourhood today? I've heard the gypsies were dealing drugs out of the bar. I've heard that "those gypsies at the Tavern del Born" have launched into one of their vendettas. Imagine the effect that's going to have on the people who are already complaining about the infernal noise.'

'Yes, rude of the poor bastard to get himself shot like that.'

Something penetrates at last and Enric stands peering at him. 'All right, point taken. It couldn't have been too pleasant, eh?'

'I believe that I was the target, in fact.'

'*No fotis.*' Enric gapes at him for a moment and then gives up on the broom. He pulls down a bottle of whisky and sets two glasses on the bar. 'Here, take a dose of this.'

Pascual quails. 'No, many thanks.'

'So it should have been you, eh?' Enric, apparently shaken to the core, medicates himself generously with Glenlivet. 'Curious, but I can't say I'm too surprised. Do I get the story at last?'

'I don't know the story. But I think it was me that was supposed to die. And what happens when the newspapers publish that the man killed in the Tavern del Born was named Gabriel Heredia?'

'Ah. Somebody will know he's made a mistake.'

'Precisely. And if he comes back for a second try I'd prefer not to be here.'

'You're going away?'

'Avoiding this place, anyway. For a while. Until the police grab whoever it was who killed Gabriel.'

Enric scowls at him. 'And who's going to tend the bar while you're off on your little holiday? Good barmen don't just wander in off the street.'

'You've got Sara. You said last night you'd rather have her anyway.'

'She can't handle it alone. I'll have to get somebody else in. And then you'll want me to sack your replacement when you feel like coming back, no doubt.'

'Sorry if it complicates your life a little. It's complicating mine quite a bit, actually.'

Enric concedes the point with a heft of the glass. 'Fine, all right. Off you go then, glad to be of service. Drop us a postcard, will you?'

'Any chance of me touching the last week's wages before I go? I'm going to need it.'

Enric parts with money the way most people part with limbs, but he opens the register and comes up with the cash. 'Who's trying to kill you?'

'If I knew, I'd be up the Via Laietana talking to Serrano instead of you.'

Enric's eyes narrow. 'You're probably taking a risk being here right now, aren't you?'

'Probably.'

The ensuing silence is interrupted by a loud '*Bon dia*' from the street door. Pascual nearly leaps clear of his chair. The postman comes in with his shoulder bag and a letter in his hand. He stands looking about avidly for signs of debauchery and carnage. 'Had a bit of trouble in here last night, eh? One of your gypsies got shot?'

'My gypsies? Since when are they mine? Look, it was a fellow who'd been in here once or twice, they say. Didn't know him at all.'

'Bad for business, eh? Clients getting shot?'

'One fatality in six months, I don't think that's so bad.'

'Some gypsy intrigue, no doubt. I'm surprised you let them in the place. Can't keep them out, I suppose, nowadays. Here, somebody's got a letter.'

Enric takes the envelope. 'I'm telling you, it was nothing at all to do with us.'

'Well, then. You want to watch out, you know. Next thing you know they'll be peddling drugs in here under your nose and you'll get a reputation.'

Enric glances at the envelope and tosses it on the bar. 'Here, it's for you.' Pascual stands and picks up the envelope as Enric sees the postman out, in furious denial. The envelope bears the return address of the Hotel Colón. On it is written *Mr Pascual Rose, c/o Tavern del Born* with the address of the bar beneath. It has a Barcelona postmark and a thirty-five peseta stamp. Pascual reaches for the paring knife and slips it under the flap of the envelope, moving with great deliberation. It is not often he receives mail from dead men. The letter is hand-written in black ink on three sheets of hotel stationery, in English. Another of Weiss's calling cards falls on to the bar when Pascual unfolds the letter. *Dear Mr Rose*, it begins. *Please believe I have no wish to endanger you or embarrass you.*

'See what we're in for?' says Enric, returning. 'I'll have to close the bloody place and re-open as a tea room.'

'Shut up, will you?' *I understand that in your position you would be reluctant to talk to a stranger about your former activities or even to admit who you are. However, I am certain that I have found the right man and I hope to persuade you to co-operate with me in bringing to light some matters that have been kept under wraps for far too long.*

I am a journalist and author with three books to my credit (see my bibliography below). My field of interest is our intelligence agencies and the crimes and follies they indulge in when not adequately monitored. I am currently researching certain things that occurred in Europe during the period 1985–8. I have learned that you were active in this period as a courier and liaison agent for the Palestinian PFLP and other groups. This is a matter of record in archives to which I have gained access and is confirmed by informed sources with whom I have spoken.

My researches so far have convinced me of two things: First, the truth has never been told about certain events that took place in Frankfurt, Germany, in 1988, which would cause considerable outrage if known. Secondly, you are the only person who is in a position to testify conclusively to the truth in these matters and thus insure that individuals guilty of extraordinary subversion of the rule of law are held accountable. Some of these people are now poised to attain positions of tremendous influence. You can expose them IF YOU WILL AGREE TO HELP ME.

What I propose is that we meet, with guarantees of your security and current anonymity, and that you recount your role in these events, to the best of your ability. I can offer you nothing in exchange for your co-operation and can only appeal to the sense of justice and morality you displayed by your defection and subsequent activities. Without your testimony I have nothing but circumstantial evidence and these matters will remain in the shadows.

As I said when we met, you may contact me at any time; I am scheduled to return to New York on the 8th of May. I hope very much to hear from you.

At the bottom of the third sheet is a list of Morris Weiss's books and a scrawled signature. Pascual lays the letter on the bar next to the card. He rubs his face with both hands.

'What's the matter with you?' says Enric, who has slunk off affronted to pick up the broom again. 'Creditors caught up with you at last?'

'Something like that,' says Pascual.

For a man who knows no English, Serrano takes a long time over the letter. A typewriter is clattering just behind Pascual; men are laughing in the hallway. Faintly, traffic noise from the Via Laietana can be heard. Pascual studies the photographs on the wall: the homicide squad, all ten or twelve of them, at their annual dinners for the last few years, dressed up and smiling for the camera. Serrano appears in each photograph, his hair going whiter as the years go by, looking like somebody's old dad among the new generation of university-trained inspectors.

'Not that I don't believe you, but I'll have to get it officially translated,' says Serrano, tossing the letter on his desk. He stares at Pascual for a while and says, 'It was posted the day he died. Why do you suppose he didn't just drop it in at the bar?'

'Maybe he figured I'd refuse to take it. This was a way of getting through my defences. Or maybe he thought somebody was following him and didn't want to lead them to me.'

'You've already gone through all the possibilities, eh?'

'It gets to be a habit.'

Serrano nods, musing. 'So what's it all about?'

'I don't know. And don't give me that look. Frankfurt in 1988 is pretty vague. If I recall correctly I passed through Frankfurt at least three times that year. And my recollection of things has gone a little hazy over the years. I didn't keep a diary, you know.'

'No, I can see that wouldn't have been wise.'

'I'll think about it. But I have to tell you, right now I don't know what the man's talking about. I think Weiss had his wires crossed.'

'Those crossed wires seem to have got him killed. I'd say that lends his claim a little credibility.'

Pascual can only nod miserably. '*De acuerdo.*'

Serrano folds the letter and replaces it in the envelope. 'His wife's flying in, poor woman, and I'm hoping she'll be able to cast a little light on what he was up to. None of the papers we found on him or in his hotel room seems to amount to much.'

'He'd be careful what he wrote down if he suspected the danger.'

'Yes.' Serrano contemplates him in silence for a moment. 'Have you thought about how Weiss found you?'

'A little.'

'And?'

Pascual lets out a long breath; it is time to face it. 'He knew I had two fingers missing.'

'All right, so what?'

'So that's a fairly recent development in my life. That wouldn't be part of any description any intelligence agency I've dealt with might have. As far as I know, all their information dates from the days when I could play a scale on the piano and hit all the notes.'

Serrano sees the point and smiles his icy smile. '*Caray*. And you thought you were safely tucked away here.'

Pascual is starting to reel from the effects of a sleepless night and too much to think about. He rubs his face with both hands. 'Wishful thinking,' he says. 'One of my greatest failings.'

7

When Pascual descends the stairs, Campos is leaning on the desk at the side entrance, chatting up the sergeant on duty. The journalist follows him out of the door and Pascual feels like a man pestered by a stray dog. He wants to turn and give him a kick.

Over his shoulder he snarls, 'Have you got anything to tell me? If not, you're wasting your time.'

'I'm working on it. What about you? You've been up there a long time.'

'Serrano gets lonely. He invites me up for tea.'

'If you've been drinking tea you'll be needing an antidote. I'm buying.'

'Not for me, you're not. I'm a busy man.' Pascual is striding down the Via Laietana at speed, hands jammed in his pockets and head down, shouldering through crowds, hoping Campos will peel off and fall by the wayside.

Just off his left shoulder he hears Campos say, 'Did you know that Weiss and Heredia were killed with two different weapons?'

'How would you know that?'

'I've got great sources in that building back there. Did you know that nobody seems to think the two killings are related?'

'Maybe they're not.'

'You don't believe that, do you? And neither does Serrano, though he's playing it close to the chest, as usual. Two completely unrelated killings, nothing to connect them, that's the story. And as you're a witness, your name of course is not being released.'

'And it doesn't have to hit the papers as long as I co-operate with you, is that the game?'

'You do me an injustice.' Panting a little, almost running to keep up, Campos says, 'You know what the two links between these killings are?'

In spite of himself Pascual glances back at Campos. 'Two?'

'Two. First there's you, of course.'

'And the other?'

'The second man killed with Weiss was a gypsy. A habitual petty criminal named Fernández.'

'So?'

'So Heredia was a gypsy. That's a link.'

'There are a lot of gypsies about.'

'Yes. You know a woman named Sara Muñoz? She works at the bar as well, I'm told.'

'I know her.'

'She spent a long time with Serrano this morning.'

'You don't say.' Pascual clenches his teeth.

'Yes. Do you have any idea how she might be involved?'

'Heredia was her manager.'

'Her manager?'

'She's a *cantaora*. He handled her bookings and such. It's natural they'd interview her.'

'A flamenco singer? A gypsy then, no doubt. I have to say, this is getting quite interesting. You and the gypsies.'

Pascual stops dead, causing Campos to ram into him. 'You're on better terms with Serrano than I am. Why are you wasting your time with me?'

Campos grins at him. 'Because neither Serrano nor I have the key. Only you have that, whether you know it or not. And when you find it you and I are going to write a great story.'

Pascual cannot summon the energy to glare and he merely blinks wearily at Campos as people brush past them. 'Dead men make poor sources,' he says. 'Try to keep that in mind.'

Pascual lets gravity dictate his path, crossing to the Rambla dels Caputxins opposite the Boqueria and drifting gently down towards the port beneath the plane trees. It is a fine afternoon, just turning cool as the sun declines. The promenade is crowded, upstream and downstream traffic passing frictionless through each other, ten thousand souls mingling. Pascual is looking at faces in their infinite variety and feeling cut out from the herd again. He will carry the mark of Cain to the grave, he fears.

He is keenly aware that he owes his life to a chance misperception. He cannot, however, face the idea of flight. Pascual has decided that his best option is to keep his head down and keep talking to Serrano.

In the Carrer Nou de la Rambla the sun has made its brief midday appearance and gone, leaving a foretaste of night. Pascual muses on this narrow street's fitness for ambush. He fumbles with his key at the door of the *pensión*.

Upstairs the rotund Senyora Prat in her apron is scowling at the telly, arms folded in judgement. Pascual's entrance rouses her abruptly; with a flailing of arms she comes up off the chair, bleating about telephones. It is so rare for Pascual to receive telephone messages here that for a moment he thinks there must be a mistake. Senyora Prat has disappeared into her chamber. '*Molt urgent*,' she is crying. Who it is that is in urgencies Pascual cannot make out until she emerges to press a slip of paper into his hand.

Lola, he reads, and then a number. The prefix indicates a mobile phone, but the image of Lola toting a mobile is comical. 'I told her you sneak in and out at all hours,' the senyora is pleading. 'I had no way to reach you.'

'*Vale, vale, gracies.*' Pascual refrains from clapping his hand over her mouth and makes for the telephone on the wall. Sara, he is thinking. Catastrophe, hysteria, suicide. He remembers the look on her face as she ran, the morbid history of the household. His hand trembles as he punches in the number.

After two rings a male voice answers with a terse '*Diga.*' Pascual hesitates; has he misdialled?

'I'm calling for Lola. She left a message,' he produces finally.

'Are you Pascual?'

'Yes.'

'Where are you?'

Pascual bristles. 'Look, who the hell are you? It's Lola I want.'

'*Momento.*'

In two seconds Lola is there. 'Pascual. This bloke wants to talk to you,' she says. 'Can you come and talk to him, please?'

'What's going on?'

'You've got to come.' Her voice is calm but full of things suppressed.

'Are you all right?'

'I'm all right. But please come.'

There is a confusion of noises at the other end and the man's voice returns. 'Now. Are you ready to answer my question?'

Running cold inside, Pascual says finally, 'Carrer Nou de la Rambla.'

'Your *pensión*? Be waiting in front in five minutes.'

In the event it is a bad seven minutes before the car appears, creeping slowly, and in that time Pascual has been through all the scenarios, beginning with the notion that he makes a very fine target in the lighted doorway of the *pensión*. Only the memory of the unquiet note in Lola's voice keeps him nailed to the spot. The car is a Honda, dark in colour, and the driver is nothing but a moustache beneath the brim of a panama hat. 'Pascual?' he says through the open window as he draws up at the kerb. Pascual nods and climbs in.

'Where the hell have you been all day?' says the driver, taking shape now as a sizeable villain with an indifferently shaved jaw and merciless eyes.

'If Lola's hurt I'll kill you,' Pascual tells him.

This brings only a puff of laughter. 'You're in no position to make threats. Anyway, I'm just the *chofer*. So keep a civil tongue in your head.' The driver is jocular and at ease, steering through pedestrian traffic with one hand. He turns on to the Ramblas and heads for the port.

Pascual is trying to figure the odds of living out the hour. 'Did you notice the old man at the door of the bar across from my *pensión*?' he says.

'What old man?'

'The one I told to jot down your licence number. If I'm not back tonight, he calls the police.' Pascual wishes desperately he had thought of something like this in time to make it real.

The driver laughs again, showing bright healthy teeth beneath the moustache, and says, 'What's the matter? Worried you're going to wind up at the bottom of the harbour?'

'It's been that kind of day.'

67

'So I hear. Don't worry, the man I'm taking you to see is famous for his hospitality.'

'And who would that be?'

'You ask a lot of questions, you know that?'

'And I get no fucking answers, have you noticed?'

'Where we're going you'll hear all you need to hear.'

'And where's that?'

'Castelldefels. Feel like a seaside holiday?'

Nestled at the base of the hulking Garraf crags, Castelldefels is a formerly sleepy seaside town that is either blessed or cursed with six kilometres of fine sandy beach and proximity to the huge city just up the coast; this jumble of getaway villas behind white walls, shaded by twisted Mediterranean pines, time-share condos, cheap hotels, bistros and nightspots straggling along the Paseo Marítimo could be any of a number of Catalan towns whose charm has been obliterated by the excrescences of mass amusement seeking. As the Honda rolls through empty streets the sun has gone behind the bluffs looming above the town and a chill is setting in with the sea breeze. Pascual has spent the ride puzzling out implications and trying to anticipate.

'You like to sail?' says the driver as he eases into a parking space at the Port Ginesta marina just south of the town proper. Pascual can see a forest of masts beyond the long line of low white buildings fronting on to the marina.

'I get seasick.' Pascual gets out of the car and follows the driver through a short passage to the terrace of a restaurant with a fine view of the rich men's yachts moored in the basin, protected by a high concrete wall. Sitting at a table on the terrace is a weathered unkempt man in a blue turtleneck sweater, head propped on one hand and a cigarette going in the other, staring at an empty glass with the look of a man hoping for a quick death.

'Had an exciting day, then?' says Pascual's chauffeur.

The solitary drinker turns bleary eyes on them. '*Joder.* Where have you been?' Pascual can hear several hours' worth of drinks in his voice.

'Looking for him. Now we've found him, it's time to go. Can you walk?'

'I can steer a fucking boat. Don't you worry about me. *Jefe*, what do I owe you?'

The drunk settles up with a white-shirted waiter who is plainly relieved to see the back of him, and Pascual and his minder follow him to the edge of the dock. He weaves only slightly, apparently invigorated by the fresh sea air. Pascual is beginning to suspect that the reference to sailing was not entirely fantastical and his heart sinks. He follows the two men along the edge of the marina to a point where a small dinghy with an outboard motor is moored. 'You first,' says the driver, waving Pascual to the ladder that descends to the water. 'Don't fall in.'

'He's the one to worry about,' says Pascual, nodding at the drunk. 'And I'm not going in after him.'

'You just worry about yourself, mate,' growls the drunk. The driver laughs. Pascual steps into the boat and sits immediately as it rocks alarmingly. He hangs on as the other two men descend with a marked lack of nautical ease, increasing the wild tossing of the flimsy craft. Things stabilize somewhat as the drunken sailor bullies the motor to life and casts off.

Pascual has been expecting to be ferried across the placid enclosed harbour to one of the boats moored at the far side, but instead the prow is headed out along the breakwater towards the open sea. Pascual shivers. Large expanses of cold water have never been his idea of a hospitable environment. The sea is relatively calm, but such a small boat would toss wildly in a bathtub. Pascual is already yearning for terra firma. They round the end of the breakwater and suddenly the penny drops for Pascual: what better way to dispose of a fresh corpse than to shove it over the side of a small boat? The vision is so clear that Pascual gets the full adrenaline treatment, the electrifying chemical surge that sets his heart thumping. The other two are being careful not to look at him; how has he let them lure him out here? He has stiffened and started to judge swimming distances when the man in the hat stretches out his hand, pointing.

In spite of himself Pascual looks, and there it is, revealed now as they clear the marina, a sleek white motor yacht riding at anchor a few hundred metres out. 'That's where we're going,' says the chauffeur, one hand clapped on top of his panama to keep it from blowing away.

'Is that where the girl is?'

'Unless she can swim a lot better than I can.'

Pascual sits in ghastly indecision as they bump over the waves, the yacht drawing closer and the comfort of the shore receding. The appearance of the yacht lends credibility to the pretext upon which he was lured on to the water, and of course he cannot abandon Lola. His aversion to cold water proves to be the deciding factor; if he leapt over the side they would only shoot him anyway, he decides, floundering in the frigid sea.

The boat is gleaming white, a good thirty metres long with a flybridge riding high on top and walk-around sidedecks, a serious sea-going boat. As they draw near Pascual strains to read the name on the stern. He can just make out *María Isabel – Puerto Banús*. He has to think for a moment where Puerto Banús is; someone has come a long way, half-way around the Iberian peninsula from the Costa del Sol.

Drunk or not, the sailor brings them smartly up at the stern of the yacht and makes fast. He steps a little unsteadily on to a narrow platform just above the water and thence up and over the stern bulwark with the aid of a short ladder. Pascual follows. 'So much for the lookout,' the panama hat says, thumping on to the deck after him. 'We could board her with cutlasses drawn and no-body'd be the wiser.'

'Lazy bastards,' growls the sailor. 'They're in there drinking down the liquor stocks again. Or maybe the girl's entertaining them down in the stateroom, eh?' He winks and leers in classic fashion, making for a steep companionway leading up from the small afterdeck.

Pascual spins him with a hand on the shoulder and hauls him up short with double handfuls of turtleneck sweater. 'If anybody's laid a hand on her I'll split your fucking skull.'

'You're not fast enough,' says the man in the panama hat. Pascual feels the muzzle of a pistol at his temple. He sends the sailor staggering backwards against a bulkhead. 'Nobody's hurt her,' says the voice in his ear. 'Now mind your manners.'

The drunk is in no shape to return the glare Pascual is giving him and he gives up quickly. Pascual watches as he climbs the companionway. 'After you,' says the man in the hat, stashing the pistol inside his jacket and giving Pascual a shove. Pascual grasps the rail and climbs. At the top he steps on to the main deck of the boat, roofed but open to the stern; to the right is a curving stairway to the flying bridge above and ahead is a door leading to the enclosed deckhouse. The sailor is opening the door, calling out in an aggressive tone. Near at hand are padded chairs, a table bearing ashtrays and a couple of glasses; a pleasant place to sit and count one's money while tossing placidly at anchor off Portofino or St Tropez. The sailor is hustling back towards him now, blanched and wide-eyed and instantly sober, and Pascual has noted something else in a glimpse through the door: a motionless hand on a carpeted deck. He stands frozen just long enough for the sailor to knock him against the rail, and by the time he has recovered his balance, it is too late.

'*Están muertos*,' is all the explanation the sailor sees fit to give, tearing feverishly at the line.

'What?'

'Dead, all of them.' The drunk tumbles into the dinghy, the line dropping into the water.

'*Mierda*.' The other man shoots Pascual a brief look and turns to the rail.

'Wait!' Pascual cries. 'What about the girl?'

'She's all yours,' says the man in the hat. He has one leg up on the rail, but now he wheels as Pascual leaps down the companion-way. He delivers a pile-driver blow to Pascual's face that instantly severs his connection with reality and replaces thoughts of escape with intense cranial pain, chronological dislocation and specta-cular if confusing visual phenomena. The agonizing jar as Pascual hits the deck is his first reminder of the world outside his head. He does not actually lose consciousness, but by the time he is able to haul himself up and look over the stern, the little dinghy is twenty metres away and making madly for shore with an angry high-pitched whine. A panama hat flies off in the wind and plops into the waves. Pascual draws breath to scream insults, but he cuts off the effort abruptly because it sends a sharp pain from the crown of his head to the nape of his neck. He hears himself groan raggedly as he slides to a sitting position, back against the bulwark.

When he is capable of standing, several centuries later, the sky is going a deep blue above him and the air is growing cool. The boat is still rising and falling very gently on the offshore swell and there

71

is nothing to hear but the cries of gulls and the vast murmur of air and sea. On land, tantalizingly near, Castelldefels sprawls mute and undisturbed, rising on to the hills beyond its beach; there are no sirens, no helicopters, no men–of–war bearing down with loudspeakers blaring. Most crucially there are no sounds of continuing homicidal activity aboard the boat. Pascual lurches to the companionway and hangs on to the rail for dear life, pain beginning to cede to nausea. Here on the afterdeck there is no salvation, nothing at all that might bear him to shore or allow him to call for help. One way or another, he is going to have to climb this ladder and see what horrors await him.

His psyche in screaming rebellion, Pascual clambers back up the companionway. He stops in the doorway and stares dumbly at the scene in the deckhouse. On the top step but one of a curving flight of stairs leading below, a man is sitting, his head and shoulders lolling back against the bulkhead, left hand trailing on the carpet. He wears a startled expression, bared teeth and open eyes, frozen in alarm. As Pascual approaches he can see the glistening crimson mess in the man's lap. An automatic lies next to his right hand on the third step down.

Pascual knows he must go below. He is pleading silently with powers he does not even believe in for miracles he knows are impossible. The dead man has thoughtlessly bled on the steps, and Pascual has trouble keeping his shoes clean as he picks his way past, clinging to the rail. He descends into a galley larger than many kitchens he has seen on land. There are glasses in the sink and an array of empty bottles next to it, but there are no bodies. A door at the bow end yields at the turn of the handle and Pascual looks into a compartment that narrows with the tapering of the hull. Crew quarters, evidently, with two bunks stacked on the starboard side and lockers opposite, boots on the floor and a smell of unwashed laundry. Pascual hurries back through the galley. Down a short flight of steps leading aft is a cramped hallway with three doors opening off it. In the passage lies another man in a vast extravagant spill of blood, pooling on the deck. Here the smell of cordite is strong. He steps carefully over the body. At the stern end of the corridor a door stands half-open and Pascual needs only a gentle shove with his foot to reveal a spacious stateroom with teak panelling and rumpled bedclothes. Something else rumpled lies jammed between the bed and the base of the wall. Pascual moves far enough into the room to identify it as a man who is beyond caring about the discomfort of his position. There is a bald pate and eyes nearly closed and a double chin sunk into a pool of blood already congealing on a hairy chest bared by an open shirt. Pascual backs out fast. He feels a powerful urge to charge up the stairs regardless of what he may step in and fling himself directly over the side, but there are doors remaining to be opened. On one side of the hall are the heads: toilet and sink and shower stall jammed together. Across from it is a cabin, smaller than the main stateroom but still ample; there is room for twin berths and the same dark polished wood all round, dimly visible in the light coming in through the small portholes at eye-level. The room is empty and Pascual stands in confusion; he would love to believe in miracles, but he cannot think why anyone would lie to him about Lola being here. At his wit's end he can think of nothing better to do than the obvious.

'Lola,' he calls out. There is no answer and after three seconds Pascual is ready at last to abandon ship. He is rocking on his heels when there is something, just audible, or maybe not quite, a mere tremor in some medium he cannot identify, just enough to make him stop. He scans and fixes on the narrow closet door before him. A step and he is there, wrenching at the brass handle. The door swings open and all he can see is clothing, hung neatly on a bar. He must tear apart the shirts and trousers before he finds Lola, huddled in foetal position on the floor, unmoving, her haunted eyes just visible above her knuckles the only sign she is alive.

8

'There's got to be a telephone, a radio, something.' Pascual is scanning the space-age array of controls on the console on the main bridge, making sense of nothing. He has propped Lola against the bulkhead behind him after shepherding her up the spiral stair through the carnage. She has said nothing, not a word since he pulled her out of the closet, though her fingers dug painfully into his arm at the sight of the dead men. Pascual has found a handset, but can raise no sound from it, jabbing at buttons. 'We'll call the police,' he says. 'They'll come and take us off of this thing.'

'No.' At the sound of her voice Pascual wheels to see her steadier on her feet but with her hands held on either side of her face like blinkers, shielding her eyes from unpleasant views or perhaps an impending beating. She looks like a child whose kitten has just been crushed by a lorry.

'What do you mean, no? Lola, it's a fucking abattoir. We have to talk to the police.'

Lola gazes at him. The fuzz on her skull is matted and ruffled and her eyes are hollow with dread. 'How did you get here?' she says, her eyes narrowing a little.

'They brought me out in a boat. What do you think? They clubbed me and ran when they saw the bodies. How did you get here?'

She blinks at him. 'They didn't tell you?'

'They didn't tell me a fucking thing. You've got a lot of explaining to do. Get used to the idea, Lola. You're going to be spending a lot of time with policemen in the next day or two.'

74

'But I didn't see a thing. They shoved me in that room and I hid when I heard the shots.'

'They still need to talk to you. What are you afraid of?'

He sees something happen in Lola's eyes and before he can react she ducks through the doorway towards the stern. Pascual is frozen with surprise for an instant and then rams his thigh painfully into the captain's chair in going after her, and by the time he has emerged from the deckhouse she is disappearing down the companionway to the afterdeck. He reaches the top of the companionway in time to see her slip over the starboard rail into the sea.

Pascual shouts her name and leaps the metre and a half down on to the afterdeck. Lola is thrashing in the water, only her head visible, gasping. 'Give me your hand,' says Pascual, leaning over the rail, stretching to the limit. 'Lola! Give me your hand.'

'Leave me alone.' Lola finds breath for the words and manages two or three strong strokes away from the boat. She has gone in on the seaward side, shielded from view on land. '*You* talk to the police.' She displays a very competent side stroke, putting more distance between her and the boat, and Pascual's panic abates; at least she is not about to drown.

'What are you doing?' he cries.

'Swimming to shore.' Lola is on her back now, holding her own in the chilly water, looking saner than she has since he found her. 'Can't you swim?' she calls.

'You're mad.'

'*Adios, pues.*' She twists and plunges, fighting through the swell in a crawl stroke.

'Wait!' Pascual can swim but knows that cold water and fatigue will defeat all but the most hardened athletes. 'Give me a minute to find something we can hang on to.' Lola is rounding the stern now, arms wheeling, drawing breath with each stroke. Pascual looks shoreward; what was a quick trip in the motor dinghy looks like a thousand miles for the indifferent swimmer he is. He looks wildly about the empty afterdeck and then flings himself up the companionway. Somewhere there must be a life preserver, an inflatable raft, an empty barrel, something that will float.

The best he can do is a cluster of life jackets in a locker in the deckhouse. By the time he has grabbed a handful and returned to

75

the afterdeck, he has to scan the water for agonizing seconds before he spots Lola, a speck of flotsam on the foam-flecked billows. He can see her arms working for a moment and then she disappears, sliding down the trough of a wave. Pascual curses eloquently and bitterly. He is considering letting the silly bitch swim and trying to hail a passing pleasure boat when it occurs to him that Lola ought to have bobbed up again by now. Alarm grows as the seconds tick off and suddenly there is no longer any question of what to do: here he stands with a handful of life jackets, and Lola is out there in the cold, cold sea, struggling. 'Lola!' he screams, tottering on the rail.

Pascual does not even notice the cold past the first shock of entry; he splashes wildly, quickly abandoning the attempt to hold on to more than a single life jacket, and strikes out for shore, kicking desperately. He quickly finds that a life jacket is not made to aid swimming, but he is afraid to let go. He manages a primitive one-handed doggy paddle which plunges his face into the water with annoying regularity. With his head just above water he can see nothing at all of Lola, if she is still there; after a couple of minutes his panting impedes his sobbing attempts to call her name, and finally it is all he can do to breathe more air than water and keep himself from going under once too often.

'What was I going to do, fire up the engines and take her into the marina? You might as well ask me to fly a 747,' says Pascual. He is sequestered with Serrano in the interview room while out in the main office coffee is drunk and banter is exchanged. Pascual rests his face on his hands, prey to a vile headache and worse. He has survived hypothermia, exhaustion and ingestion of seawater; he has come through two bouts of police interrogation, a confrontation with officious physicians, and an agonizing midnight telephone conversation with Pilar, but the memory of his last sight of Lola is driving a stake through his heart. If this is what the world is going to feel like from now on, Pascual would rather die.

'A pity you didn't. We might still have our witness.' Serrano puts match to cigarette and scowls through the smoke at Pascual.

'She was more than a witness. She was my friend.'

Serrano smokes in silence for a while and says in a softer tone, 'They haven't found a body yet. Until they do, there's hope.'

Pascual appreciates the attempt, but does not believe it for an instant. 'Could I have a cigarette?'

Serrano throws him the packet and the box of matches. 'Now, I know you went through it with the Mossos down in Castelldefels, but I want you to tell me exactly what you saw on the boat.'

'I saw three dead men.' Pascual labours over the cigarette with clumsy fingers. 'One on the stairway to the lower deck. I think he'd been coming up from below. He had a gun lying near him. I don't know if he'd managed to get off any shots. I didn't see any bullet holes, no smashed windows or anything, no damage except to the two on the floor.'

'And the others?'

'Both below, one in a passage and one in a stateroom.'

'And the girl.'

Pascual nods. 'Hidden in a closet.'

'And who was she?'

'A girl named Lola, a friend of the Sara Muñoz you've already talked to.'

'And how does she come into it?'

'That's how they found me. Somehow they got hold of her and made her phone me. They might have grabbed her off the street. She sells her drawings on the Ramblas or in front of the cathedral and she'd be easy to find.'

Serrano nods. 'You saw no other boats in the vicinity?'

The last thing on earth Pascual is concerned about today is dead villains, but he makes an effort. 'I have a vague impression there were others – there are always boats about off a place like Castelldefels. But I don't remember one nearby.'

Serrano gives him a long, impenetrable look. 'Do you have any conception of what's happening around you? You're a wonder of nature.'

Stung in spite of himself, Pascual snarls. 'I haven't done a thing. Except exist.'

'That seems to be all your role requires. This time your careless occupation of space seems really to have stirred things up. The boat's tied up at Castelldefels with forensic teams swarming all over it and half the media crews in Spain milling on the quay. There's another magistrate down there smelling headlines and you are going to have to talk to him.'

77

Pascual finds he cares very little. By way of refuge from thinking about Lola he tries to regain an interest in his own fate. 'Have they identified the victims yet?' he manages.

'That I don't know,' says Serrano, reaching for the phone, 'but the type of person who travels on a yacht like that doesn't usually die in anonymity. It should be very interesting.'

'Yes,' says Pascual. 'I'm sure it will be.'

The magistrate in charge of the Castelldefels inquiry is the very model of a modern *juez de instrucción*, nicely turned out in a blue blazer and thin black tie, lean and intent. His name is Espinoza and Pascual can tell by his demeanour that he is keenly aware that the case of his career has just landed in his lap. Pascual has been walked painstakingly through the same story he gave Serrano. 'You seem to be the centre of attention suddenly,' says Espinoza.

'I've done nothing but mind my own business.'

'That seems to be a fairly dangerous proposition. Inspector Serrano has filled me in on your background.'

'What do you want me to do? I'm co-operating with you.'

'Very well. Any idea who that is on that boat?'

'None. I wasn't given a name. You can look up the registration, can't you?'

'Of course.' Espinoza gives him a keen look. 'Did you see what their home port was?'

'Puerto Banús. That's next to Marbella, isn't it? From what I understand there's quite a roster of villains down there to choose from.'

'Yes. Well, I expect I'll be talking to you again. Meanwhile I'll leave you in the competent hands of Inspector Serrano.'

The man with the competent hands drifts into the vacuum left in the interview room by the departure of Espinoza and his small retinue of scribes and counsellors. Pascual has been in this room or in a cell four floors down for eight hours. Empty cups and the remains of a *bocadillo* on greasy paper litter the desk. 'So who's the dead man?' Pascual says.

Serrano gives him a blank look. 'It's not my case. I'm not the man to ask.'

'What's Marbella got to do with it? Your judge was dropping some heavy hints.'

'You'll have to ask him, I'm afraid.'

Pascual shrugs. 'So am I free to go?'

Serrano makes a rueful face. 'Ah no, I'm afraid not. You see, we're going to have to hold you until somebody comes along who can prove you didn't kill those men,' he shrugs, 'or until we prove you did. We've got seventy-two hours to do it.'

Pascual gapes at him. 'Why in God's name would I be sitting here if I'd killed them? I'd be in France or Morocco by now.'

'It's happened,' says Serrano. 'People report crimes they've committed all the time. On the theory that nobody will expect them to do so, I suppose. Or to protect someone else. I've seen it many times.'

'But I've got two witnesses who can say they were dead when we got there.'

'Ah, that's the problem, isn't it? You don't have them. They've vanished. We've only your word that you found the dirty work already done. You and your phantom in the panama hat could perfectly well have done it yourselves, pitched the weapons into the sea and got your stories straight before splitting up. Even your poor drowned girl is a phantom. Nobody else saw her.'

Pascual goggles at him. 'Why would I invent her?'

'To explain why you went out to the boat. The damsel in distress is always a good one.'

'You can't possibly think I did it.'

Serrano gives an exaggerated look of affronted dignity, palms raised. 'And you can't possibly think I could release you.'

Pascual has no riposte to this and merely sags lower on his chair. 'Is it time for me to request a lawyer?'

'It might be. But before you get a lawyer in here and he tells you to stitch your lips shut, you might wish to show your good faith by helping me with my inquiries a little further.'

Pascual considers this and finds that like everything else at the moment, the choice makes little difference to him. With a shrug he says, 'What do you want to know?'

Serrano reaches into a file he has been holding and pulls out a sheet of paper. 'Have you ever seen this man before?' He tosses the paper on the desk in front of Pascual. It is a single sheet with the photo of a man in the upper right corner, blank elsewhere, obviously a photocopy made with the information on the rest of the original blocked out. The man in the photo is balding, portly, middle-aged, a Mediterranean type, with the dazed look of a man in a police mug shot. There is something familiar about the face and it takes Pascual only a few seconds to put his finger on it. 'I think I saw him dead last night. In the stateroom.'

'Very good. Never seen him before last night?'

There is something else, the real reason the face set some string throbbing far in the back of Pascual's mind. Pennies drop and cylinders click into place. Pascual lays the paper on the desk. 'Yes. A long time ago.'

'Where?'

Pascual looks up at Serrano, standing impassive above him. 'Frankfurt, I think. 1988.'

9

'I've spent years trying to forget these things. After I was debriefed I just tried to put it all out of my mind. It's going to be hard to reconstruct it.' Pascual scratches at the stubble on his cheeks, rubs vigorously at his eyes.

'Just tell me what you can dredge up.' Serrano is lounging on his chair across the desk from him, looking like a *catedrático* putting an ill-prepared student through his paces. 'Who was he, for starters?'

Pascual squeezes his eyes shut, feeling for synapses he hoped had atrophied for ever. 'I think he was called Rafik.'

Frankfurt, 1988. Pascual's recollection of the period is hazy: a jumble of furtive comings and goings, forged papers and third-rate eastern bloc airlines, shabby hotel rooms and empty safe houses in dreary streets. He remembers endless stress and corrosive solitude. He was already doubting, already beginning to sense that the endeavour he had devoted half a decade to was a malicious juvenile fantasy. He was running on inertia, beginning to yearn for connection with the masses he had despised. He remembers a pretty girl on a park bench, his bitter grief as she walked away, realizing how much of his life he had squandered.

He remembers the man behind the desk in the cluttered office of a garage in a desolate industrial zone near the river. Out on the shopfloor someone was welding, someone else hammering; banter in Turkish was shouted above the noise. Rafik was an Arab, Lebanese from his accent, Beiruti probably; one did not make small talk in such situations but after three years based in

Damascus Pascual's skills in colloquial Levantine were at their height. He remembers Rafik's compliments on his prowess. '*Ya salaam*. So few foreigners bother to learn it.' A smallish man, bald and moustachioed, on the corpulent side with a round belly straining at his pullover: a jolly restaurateur or somebody's favourite uncle but for the eyes full of irony and contempt.

First there was an errand to run: Pascual can see Rafik shoving a suitcase across the desk towards him. 'You get the key when you get to Geneva. Somebody will call you at the hotel. If you don't show up this evening, we come looking for you.' He remembers half a day's drive in a car Rafik assured him was not stolen, another hotel. Pascual remembers the lake, fractured sheets of ice quiescent under a grey sky. He remembers the reverent hush with which the two officials in the private conference room handled the bundled stacks of hundred-dollar bills. Operational funds, Pascual has always assumed, sustenance for one of the teams of thugs whose homicidal campaigns it was his job to facilitate, though at the time he wondered at the quantity: enough to spread mayhem across half Europe.

The second phase of the operation involved setting up safe houses. Pascual had money and papers and an idea of where in Frankfurt's immigrant quarters a man might swing a quick deal for a shabby tenement room, few questions asked. He was long accustomed to the work and had his own special criteria for house-hunting, quite apart from adequate hot water and storage space: absentee or elderly landlords, clear views and access to escape routes. The men who would ultimately occupy the flat were unknown to him. Pascual neither knew nor wanted to know what would be done inside; the effort of denial was already costing him precious psychic energy.

Rafik was the local boss of this intrigue and Pascual reported to him after each step, meeting in dingy smoke-filled bars or, after taking pains to check that his back was clear, slipping into the garage near the river and nodding at the Turks as he made his way back to the office. It did not take Pascual long to suss out what was happening there: the Lebanese connection, bodywork going on in dark corners of the shop and cars moving in and out at odd hours all added up to one thing. Pascual's puritan instincts were offended, but this was one more thing not to question; he was still clinging desperately to the notion that all this dirty business was in the service of a better world somewhere down the road. It would take him another year to decide that he wanted no part of a world created by people like Rafik.

What Pascual remembers principally about Frankfurt is the sense of vulnerability gnawing at his nerves. By this phase of his career his instincts for self-preservation were honed to a knife edge; with freedom and maybe life itself depending on his awareness, he moved through each day on high alert, the effort of constant observation, back-checking and furtive manoeuvres leaving him exhausted and unable to sleep, peering out past blinds in darkened rooms.

It was his professional paranoia that prevented disaster this time, one of half a dozen narrow escapes in his career. Pascual knew better than to trust anyone, fully aware of the possibilities of infiltration, co-optation and naked treachery inherent in his trade. He had made it routine practice to take nothing at face value, double-check everything, and slip an ace up his sleeve whenever possible. Thus it was that he made a minor hobby of tailing Rafik in the long stretches of idleness involved in this or any operation, making good use of the cars he was lent from the garage to facilitate his movements. He quickly identified Rafik's favourite Sachsenhausen watering holes and a flat near the university that appeared to house a mistress, but Rafik's own quarters remained a mystery. One afternoon the Lebanese began to display all the signs of a man being cautious about his back, but his tradecraft was sloppy and with the help of a couple of inspired guesses Pascual managed to stick close enough to see him turn into the gate of a house in Offenbach.

The trip wire was the second suitcase. Seeing it on Rafik's desk he felt ice in the stomach; he had grown used to hauling cash about the continent, but baggage like this made border crossings fraught with stress. The instructions, however, were easy. 'Get this to the man in Bockenheim. He's expecting you, but you'll need to ring three short and one long.' This was the first indication that the safe house had been occupied. Rafik tossed him the keys to a battered BMW sedan and Pascual loaded the suitcase into the boot. It was heavy enough to be a fortune in drug-tainted dollars, but Pascual wondered about the destination;

for all he knew it could also hold enough morphine base to kill every junkie from Amsterdam to Madrid. His not to wonder why, he cruised the streets under a leaden sky with great attention to his mirrors, making his way cautiously through streets where forlorn *Gastarbeiter* clustered at the corners, collars turned up against the cold.

His sensors on high alert, he spotted the men in the parked car just shy of the safe house and drove on past, knowing they could be innocuous but not willing to bet on it. He found a place to stash the car three streets over and walked back, hair rising on his neck, for a casual stroll past, hands in his pockets. This pass set the alarms screaming even before he came in sight of the flat; too many closed vans at the kerb. Pascual kept on walking. His own tradecraft was solid, learned not from intelligence professionals but from their quarry: sound, battle-tested stratagems acquired from people who had survived in underground Europe for years.

Doubling back to the car, he made snap decisions: it was just possibly safe to drive the thing back to the garage and opt out of further manoeuvres. For safety's sake he stopped half-way and bought cigarettes, watching from inside the shop for anyone pulling over at a discreet distance behind him.

On his first pass he could see the garage was deserted; he saw the padlock on the door, the lights extinguished behind filthy windows. His foot grew heavy on the accelerator; when the GHQ shuts down the situation has reached critical. Behind him a blue Opel pulled away from the kerb. Beginning to sweat, he drove, his attention to the mirrors nearly causing him to leave a fatality or two in his wake. After a few turns the blue Opel was no longer with him, but that was no guarantee he was clear; the BMW had become a liability. He rounded the corner past the first U-bahn station he found and dropped the car quite illegally at a bus stop. He gave three seconds' thought to the suitcase, thinking Rafik could salvage the bleeding thing himself if he was not in jail by nightfall, but he could still hear Rafik saying *we come looking for you* and tried to imagine himself explaining the loss of twenty kilos of banknotes or pure heroin to the people he had to report to. He hauled the suitcase out of the boot and put distance between himself and the car; after a minute's observation of traffic from the shelter of a news kiosk he ducked down into the U-bahn.

He came out at the Hauptbahnhof and walked into the station, then out again to the ṭaxi stand. It was growing dark. He had no good options but the least bad was the house in Offenbach. He had not noted the address but could describe the route to the driver; his sense of direction was a survival skill. He had the driver cruise down the street slowly in the dusk, pretending to look for the right house; when he was satisfied that there were no GSG 9 commando teams lurking in the trees he had the driver drop him at the next-to-last house and paid him off. It was a leafy street of detached houses behind stone walls. Pascual walked, lugging the suitcase, around a bend. There was a lane that ran between head-high walls behind the gardens of the houses he had passed, and Pascual turned into it and started counting houses. When he reached the right one he heaved the suitcase over the wall and then pulled himself up and over. He dropped into a small garden shaded by an oak and leading to the back of a squat villa with light showing inside. There was a shed in the angle of the wall, unlocked, and Pascual left the suitcase there before going to tap on the back door of the house and then duck into the shadows beneath the tree.

The man who came to the door was prudent. He opened the door and stood back in a darkened hall, barely visible, until Pascual called out gently, '*Wayn Rafiq?*' It was the best water-testing stratagem he could think of and it gave results; the man went away and in a few seconds Rafik appeared in the doorway, calling back in Arabic, 'Who's there?'

Inside, nobody was happy to see him. Pascual's explanation of how he had found the house caused a moment of distinct tension between Rafik and the other man. This one was somewhere in his forties, bearded with his hair gone on top except for a tuft in the middle, and his displeasure was clear. He stood glaring at Pascual in the lamplight, arms folded, the householder confronted with unwanted guests. He was no Arab, though his German had a very faint accent that could have been just about anything; Pascual devoted little thought to it, having more pressing matters on his mind. 'There are *polizei* all over Bocken-heim,' he said.

Rafik was clearly shaken, but fighting to maintain his bravado. 'Don't worry, we got the boys out in time. Where's the suitcase?'

'In the garden shed. What the hell happened?'

Rafik and the bearded man traded a look and the bearded man headed for the back, moving slowly. 'Never mind. How did you get here?'

As Pascual was giving a précis of his movements the bearded man came in with the suitcase and set it gently on the floor. The look he gave Rafik was murderous, aided by his natural physiognomy: dark eyebrows with a slight upturn at the ends gave him a vaguely Satanic look despite his buttoned cardigan and fraying house slippers. Pascual was revising his assumptions; this was not Rafik's house but the other man's and their host was getting more than he had bargained for.

'We've got to get over a border,' said Rafik. 'He can drive us.'

'What about this?' said the bearded man, cocking a thumb at the suitcase.

'I'll phone you,' said Rafik. 'I'll need a couple of days to make arrangements.'

Pascual was not particularly concerned about Rafik's relations with his civilian dupes except in so far as they affected his survival odds. He observed the tersely suppressed clash of wills that followed, slumped on his chair. When the bearded man sullenly dragged the suitcase out of the room Pascual reverted to Arabic, murmuring, 'He's a weak link. He'll crack if there's any pressure.'

He remembers Rafik smiling his superior smile. 'Oh, no. That's one man we don't have to worry about.'

It was decided that a quick stop at Pascual's hotel was a good risk. Calling police attention to a vanished guest was never a good idea, not to mention abandoning physical traces like clothing purchased in Damascus. His abrupt departure caused only mild surprise at the desk and he was cheerfully charged for the coming night. The drive south was made mostly in silence in the bearded man's Mercedes, the world reduced to the firefly dance of tail lights on the autobahn. Rafik had ways and means in Strasbourg but could offer Pascual nothing; in any event Pascual wanted nothing more than to be quit of Rafik. They crossed the brooding Rhine at Kehl without incident and Pascual was ejected on to a dreary Strasbourg street without so much as a handshake. He watched the Mercedes roll away, too weary for resentment and thinking only of the need to find another room, arrange more transport, report once again to men with suspicion in their eyes in shabby Damascus offices. The idea of flight was beginning to germinate at the back of his head, but it would take another year to blossom. In three months he would be back in Frankfurt on another pointless intrigue, but he never saw Rafik or the bearded man again.

Pascual stubs out his cigarette, eyes stinging from smoke and fatigue. 'We all went by false names. Rafik might have been his real first name, but even that's long odds. You get used to changing names the way you change socks.'

Serrano nods. He looks at Pascual for a long moment, hands clasped behind his head, musing. 'I wonder if we don't know his real name,' he says finally.

There is a rap on the glass that separates the interview room from the office and a man is holding up a telephone receiver and motioning to Serrano. He goes to take the call; through the window Pascual watches him speak at length, hang up and exchange a few words with a colleague and then wander to a desk, where he opens a drawer and takes out a newspaper. He comes back into the interview room and tosses it on the desk in front of Pascual. 'Did you see this?'

The paper is *El País* from two days ago and in the lower right-hand quarter of the front page a headline reads *Tiroteo en un club de Marbella*. Pascual scans. 'I haven't been paying much attention to the papers. What happened?'

'Somebody tried to kill one of Marbella's leading citizens last Saturday night. There was a shootout and a bodyguard was killed, along with one of the attackers. After talking to the police, the target disappeared.'

Pascual's eye has halted on the name. 'Hussein Ilmeddin,' he reads aloud. He stares at nothing for a moment, prey to an impression of great wheels turning, dragging him into the mechanism. He shoves the paper away. 'The identification's definite, is it?'

'As definite as it can be. The mobile phone number you called is registered to him. The boat belongs to a friend of his. The word is they sailed in the wee hours of Sunday morning, a few hours after the shooting and about thirty-six hours before they were first spotted off Castelldefels. They'd just have time to make it, sailing non-stop.'

'Who was he?'

'A gangster, some people said. A very wealthy man by all accounts.' Serrano eases back on his chair, letting out a sigh. 'Must be a funny place, Marbella. The fact that a crusading magistrate has been trying to indict him doesn't seem to have affected his standing in the community.'

'From what I've heard that would put him in pretty good company down there. What was the magistrate after him for?'

'Specifically, accessory to homicide. He allegedly supplied the weapon for a killing in Madrid a number of years ago, though the original witness has recanted and others have shown a frustrating tendency to disappear. Hence the difficulty in indicting him. But the broader agenda was to bring him to heel for his role in keeping Europe amply supplied with Middle Eastern heroin. There's some question as to how a Lebanese auto mechanic who emigrated to France in the late sixties made enough money to buy himself a villa in Marbella. There are also, strangely enough, whispers of involvement in terrorism, dating back to days when you were still . . . active.'

Pascual nods once, wearily. 'So we've found Rafik.'

'Perhaps.' Serrano folds the newspaper and slowly rolls it into a club. 'We've also found your drunken sailor.'

'What?'

'Your witness. He made it as far as Tarragona, trying to hitch-hike back to Marbella apparently. Then he got impatient and tried to steal a car. They had him in their *comisaría* when we put out the bulletin on him. Espinoza's just had an intimate talk with him. A bloke named Padilla, sober now, and eager to please. He must be hoping for a break on the car theft because he's talking so fast we can hardly keep up.' Serrano taps on his leg with the rolled-up paper. 'You seem to be telling the truth.'

Sullenly, Pascual says, 'Disappointed?'

'Disappointment would indicate the existence of bias.' Serrano pauses. 'Where are you planning to sleep tonight?'

Startled, Pascual says, 'You're not holding me?'

'Why? Padilla confirms your story in every detail. You've committed no crime, have you?'

Pascual finds this nonchalance highly suspicious. 'Espinoza said he'd be wanting to talk to me again.'

'He's not going to have the chance, I'm afraid.'

'Why?'

'The crusading magistrate I mentioned? Perhaps you've heard of him, the illustrious Pinzón of the Audiencia Nacional. The word has come down from Madrid that he's insisting on taking over the case. Weiss's as well, as it must certainly be related. He seems to feel some sort of proprietary right to Ilmeddin, and he pulls a lot of weight. So Espinoza's out, and he's not happy about it. He's dumped the file in my lap until our eminence gets around to demanding it. God knows when that will be, the burdens of power being what they are. You're a material witness and we may have to pack you off to Madrid at some point, but I'm not sure what to do with you in the meantime. Nobody's given me any orders about protective custody and I don't have the manpower at my disposal to babysit witnesses on my own authority. Are you planning to do a bunk?'

'You think I'd tell you if I were?'

Serrano's head is tilted again, the philosopher pondering. 'I think if you were going to run you'd have run by now. I think the fact that you're sitting here means you plan to stick it out. Don't prove me wrong.'

Pascual shrugs. 'I'm not sure where I'd go, anyway.'

'Well, you might want to steer clear of your usual haunts for a while. Find a hotel room or a friend with a spare bed and leave me a number where I can reach you. So far we've kept you out of the papers precisely because you are a material witness. But if you do run, I'll see that your name and face get into every newspaper in Europe and I don't think you want that.'

'No. I don't want that.'

Serrano rises and stands looking down at him. 'You'd be surprised at how many people fail to run and hide when it would save them a beating, save their lives maybe. And they all say the same. Where would I go? Most people will risk everything to go on clinging to the life they've known.'

Pascual ponders in turn. 'It's all I've got.'

89

IO

Pascual creeps warily out of the Jefatura into the deepening gloom of evening. 'Don't worry,' says a voice at his shoulder. 'The others swallowed everything the press officer gave them and went off to meet deadlines.' Campos grins at him, white teeth and spectacles gleaming in the shadows.

'Don't you have a deadline to meet?'

'I've already filed a story. This is overtime. And my compensation is the pleasure of having a drink with my favourite source.'

Pascual, weakened by hunger and thirst, finds no strength to resist. In addition he is grateful for anything that postpones the visit he must make to the flat in Carrer Princesa. 'I'll bet you can tell me all about the dead man,' he says a minute later over the din of a bar in Laietana at the height of the early-evening rush.

Campos shoves money across the bar as their beers arrive. 'Hussein Ilmeddin. Lebanese, fifty or so, filthy rich reputedly because of his control of one of the major heroin routes from the Bekáa into Europe back in the seventies and eighties. Long reputed to have close ties to the Syrian regime.'

Pascual drains half the glass. 'You don't run heroin out of the Bekáa without the blessing of the people who run Lebanon. How did he wind up in Marbella?'

Campos's eyes are alive with the fervour of the enthusiast. 'He had to flee Germany in the late eighties because the Germans finally broke up his networks. He'd owned a house in Marbella for some time and he went to earth there. The Germans have made some attempts to extradite him, but nothing ever comes of it. Witnesses tend to die or recant and the word is he's got protection in obscure circles in Madrid. Probably a simple case of blackmail, as he may know too much about some of the deals that were struck back when your lot was running around perpetrating outrages at every turn. Then along came Anselmo Pinzón. He'd made a name for himself taking on the high and mighty and he was willing to risk irritating people. All it did was precipitate some murky infighting in Madrid, but Ilmeddin was supposedly feeling the net closing for the first time. In any event he fitted right in down there in Marbella, with Kashoggi and that jet-set lot. Nothing like a complaisant local administration to encourage the more colourful type of international crook to call a place home. The nightlife scene in Marbella is quite extraordinary, by all accounts.'

'One hears interesting things.'

'Yes. You have to be careful whose elbow you jostle at the bar, they say. According to the reports, Ilmeddin had his usual small army with him the other night. He must hire good people because the word is that the bodyguard shot first. He spotted a fellow on his way back from the toilet who seemed a little too interested in Ilmeddin. The bodyguard bagged him when he came up with a gun, but he wasn't alone – a second man popped up out of nowhere and killed the bodyguard. He would have killed Ilmeddin too if another of his men hadn't shoved him under the table while a third returned fire. It was quite a little dust up, they say, with a full-fledged panic ensuing, screaming girls and toppled tables and all. The second attacker got away, so the score was tied at one apiece when all was said and done. The dead *sicario* had no papers whatsoever, but they're checking his prints. A good professional hit team, it seems, who just happened to meet their match that evening. The telly showed images of the place afterwards. Lots of glass lying about, mirrors shot to hell, blood all over the nice upholstery. Ilmeddin hung about long enough to talk to the police – even he couldn't just leave a generous tip and apologize for the mess – but then he vanished. And now we know how.'

'A lot of good it did him.'

'Yes. And that's the intriguing part, isn't it? How did the killers find him?'

'And how did he find me? I have to say, that's even more intriguing to me personally.'

Campos reaches for his beer. 'Somebody's desperate, wouldn't you say?'

Pascual sets down his glass and catches sight of himself in the mirror behind the bar, haggard and hollow-eyed. 'Or perhaps just used to getting his own way.'

Joselito sticks his head out of the *conserje*'s office under the stairs before Pascual can mount them. Joselito freezes at the sight of him and then approaches slowly, hands in the pockets of his blue coverall. Pascual steels himself. Joselito comes to a halt a metre away and regards him gravely, his wizened face unreadable. '*¿Cómo estás, chico?*'

Pascual's arms flap helplessly. 'I couldn't stop her.' Suddenly he is a blink away from breaking down completely, the effort of suppression crumbling under fatigue and cranial pain. 'I tried to reach her. I'm a poor swimmer myself, I couldn't . . .' His throat seizes up.

'I don't blame you,' Joselito growls. Pascual is so astonished to hear the words that he merely stares, and Joselito says it again, 'I don't blame you. I know you did what you could.'

It is a few seconds before Pascual can speak. 'She panicked,' he murmurs.

'*Mira.*' Joselito strolls to the street door and stands looking out. 'They haven't found her yet, and until they do, as far as I'm concerned she's alive. She probably crawled out a few hundred metres down the beach and went to earth somewhere. You shouldn't have mentioned the police to her. She was terrified of the police. What Lola went through with the police after the rape was nearly as hard for her as what happened in the back of that van. I think she's found a place to hide and won't come out until she's sure there are no coppers waiting.'

Pascual recognizes deep denial but has no desire to puncture it. There are long, long nights ahead for everyone. 'Are Sara and Pilar at home?'

'Sara's up there, sitting by the phone.' Joselito turns from the door and scowls at Pascual. 'Pilar's down in Castelldefels, walking up and down the beach.' He brushes past Pascual on his way to the office.

Pascual labours up the stairs. To spend eternity climbing these steps would spare him the agony that awaits at the top. Sara opens the door and he cannot read the look in her eyes. Her hair hangs free, framing the long melancholy face dominated by the black eyes. She is dressed in jeans and a dark blue pullover and to Pascual she is water in the desert, but he fears this oasis is poisoned. He stands wary and unmoving. 'No word yet?' he says after a few seconds.

'Nothing.' She steps back, inviting him in, and as he steps through the doorway she reaches for him. They stand for a long moment, swaying slightly. 'Forgive me,' Pascual breathes, releasing her.

'Don't blame yourself,' says Sara, closing the door. 'You didn't kidnap her, did you?'

Pascual reels a little following her down the hall; he would prefer a beating to this careful solicitude for his feelings. 'It's my fault. I should have run like the devil when that reporter showed up.'

'That wouldn't have changed a thing.' Sara drifts to the window overlooking the street and stands looking out.

Nobody wants to look him in the eye tonight, Pascual sees. He collapses on a chair at the dining table. To Sara's back he says, 'How? How did they get Lola?'

'I don't know. Didn't they tell you?'

'No. The man who picked me up didn't say a thing.'

'Does it matter?'

'Yes.' Pascual reaches for a pack of cigarettes lying on the table and gets one going. Under the restorative effects of the tobacco he manages to order his thoughts. 'There are two different parties at work here. Whoever killed Gabriel was really gunning for me. That's one party, and I think it's the same party that killed the American. But this bunch on the boat didn't want to kill me. Not right away, anyway, or they'd have shot me in the doorway of my *pensión*. They wanted to talk to me. But party number one got to them first. I think party number one's trying to eliminate anyone who can testify to what the American had uncovered, which includes me and the fellow on the boat. And the frightening thing is, I think we must have seen people from both parties, talked to them, served them drinks. We just didn't know who they were.'

'At the bar.'

'That's right. We all practically live there, and there's been any number of strangers about in the last week. However Weiss found out about me, they could have, too. Or maybe they followed him. Any one of those strangers could have been scouting the place out, watching us all and trying to figure out who was who. Can you remember them all? Any of them? The first bunch got it wrong and killed Gabriel. By now they'll know they got it wrong. The second bunch knows, too, and after Gabriel got killed they knew they had to get to me fast. They'd seen us all together at the bar and they probably saw Lola on the Ramblas and recognized her. All they had to do was get her into a car somehow.'

Sara leans against the window frame, arms folded. 'Is that what the police think?'

'I'm never sure what the police think. I've been over everything with Serrano, for what that's worth. I think he holds me responsible for losing Lola, too.'

'You didn't lose Lola.' Sara's voice is barely audible.

Pascual lays the cigarette carefully on the edge of an ashtray. He rises slowly and paces across the room to stand at Sara's shoulder. 'You don't have to spare my feelings. The whole thing starts with me. I carry the plague, Sara. I contaminate everyone I come in contact with.'

She looks at him, and in her eyes he can see the patient numbness of long familiarity with pain. 'We've all got the plague around here. We had it a long time before you showed up.'

Pascual is waiting for signals, a shift in body language that would invite an embrace, a touch that would offer comfort, but Sara's stance tells him he is a stranger. His spirits touch bottom. 'I wouldn't blame you if you wanted to see the back of me. My whole life's a lie and I didn't have the balls to tell you. Say the word and I'll go.'

Something like panic flashes in Sara's eyes, but he can see her suppress it. She closes her eyes and when she opens them she is calm. 'Pascual. That's the last thing in the world I want. But right now I'm confused. I'm going to ask for a few days to deal with all of this, and then . . .'

Pascual waits for a promise, but it doesn't come. He pulls away.

Sara catches his arm. 'For a while things are going to be ghastly around here, and I don't think you're going to be welcome. Forgive me.'

Pascual notes with some bitterness that she has deftly left open the question of just who it is who would object to his presence. '*Vale*,' he says. 'You know where to find me.'

Her look freezes him, her lips parted, something on the verge of being said, and then a key rattles in the lock. Sara's eyes widen. 'Pilar,' she breathes. Immediately she is putting distance between herself and Pascual, making for the foyer. Trapped, Pascual can only listen as Sara greets her friend quietly. He hears murmurs, a shuffling of feet. Pilar comes into the room, trailed by Sara, and sits at the table. She looks utterly spent. She stares vacantly into a corner. Pascual paces half-way around the room before her eyes rise to meet his. She is the most beautiful of the three, and Pascual is terrified by the look he sees in her exquisite eyes. He stands groping for a word and finally can produce only, 'I'm sorry.'

'Me too.' Pilar lights a cigarette and exhales, watching the smoke rise in the lamplight. 'I'm very sorry.'

'I'll be on my way, then.' If he expects anyone to stop him, he is disappointed. He shambles towards the door.

'Pascual,' Pilar has turned to look at him. 'Lola will show up. I'm sure of it.'

Until now Pascual has avoided anything so craven as tears, but the quiet assurance in Pilar's voice, a child singing to herself in the dark, nearly pushes him over the edge. '*Esperemos*,' he squeezes out.

Downstairs, Joselito is nowhere to be seen. In the street there are lovers and vagabonds, tourists and drunks. Pascual lights a cigarette and wonders where the hell he is going. Not the Tavern del Born, though he would give anything to be able to while away the evening there; the bar is the one place that everyone, friend, foe or policeman, seems to know about. The status of his *pensión* is uncertain; as far as he knows the only party that has located him there has been decimated. There are no safe bets, but it may be a decent risk and he does not want to spend the night on the street. He shakes out the match and tosses it into the gutter.

He walks up Princesa to the bright lights of Laietana and crosses, then continues up Ferran into the Gothic Quarter. Here the tourists and the pub crawlers are thick on the ground. He crosses the Plaça Sant Jaume under the gaze of the police guards in front of the Ajuntament and dawdles down the gentle slope towards the Ramblas, looking in shop windows, hesitating on the thresholds of bars. He is hungry, but there are other things on his mind. By the time he reaches the Rambla dels Caputxins he is sure he is being followed.

Instinct has nothing to do with it; it takes an effort of observation and memory and Pascual is surprised to find how easily old habits have come back to him. Standing in the doorway of Sara's building lighting his cigarette, he catalogued the few unmoving figures in the street, and one of them has come all the way across the Gothic Quarter with him, fifty metres behind, as studiously unhurried as Pascual himself. Jeans and leather jacket, a generic look, dark hair and not much else to be seen at this distance except the fit athletic carriage.

Pascual pauses at the Rambla, traffic tearing by in front of him, poised to cross to the central promenade. With sudden decision he turns to his right. The back door of the Café de la Opera is the oldest wheeze there is, having served trapped adulterers, penniless drunks and anyone else needing a quick discreet exit since time began, but if this is foreign rather than domestic talent behind him, it may be worth a try. Pascual pauses at the front entrance, making a production of it, a man fighting temptation and losing. When he is sure his tail has had time to come around the corner, he plunges in.

The café is doing its usual frantic business, white-jacketed waiters sweating their way through clouds of smoke with trays held high. Pascual pushes quickly through the narrow front room and down the long bar into the spacious back chamber. Normally he would stop and greet all these people who are waving, calling his name, but if the wheeze is to work it must be fast.

Without a glance behind he makes for the back door. There is a short flight of steps down into a narrow lane with a high blank wall opposite and he will have a decision to make: up towards Boqueria or down to Ferran, a few metres to the right. Pascual is weighing the choice when he goes through the door to find his tail at the bottom of the steps, looking up at him with a startled expression on a face that has survived a few prize fights or perhaps a couple of nasty accidents.

Recognition is instant on both sides, and there is a second of almost banal embarrassment before Pascual becomes aware of the stakes. What was almost a tactical exercise is suddenly much more, and all Pascual can see is Gabriel's brains going splat across the bar. The man at the bottom of the steps has had no time for gestures, conciliatory or otherwise; all Pascual can see is the sudden narrowing of his eyes, and this is enough to make him lash out with his foot and catch his opponent in the face. The man crumples backwards with a grunt, but he has taken heavy punishment before and his hand is inside his jacket before his buttocks have smacked into the pavement. Pascual does not wait to see what variety of modern ordnance will emerge; he spins and heads back into the café.

He is aware as he runs that he is causing outrage: the noise of spilled trays crashing to the floor, flecks of warm liquid in his face, fleeting glimpses of wide eyes and bared teeth all indicate that his passage through the room will be remembered, and not just because he sets a speed record for traversing the Café de la Opera that will stand for a long time. His attention, however, is overwhelmingly engaged by the possibility of lead catching him from behind.

He fights his way out on to the Ramblas and with only a glance at the cars bearing down on him sprints into the street. He gains the crowded promenade in a squeal of brakes and makes more enemies crossing to the far side; the downhill lane is easier and he makes the mouth of the first street leading into the Raval without further devastation.

Pascual runs until he can run no further. He heaves to in a deserted alley in the heart of the Raval and vomits a thin bitter gruel on to the paving stones.

The Bar Melilla is small and squalid, with banknotes from Arab countries taped to the tiled walls along with posters in florid Arabic script touting concerts given by Moroccan singers portrayed in mannered poses.

'They're all *argelinos*,' Mohammed says, holding court behind the bar. 'You don't want to spend the night up there.' Mohammed has the leathery face of a Rifian bandit and a reputation as a minor tycoon among the *moros* of the Raval. 'Thieves and ruffians.' Mohammed speaks with the disdain of the long-established immigrant for the newcomer. 'Besides, they're dirty.'

'Will I have a bed of my own?' says Pascual.

'For an extra five hundred pesetas.'

'Will anybody cut my throat in the night?'

Mohammed smiles. 'That I can't guarantee.'

Pascual shrugs. 'I'll take my chances with the Algerians. I've got bigger problems out on the street.'

Mohammed shakes his head and slides off his stool, motioning to Pascual to follow him. 'A Christian willing to lie down with *moros*. Now I've seen it all.'

Upstairs the squatter toilet is hopelessly clogged, a reeking basin of excrement without even a clear spot to place one's feet. Pascual pisses delicately into the mess, holding his breath, and withdraws, sunk in depression. He had long thought this phase of his life was behind him. He tiptoes down the hall and eases through a creaking door into the room at the end. In the darkness somebody stirs. Pascual does not need light to sense the bodies stacked floor to ceiling; eight to ten, he estimates, listening to laboured breathing in the dark, his room-mates till morning. As he gropes his way towards the empty bunk Mohammed has assured him is to be found in the corner, there is a thrashing noise and a burst of anxious Maghrebi Arabic. '*T'en fais pas*,' he essays in whispered French. 'Just looking for a bed.'

Prone on a filthy mattress, his head resting on a pillowcase that has not been changed since the *moros* took over this ancient Catalan house, Pascual listens to the uneasy night murmurs of the disinherited, the desperate and the damned. Like a dagger in his heart the thought crystallizes that it is here, and not in the airy flat in Princesa where Sara sleeps alone, that he is truly at home.

I I

'We should give you your own desk,' says Serrano. 'You've certainly spent enough time here.'

'I thought you might appreciate my reporting it. This time I can give you a good description. I got a good look at him, the ugly bastard.'

'Oh, I appreciate it. You're sure he was about to shoot you?'

'His hand went inside his jacket.'

'Before or after you kicked him?'

Pascual reflects. 'After, perhaps. But you can understand my not wanting to take chances.'

Serrano is giving him the kind of look a primatologist gives a fractious ape. He stares for nearly half a minute, then rises wearily to his feet and walks to the wall where the group photos hang. He peers at one of them and then turns to Pascual, pointing at the picture. 'Did he look anything like this fellow?'

Pascual closes his eyes, sighs, breathes obscenities. Finally he stands and goes to look at the picture. Midway along the back row, smiling at the camera and dressed up in a suit, is his assailant of the previous night. Pascual shakes his head, returning to his seat. 'You put a fucking tail on me.'

'Of course. I'm not a bloody idiot.'

'Good God, I kicked a policeman in the teeth.'

'You missed his teeth, actually, though he's got a lovely purple eye today. He wanted to pick you up and charge you. I had to talk him out of it.'

'I'm very grateful.' Pascual slams the desk. '*Coño*, can you blame me for being nervous?'

'I suppose not. Where did you go after you wreaked havoc on the Ramblas?'

'I found a place to hide.'

'I'll need an address. And phone number.'

'If you need to contact me you can always leave a message at my *pensión*. I'll check there for messages even if I'm not sleeping there. Am I going to talk to your judge any time soon?'

'I really couldn't say. Apparently he's decided to concentrate on the Marbella end of things. That's where the action is, apparently. When he's likely to summon you, I don't know. But I think for the moment you've been overlooked. I have no orders to hold you and for that matter no reason to believe you'll flee. And I think you just might get to the heart of things before he does, if only in the way a goat tied to a stake gets to the heart of things.'

'*Gracias*. I'm glad my well-being is so important to you.'

'What's important to me is to clear up these homicides.'

'And you won't mind my being the next victim as long as you're there to grab the killer, is that it?'

Serrano shrugs. 'Mind you, I'll do my best to keep you alive. Another murder on my patch wouldn't look good. We're far ahead of the normal rate this year, thanks largely to you.'

Pascual blinks at him for a moment. 'You really don't like me, do you?'

'I have no feelings for you one way or another. To me you're a problem to be solved. That's all.'

'I've a good mind to skip town just to land you in the shit with your higher-ups.'

'Suit yourself. As I believe I've mentioned, the instant I can't lay my hand on you, your name and face go out on the wires.'

'You're not going to keep the tail on me?'

'After last night? I doubt I could find any officers with the patience to take on the job. Though I'm sure I could find a few volunteers to haul you down a cul-de-sac and teach you to mind your manners. No, it was a bit of an experiment and not a very successful one. Frankly I was rather hoping to catch you in a lie or two, but all I've done is make you more careful.'

'What would I lie about?'

'Anything. The dead girl, for example. Until I see a bloated corpse I don't believe she drowned.'

Pascual seethes. Finally he sighs and says, 'So what do you want from me?'

Serrano leans forward, a thin smile deepening the creases around his eyes. He looks like a vulture settling in for a feed. 'I want you to tell me who's killing people in my district before that prima donna down in Madrid does. Do that and I promise you I'll be fond of you. A little bit, anyway.'

Pascual nods, slowly. 'Well, that's quite an incentive.'

Serrano straightens and paces to a desk. 'I've got something else for you to look at.' He pulls a leather briefcase from beneath the desk and opens it. He takes out a handful of papers and slides them across to Pascual. 'We found this in Weiss's hotel room. The original's being held under lock and key for the judge, but I managed to have a copy made. I've had one of our young anglophone geniuses take a look at it, but I'm not sure what he's going to be able to make of it.'

Pascual pulls the photocopies towards him. They are evidently taken from the kind of notebook he remembers from his unhappy high-school days in Brooklyn, with paper lined in blue in the American fashion with a red line to mark the left-hand margin. 'What do you want me to do?'

'Read it, decipher it, puzzle it out. See if you can find anything there that tells you why Weiss's coming to Barcelona set off a bout of mass slaughter. I'm giving you this because it may mean more to you than to us. It doesn't go out of this room, and anything you find there you tell me first. Is that clear?'

'Perfectly.' Pascual scans, making out words. 'It may take some time.'

Serrano smiles. 'You've got plenty of that. Shall I get you some coffee?'

Here it is in black and white: *Pascual (formerly Rose – current name?).* Pascual stares at his name in Weiss's neat hand, half-way down a page. *PFLP liaison w/RAF et al – defected June 89 – debriefed by S in Athens.* Pascual's skin crawls as he deciphers the shorthand account of his career in the service of death. A phrase from Weiss's letter is still echoing in his head – *the sense of justice and morality you displayed by your defection and subsequent activities.* He can hear the mockery in Weiss's voice.

He has picked out all references to *P*, himself presumably. None of the other initials in the outline is so helpfully identified in margin notes, possibly because they were all well known to Weiss from previous research. *P flew to Frankfurt 2/88.* Weiss has talked to someone who knows, clearly; S himself perhaps. *Sources with whom I have spoken*, his letter said.

Pascual closes his eyes, trying to bring back February 1988. He remembers flying into Frankfurt from Athens, bearing orders from a PFLP higher-up he had met in a hotel just off Syntagma Square. His instructions were to check into a hotel near the Hauptbahnhof and wait for a call; Pascual remembers bolting the door and sitting on the bed, staring bleakly about the room and listening to harsh male laughter in the Kaiserstrasse below.

He flips over a page. The notebook appears to be a haphazard collection of random jottings, heavy with abbreviation and initials, with occasional beacons of relative clarity like *I met H in Geneva, 6/85.* As far as Pascual can tell, it is a sort of working journal of Weiss's progress in his enquiry, the minimal outline needed for him to keep the strands untangled in his head while gathering more. *I reported to GRU while working for M.* The one pitiful advance he can claim is to have figured out in fairly short order that Weiss's apparent account of his own doings is not that at all but rather the use of the initial *I*, written like all the others without a period. *H flipped I, tracked $ thru him.* Ilmeddin? Pascual goes with the obvious and marvels as the picture takes shape. *I gave P $ to deposit in Geneva — portion drawn by PFLP operatives, remainder transferred to accounts controlled by I.*

Pascual is beginning to understand. He has remembered the name of the bank in Geneva: an outfit called BCCI. The BCCI would have been a good port of entry for a laundering operation that would see the money to safe and respectable accounts in Zurich, minus the PFLP's cut.

G says P can prove M protected I. Pascual stares at the sentence. This is the key, the red flag, the tiny nugget of gold glistening in the muddy stream bed. He rubs his face vigorously, exhales. *G says P can prove M protected I.* Pascual struggles to concentrate through his fatigue, to make sense of the alphabetic jumble. He stubs out the cigarette, rubs his eyes, turns over a page. *H touted I to M. M knew of I's operation but let him go on, needed him to run stings.*

Pascual scans, backtracks, reads and rereads, putting together a picture. *I blew Cyprus operation, agents lost.* At the bottom of a page is a single sentence underlined twice: *P can identify M???*

Not a chance, thinks Pascual, but that is not what matters, he is beginning to see. What matters is that G, and Weiss, and others, think he can. And if P can prove that M protected I, then P has to go.

Looking at it from M's point of view, even Pascual must concede the point.

'Got it all sorted out?' Serrano has come quietly up behind him, the examination invigilator sneaking about the classroom.

'Not exactly.' Pascual shoves the papers away, rubs his face. 'Weiss did his homework, that's for sure. But he wasn't considerate enough to write down names. Only initials. I think *I* must refer to Ilmeddin. Now you need to find a *G* and an *M*.'

'A *G* and an *M*. Well, that narrows things down.'

'It would, if you had the proper framework. If Weiss could get this far, surely you can. He must have written down more than this. Reporters write down everything. It will all be in another notebook, or on a computer, back in New York. Get somebody to look for it. Call Interpol or whomever it is you call when other countries are involved.'

'I'm sure that's occurred to the judge.'

'Yes. And even if he didn't write it all out, you could reconstruct it. You'd need a list of his sources, the people he talked to. Look for an address book or a diary perhaps. This *G* in particular must be identifiable. It looks as if he's the main source for this. Weiss had good contacts in the intelligence business. Look for alienated or resentful intelligence officers, reformers, dissidents. Somebody with an interest in undoing both Ilmeddin and the officials who protected him. Weiss will have interviewed him. There must be traces. Didn't you say he was married?'

'Yes. As it happens, Weiss's wife arrived yesterday, with a fellow from their consulate in tow. She's one of those ferocious American women, all make-up and elaborate earrings, very correct but obviously suspicious of our Latin inefficiency, which she appears to believe killed her husband.' Serrano shares a brief ironic look with Pascual. 'I try to make allowances for grief. Apparently they were separated and Weiss kept her only vaguely up to date on what he was working on, more's the pity. In any event, apparently we're not competent to handle her. The judge has dispatched someone from Madrid to take her statement.'

'I see. Being closed out of the investigation, are we?'

Serrano smiles. 'Well, affairs of state are not exactly my department. I'm an old-fashioned district policeman. Give me a nice easy knifing any day. A crime of passion, a drunken brawl, thieves falling out over the loot, that type of thing. Blood in the gutter, that's what I know. I'm out of my depth with these high-flying international crime lords and secret agents.'

Pascual admires the deadpan delivery. He has a feeling that a high-flying international crime lord would find it strangely difficult to slip anything past this plodding beat copper. 'Here's what I can tell you,' he says. 'As far as I can make out, Ilmeddin was pulling the wool over everyone's eyes. He was running drugs into Europe and paying for Syrian-directed terrorist operations at the same time. Somebody in a Western security agency, probably the CIA given Weiss's interests, found out about it, but instead of reeling him in they turned him and tried to use him to infiltrate the terrorist organizations. That meant looking the other way while he went on making money and eventually it meant protecting him from the Germans, who wanted to break up his drug operations. What they didn't know was that Ilmeddin was on the Soviet payroll as well, reporting to the GRU, Soviet military intelligence. Now, if you're a member of a security agency and word gets around that back in the Cold War you protected a notorious drug lord to run a sting operation that never went anywhere because he turned out to be a Soviet agent who tipped them off all along the way, then I'd say your reputation would suffer. And you might wish to prevent the news from getting out. Particularly if, as Weiss suggested, you were about to attain a position of power.'

Serrano nods. '*M*.'

'If Weiss had it right.'

'And where do you come in?'

'Weiss was told by this fellow *G* that I can identify *M*.'

'And can you?'

Pascual heaves a great sigh. 'Only if I work at it. I'm being forced to acquire knowledge that makes me dangerous.'

Serrano appears to enjoy the irony. 'The knowledge has to have been there all along.'

'But I never made connections. I can remember a face and deduce that that's the key face. But I don't know who it belongs to.'

'Then perhaps your role is merely to stay alive until someone else puts a name to it, so you can say yes, that's the man.'

Pascual nods, slowly. 'All right, I'll try to stay alive.'

Up in Father Costa's room, someone has died. It is not the priest, not yet, for Pascual can see the fierce light in the black eyes, but the other bed is being hurriedly remade with fresh sheets. 'He went quietly,' says the priest. 'A mercy. But it was an uncomfortable reminder. How tired you look, my boy.' The priest is propped up on pillows and strong enough to close the book he has been reading and lay it down, but his face bears traces of the beast that is slowly chewing his insides to pulp.

'I've had an active few days.'

'How I envy you. Activity is another thing I am forbidden.'

'Can I bring you anything? More books?'

The priest frowns, gearing up for the effort of speech. 'That's kind of you. But I'm not sure I have the time left to finish even this one. It is a strange thing to realize that one literally does not have time. For sixty years I've been collecting books, amassing them by the kilo, stacking them in corners and shoving them under the bed, each volume with the certainty that some day I would get to it. And then not too long ago I realized that there was simply not enough time left to me. That was the first real pang of regret.'

Father Costa closes his eyes and Pascual watches as his features gradually relax. Quietly he says, 'You may outlive me yet, Father.'

'Surely not.'

'My past seems to have come back to haunt me again.'

Time passes and Pascual thinks the priest has dropped off to sleep, but finally the old man says, 'Do you want to tell me about it?'

'I don't wish to disturb you.'

His eyes open, and there is a ghostly flash of the old humour.

'Disturb me, my boy? That would take some doing at these altitudes.'

'All right then,' says Pascual. 'Perhaps you can even help me.'

12

Phone to his ear, Pascual swivels on the chair to put his feet up on Father Costa's desk. Shelf upon shelf of books loom above; brandy from the priest's private stock swirls luminously in a *copa* in his hand. The key and the priest's handwritten note to the *conserje* downstairs giving Pascual access to his rooms for purposes of assistance in his research have admitted Pascual to this modest suite in the Industrial School student residence where Father Costa serves as chaplain. Pascual does not know how far he can stretch the priest's hospitality, but for the moment nobody seems to be questioning his right to be here.

'*Hombre*,' says Campos at the other end of the line. 'The mystery man. There's starting to be quite a lot of talk about you. Who is the man who swam to shore and reported the crime? So far Serrano hasn't released your name, but I don't know how long you'll be able to hide behind your protected witness status. I've been playing dumb, but I think some of my colleagues suspect I know.'

'Just keep your mouth shut and we'll both benefit. Have you got a moment?'

'Talk fast. I've got a deadline to meet.'

'I want you to help me.'

'*Hostia*. Wait, I think the phone's playing tricks on me. Did I hear you correctly?'

'Listen. This is naked self-interest on my part. I'm at risk until we have names and faces to give the police, and Serrano's practically written me off. A new judge has taken over the investigation and so far he's concentrating on the Marbella aspect.

Meanwhile, there's a chance the people who killed Weiss and Heredia are still around looking for me. So if you think we can really find out who's giving the orders on this, then let's put our heads together.'

Nobody says anything for a long moment. Pascual can hear tumult at Campos's end, the hum of a busy office. 'Where do we start?' says Campos.

'We start with an initial. Serrano let me have a look at Weiss's notes.'

'My God. What did you find?'

'Work for you. Find out who with the initial *M* ran a sting operation involving Ilmeddin for some intelligence agency, probably the CIA, in Frankfurt in 1988.'

'*M*. Like James Bond's superior. More and more cinematic.'

'Except this one's probably about as cinematic as a bookstore clerk. Intelligence officers don't survive long otherwise.'

'All right. I don't know if anything I've got is useful. The book I read is mainly concerned with things that happened in Latin America. I don't know how he got on to the business in Frankfurt.'

'That'll be in a notebook somewhere, one I wasn't shown. The answer will be in New York, probably. I suppose the new magistrate will get there eventually, but who knows when? What we need is a way to retrace Weiss's steps. He found out who M was, so other people can. We need a list of his sources. A principal one seems to have the initial *G*, for what that's worth.'

Campos makes a thoughtful noise. 'His wife would be a good contact, but I couldn't get close to her. She's flying home tomorrow with the body, I understand. We could make some phone calls. His editor, his agent maybe, I don't know. He must have some collaborators on the project. But I'm not sure my English is good enough for that. I can read it fairly well, but when those Yanquis start mumbling and slurring the way they do, they lose me fast.'

'I can do the talking if you'll guide me. We'll run up quite a bill, probably, but then I've got somebody else's phone to do it on and I don't think he's going to be around to worry about it.'

'There's this side of the ocean as well. I'm waiting to hear the latest on the man shot in Marbella.' Campos pauses. 'You know, everything we've talked about is just shadowing what the official investigation is going to do.'

'I don't know what else to try.'

'Look at it this way. You're in a unique position. You're the man who was there. You're on the inside. You've got to know something nobody else does. That's why they're coming after you, after all. Think about what you know that nobody else can and see if it doesn't get us there faster.'

'I've told Serrano everything I can think of.'

'Maybe so. But maybe there's something else. Work on it. Listen, I've got a story to write. I should be free by eight. Where can I contact you?'

'Better let me contact you.'

A pause, and Campos says, 'You don't even trust me, do you?'

'And what would make you different from anyone else?' says Pascual.

Pascual hates this feeling that the waters in which he swims have been poisoned. He is a creature of the streets, and in a broad arc stretching from the Esquerra de l'Eixample to the Ribera he is seldom far from a familiar watering hole, a shop where he is known or a secluded nook that evokes his childhood. Where other people have comfortable parlours Pascual has the streets. Now, however, he walks like a gazelle in lion country, stomach muscles clenched tight and scanning a landscape gone cold with menace.

Deciding what is safe and what isn't is not a trivial problem. He may, he thinks, be able to duck into his *pensión*. He craves a shower, a change of clothes, a few minutes to lie and let his mind wander. Later perhaps he will throw a toothbrush and some spare clothing into a bag, the minimum to survive a few days underground. Movement is the key, he remembers from the old days, staying a step ahead. He could be clever and send someone else up to collect his things, but he has no wish to get anyone else killed in his stead or offer another hostage. If someone is lying in wait, it is his problem and his alone. In the end he decides that a token effort at disguise is a reasonable precaution and buys a pair of sunglasses and a beaded cap from an African street vendor in Plaça de la Universitat before slipping into the alleyways of the Raval.

He makes it to the *pensión* without incident and frightens the Senyora Prat by forgetting to remove his disguise. When he succeeds in establishing his identity she sags with relief. 'What a fright. I thought you were another one.'

'Another what?'

'Another gypsy. You had a band of gypsies come round calling for you this morning.'

'A whole band?'

'Well, two of them. *Mira,* they left a number for you to call.' She fishes in a pocket and hands him a slip of paper.

Fernando, he reads, followed by a telephone number. 'Did they say what they wanted?'

'They need to speak to you urgently, they said. What a fright they gave me. Gypsies at the door, what'll it be next? What black villainous faces they have.'

Pascual sinks on to his bed. He is too tired to confront any urgent business. His feet hurt and all he wants is to expire quietly in this black cloud of depression. Out in the hallway, the telephone rings. With fatalistic certainty he listens as the Senyora Prat answers and then comes clopping down the hall to his door. '*Senyor?* You're wanted on the telephone.'

'Coming.' Pascual creaks to his feet.

'At last,' says Fernando in his ear a moment later. 'You're a hard man to reach.'

'I've been rather busy. What's going on?'

'We need to talk. Can I come by and pick you up, say in ten minutes?'

Pascual considers his current state of hygiene. 'Make it half an hour.'

In half an hour he is standing showered and shaved, just inside the door of his *pensión* looking out through the glass, having learned his lesson last time. When a monstrous bright red vintage Chevrolet almost too wide for the street hauls up outside he is not surprised to see Fernando at the wheel. The band has expanded to three, Pascual sees: Diego is on the passenger seat beside him and Antonio in the back. Pascual ducks into the back and Fernando puts it in gear.

'Like it?' says Fernando, rolling slowly towards the Ramblas as foot traffic scatters before him. 'It's a 1964 Impala. I bought it off a

Russian in San Felíu, cheap. He'd lost all his money in a card game and needed the cash.'

'What was a Russian doing in an American battleship like this?'

'Driving to Morocco. He said he was running from the Mafia. I hope he made it.'

'Not if he had to depend on RENFE, he didn't,' says Diego.

'Where the hell do you park it?' says Pascual.

'I don't. I pay a boy to drive it around all night while I sleep.'

Pascual watches the Ramblas go by as they head for the sea. There is nothing illusory about this sense of *déjà vu* and he dislikes it intensely. 'So where are we going? What's the urgent business?'

'It's a nice day, we're going for a ride. As for the business, we don't know. That's what we need you for. We need you to tell us what's going on.'

Pascual has known these men for months and has not the slightest fear of them, but there is a faint tinge of intimidation beneath the banter. 'I don't know,' he says. 'Somebody's trying to kill me.'

'You?'

'Yes, me.'

'So far the only people dead are a Yanqui journalist, two gypsies, a boatload of Arab gangsters and poor Lola. But you're the one the cops are talking to. What's going on?'

'Gabriel was a mistake. The killer called my name before he fired.'

Nobody says anything while Fernando swings smoothly to the right towards Montjuïc. 'You're sure about that?'

'Completely. And the American had come looking for me. Somebody's trying to cover up what he was working on.'

'And you've got no idea what it was?'

'I've got ideas. I just don't have a name to take to the police yet.'

'I see. What happened to Lola?'

'The Arab got hold of her and used her to find me. She got caught in the middle and panicked.'

'You were there when she drowned?'

'I was trying to save her. I watched her go under.'

Silence reigns. Fernando swings on to the road that climbs in a long switchback up the side of Montjuïc. The city falls away behind. 'Pity,' says Fernando.

After a moment Pascual says, 'I know. I'm the angel of death. You think I'm having fun?'

'Nobody's blaming you.'

Pascual has grown tired of hearing these words. 'Then what's the convocation for? Why am I being taken for a ride?'

'*Coño, cálmate*. We're your friends. We're all on the same side. We're trying to get this sorted so we can get the *pestañí* off our backs.'

'What, they've been after you?'

'From the start. That's all they need to know, that a gypsy was there, and they've got their suspect. The day after Gabriel got killed they came looking for me.'

'Why you?'

'My record. I did three years in *la Modelo*, remember? And I was there when he got shot. I don't know who told them, God knows I was out that door before the smoke cleared. But that's the angle they're working. The dead man's a gypsy, to them anyway, so it must be a gypsy intrigue.'

'It was me that told them about you. They asked who was there and I told them everyone I could remember. I didn't mean to get you in trouble. What do you mean, "to them"? I thought Gabriel was a gypsy.'

Fernando shrugs. 'There are gypsies and there are gypsies. He may have had gypsy blood but he lived like a *payo*. He kept his distance from us, anyway.'

They have reached the Plaça de l'Armada overlooking the city and Fernando parks the behemoth at the side of the road. They get out and walk to the restaurant terrace that sits atop the cable-car station dug into the hillside. They sit at a table at the edge of the terrace and Fernando orders a round of drinks. Beneath them lies the rumbling city, the port close at hand and the vivid blue sheen of the sea stretching away northwards into the haze. Pascual hands round cigarettes and studies his companions as they light up. Fernando the pirate, with a face to send old Catalan women scurrying for cover, long hair in a ponytail and gold earring glinting in the sun; taciturn Diego, the darkest of complexion and the most physically imposing, thick through the chest and shoulders and with the watchful eyes of a nightclub bouncer; and Antonio, thin and graceful, with soulful eyes in an open innocent face and carefully tended hands, the artist. 'You told the police Gabriel wasn't the real target?' says Fernando.

'Of course. The whole thing revolves around me. And the Arab on that boat. It's all in the hands of a magistrate from Madrid now. It's got more to do with politics than with anything you've ever done, and they know that. They'll leave you alone now, I imagine.'

Fernando smokes, eyes narrowed. 'You know there was a second man killed with the American? A gypsy.' He cocks a thumb over his shoulder. 'Just round the other side of the mountain here.'

Pascual nods. 'I didn't think that was significant. I assumed the gypsy was lured into the set-up somehow, to make it look like a drug affair. It was a popular spot for that type of transaction, I understand.'

'And the dealers are all gypsies, are they?'

'Enough of them are for the whole thing not to strike anyone as improbable. Am I wrong?'

Fernando shrugs. 'Why you?'

'All I know is that the American wanted me to talk about dealings I had with the Arab years ago and somebody else wanted to prevent that.'

'You and the Arab?' The three of them are looking at him with keen interest.

Pascual waves his cigarette vaguely. 'You're not the only one who's been on the wrong side of the law. Maybe I'll tell you about it some day.'

'Go on.'

'I think that's what's behind all the killings. The only gypsy connection is that somebody needed a dupe for the set-up and where it happened it's not unlikely they'd get a gypsy. But at bottom it's got nothing to do with the gypsies. That's always an easy first guess for the police but I think even they've figured out by now that it's too easy.'

The gypsies exchange looks. Fernando takes a long draught of beer. '*Vale*. How's Sara taking all this?'

Pascual stalls, looking out to sea, until he can feel their gazes on him. 'She's bearing up.'

'We're counting on you to take care of her,' says Antonio. There is something close to pleading in his eyes and Pascual remembers Sara using the words brother and sister.

'That one's a real *gitana*,' says Fernando. 'She's got it in her blood and I don't care if her father was a *payo*.'

'Sara's family, see?' Diego puts in gruffly. 'And a gypsy will do anything to protect his family.'

Pascual meets each gaze in turn, trying to fight off the feeling that he has let everyone down. 'Understood,' he says. 'Message received.'

13

Pascual has resisted the temptation of alcohol; he knows it will dull his edge and it is time to muster his powers of concentration. At this dark corner table with cigarettes and strong coffee he is fortified for the effort. He has let a random walk bring him into this anonymous bar somewhere above the Gran Via and below the Diagonal, and undistracted by the inane beeping of video machines and the eruptions of laughter at the bar, he is determined to follow Campos's advice and figure out what he knows.

He knows a face to begin with, he thinks; the more he looks at it the surer he is that the man in Offenbach is M. He can picture it only hazily, but he knows that if he sees it again he will recognize it. A face, however, is nothing without a name. He needs a route to M that no one has thought of.

Find the house in Offenbach and find out who rented or owned it in 1988? Pascual has no idea of the address and doubts he could even find the street again. He closes his eyes, massaging his brow and straining to recall all he can of the place, any details that might betray the owner. It is futile; he remembers only a nondescript garden, a comfortable house with no helpful peculiarities. He cannot even recall the make of car in which he was driven to Strasbourg, much less anything so crucial as a plate number. Twelve years of purposeful neglect have eroded and blurred his memories. M was a foreigner; of that he is sure. His German was excellent, but lightly accented. American? Conceivable. If the accent had been stronger he would have a better impression of its origin, but it was faint and intermittent, the accent of a man who had lived in the country for long enough to master the language.

Intelligence officers frequently have diplomatic cover, he knows. Is there a way of looking at records of American consular officials in Frankfurt in 1988? Matching an initial and a photo? Can a reporter from a Spanish daily get him access to this information? No doubt the police can, and it is worth suggesting it to Serrano or perhaps the illustrious Pinzón when their attention returns to him, but for the moment the idea gets him no further.

Pascual gives up in frustration and orders another coffee. Weakening, as an afterthought he asks for a brandy to go with it; the caffeine he has ingested will keep him awake for a month. His stomach is complaining of stress and abuse. Pascual knows he should eat, but he knows also that food will make him drowsy and content, and contentment is his enemy.

There is another matter it is time to confront. *How did he find you?* he can hear Serrano saying. Pascual has been avoiding the implications of Weiss's reference to his missing fingers. He has assumed, when his mind has touched on it, that Weiss must have been tipped off by a casual acquaintance, that he had trolled a number of Pascual's haunts, asking after him, before running him to earth in the Tavern del Born. Now Pascual sees that this is wishful thinking. Weiss knew where to look for him and he knew he was maimed, and it is time to wonder who told him.

Logic, Pascual thinks. Who knew two things? First, that Pascual Rose the turncoat PFLP operative was lying low in Barcelona, and second, that he was missing two fingers? There is a small group of people who know the first fact and another who know the second, but for the most part the two groups do not intersect, as the loss of his fingers took place years after his defection and debriefing. The answer, therefore, should point with precision to his Judas. He can think of three people in Barcelona who know the full story of who he is: Father Costa, Serrano and Campos. Father Costa is the closest thing to family he has left and the question of betrayal simply does not arise. Serrano has long known who he is and shared the knowledge in official circles; he had also seen Pascual recently enough before the current mess to know of the missing fingers. However, he appeared surprised to hear that Pascual was working at the Tavern del Born and presumably could not have sent Weiss there. Campos knows who he is and may have bandied it about, but to Pascual's recollection he had had no contact with Campos since before the loss of his fingers two years ago. Who then? Enric may suspect much, but Pascual can think of no way he could have learned the full story. For the rest his intimates and acquaintances are ignorant of his background.

As far as he knows. Pascual's head swims. He downs a mouthful of brandy. Serrano is the most likely leak; God knows whom he might have told, in the line of business or otherwise. He might also have been feigning surprise at news of Pascual's job; but why? Campos might have been careless, but the profit motive would seem to give him an incentive to keep quiet about Pascual's identity. And how did he learn about Pascual's injury?

Rigorous logic, Pascual thinks, beginning to lose the battle for concentration. Three people could know all the necessary facts. Or possibly not. In any event, he is meeting one of them tonight.

'The dead gunman in Marbella was named Branko Matic.' Campos spells the name, peering at his notes. Tiny twin images of the computer screen are reflected in his glasses. 'According to his passport, a member of a disappearing race, the Yugoslavian.' Through a thin wall comes the muted clink of crockery as Campos's wife tidies up in the kitchen. Pascual's sense of dislocation is overpowering. Here in Campos's cramped but tidy flat in the tranquil sloping streets above the Via Augusta he feels like the new best friend from school, brought home and shown off to the family. A satisfying supper *en famille* with wine flowing liberally down his throat from the *porrón* and conversation carefully kept excruciatingly banal has given him distance from the horrors of the street but done nothing to change the impression that he has entrusted his fate to an amateur.

Pascual musters a frown. 'Employed by whom?'

'That's precisely what the police are working on. His passport says he was a mining engineer and he's got visas from half a dozen countries in Africa. But he also had an extensive record of service with the Yugoslav army and a Serbian militia unit that did a lot of nasty things in Bosnia in the early nineties. There's no indication of who might have employed him since, legally or otherwise. He had no criminal record.'

'A Serbian mercenary. Curious.'

'Yes. The police, naturally, are trying to trace his movements.' Campos lays his notebook on the desk. 'Meanwhile, they think they've found the boat used in the attack on Ilmeddin. A motor launch was stolen from a marina in Sitges and then abandoned just down the coast from Castelldefels. Somebody got a look at the men who made off with it, but the descriptions are vague.'

'More mercenaries, no doubt. Or the most expensive type of gangster. Somebody's got a lot of money to throw around.'

'Which means your death is worth a lot of money to someone.'

Pascual considers. 'Or maybe they don't have a lot of money but they have contacts. I don't know how many intelligence officers get rich, but I know they have the type of friends who can deliver favours like a quick efficient killing.'

'Our friend M.'

'Yes. Any ideas there?'

'If you can help me with the English, maybe.'

'What do you need?'

Campos digs in the papers on the desktop. 'See if you can get in touch with a man named . . . *coño*, these Yanqui names . . . *Stanley Prentice*. He seems to be the reigning expert on Ilmeddin. I found a report by him on the Internet that goes into Ilmeddin's drug-running and the deals he's allegedly made with the powers that be. Published by some watchdog outfit in the US called . . . *Beacon International*. No mention of any M or of Frankfurt beyond the fact that he set up shop there, but a talk with the man might be useful. Unfortunately there's no indication of how to get in touch with him. The site just gives his name and calls him a "*Florida attorney*". What's an *attorney*?'

'*Abogado.*'

'Ah. Well, how many of those named Stanley Prentice can there be? There must be a way to find him. What's *colegio de abogados* in English?'

'Let me think. The *bar*, that's it. There will be a Florida Bar Association or something like that. Search for that.'

Campos fumbles with the computer mouse. 'I have to say, you never know whether these Internet things are legitimate or just paranoid fantasizing. One time on the Internet I found proof that Elvis Presley was behind the assassination of Martin Luther King.'

'It makes a certain kind of sense.' He watches Campos poke at the keyboard. The computer hums and clicks and Campos leans back with his hands clasped on his head. 'Tell me something,' says Pascual.

'What?'

'That morning you came to my pension. How did you know I was living there?'

Campos stares at him blankly for a long moment while water runs through pipes in the walls and a car labours up the steep grade in low gear in the street outside. 'I asked Bonell, your *jefe* at the bar.'

Pascual scowls. 'And he told you, just like that? So much for closing ranks.'

'Why wouldn't he? Most people see no reason not to co-operate with journalists. Look, I'm sorry, I admit I've been quite aggressive. It's a professional reflex we develop.'

'*Vale, vale.* I'm just trying to work out how Weiss found me. Do you think Serrano could have told him?'

'I don't think so.' Campos is scowling at the computer screen. 'I've known Serrano a long time and he's got a reputation for playing by the rules. If your identify is supposed to be a secret he'd keep it unless the approach was official.'

'Maybe.'

Campos gives him a long look before turning back to the computer screen. 'Look, we've got a result. The Florida Bar Association, here it is. And you can search for a name. How do you spell Prentice?'

A minute later Campos sits back with a murmur of satisfaction. '*Hostia*, what a marvel, this machine. Look at that.'

Stanley Prentice, Attorney at Law. Pascual reads a name, address and telephone number in a place called Bradenton, Florida. 'What time is it over there, about five o'clock?'

'The east coast of the United States, let's see, six hours earlier. Yes.'

'Then I suppose we might just catch him.'

'I know he's dead. I heard. You're a reporter, are you?'

Pascual is speechless for a moment; he still only half-believes in modern communications, and he is amazed that fifteen minutes after Campos first mentioned Stanley Prentice he is hearing the man himself, a quarter of the way around the globe. 'Yes. I work for *El Mundo* in Barcelona,' Pascual manages.

'Well, you're lucky to catch me. I was just leaving for the day.' To judge by the voice, Prentice is middle aged, perhaps even older, and there is just the faintest hint of the American south in his diction. 'How did you get my number?'

'From the what do you call it, the website, of the Florida Bar Association.' Pascual's English is hard-wired but rusty.

'Oh, sure. You've read my book?'

'Just what's on the Internet.'

'On the *Beacon* site? I'm glad to know somebody's looked at it. Talk about a voice crying in the wilderness. So somebody got him, finally.'

'Yes. I saw the body.'

'You did? I envy you, sir. I'm just sorry we never got a chance to see him in a courtroom. Do they know who did it?'

'Not yet. Actually I'm hoping you might be able to cast some light on that.'

'Me? I doubt it. All I can do is give you a long list of people who had reason to want him dead. And I'm not sure how current I am. My work on Ilmeddin was done in the early nineties, and since nothing ever came of it in the way of prosecution or even much of an uproar, I got frustrated and quit dogging the bastard. If he's gone on making mischief, then what got him killed may have nothing to do with anything I know about.'

'Actually, what we're thinking here is that this may be connected with things that happened back in the eighties.'

There is just the slightest pause. 'We being who, exactly? You're a reporter, you said?'

'Yes, sir.'

'And what was the name?' Sounds of a man scrabbling for pencil and paper come across the wire.

'My name is Ernesto Campos.' Pascual looks at Campos, who shrugs.

'Your English is pretty good, Mr Campos.'

'I studied in New York for a while.'

'Well, I guess you could call what they speak up there English. Now, this is the thinking of the police you're giving me? The official investigation?'

'Well, no. I'm not sure quite what the police are thinking.' Pascual gropes for a formula that will work. 'I'm pursuing a line suggested to me by the notes of a writer named Weiss, who was working on a book about intelligence scandals.'

'Morris Weiss? The guy who wrote *The Shadow Agency*?'

'That's right.'

'And you talked to him?'

'Briefly. Before he was killed.'

Modern communications are capable even of transmitting a sudden chill across eight thousand kilometres of ocean. Several seconds pass before Prentice says, 'What happened?'

'He was shot here in Barcelona, last week. Apparently in some sort of drug-related dispute, but I don't think even the police buy that. He was here to research a book, and he told me personally it involved something that happened in Frankfurt in 1988. He said the truth had never come out and that somebody who was about to reach a position of great influence had been involved. Those were the words as close as I can remember them.'

'This is very disturbing.'

'Yes. There's been a third killing, too, which may be related. And I'm not sure the police will be able to get very far in connecting the three.'

'I see.'

'So anything you could tell me about Frankfurt in 1988 would be very helpful.'

A faint sigh comes over the line. 'Well, what I know is in the book.'

'To be specific, we're looking for someone with the initial M who we think protected Ilmeddin in Frankfurt in 1988. Possibly CIA, though that's not certain.'

'Look, I can't name names. Not individuals, anyway. I do know that Ilmeddin was a master at covering his ass. He swung deals with corrupt officials throughout his career. That's the scandal, the whole point of my book. And our own government wasn't blameless. They were hot on Ilmeddin's tail in 1990 for a whole range of things. But then along came the Gulf War, and we needed the Syrians on our side to go after Saddam, and Ilmeddin worked for the Syrians, so suddenly there wasn't any evidence against him. That was our government's part in letting Ilmeddin off the hook. I thought for a while a few months back that things had changed because the word was some Justice Department official was interested in going after him as part of some big push against the world heroin trade they were gearing up for, but nothing came of that either. There's only so much attention, so many resources, and everyone's competing for them.'

'I see.'

'Specifically in Frankfurt in 88, he slipped through the net when the BKA, the *Bundeskriminalamt*, busted up his drug network there. Somebody tipped him off and he got away. A mole in the BKA probably. But do I have the name of the tipster? No. I name a few names in the book, but they're all higher-ups and they've got terrific deniability. It would take better digging than I as an amateur could do to come up with the operational details. All I was trying to do with the book was get the ball rolling, and I failed miserably at that. I'm afraid M means nothing to me. I'm sorry.'

Pascual fears he is about to hear a click in his ear. 'You've been very helpful.' Desperate to keep Prentice on the line, he says, 'If you don't mind my asking, how did a Florida lawyer get involved in researching international terrorism?'

'Very simple,' says Prentice. 'Ilmeddin killed my daughter.'

'Excuse me?'

'He killed my daughter. Had her killed, anyway. Remember KLM 640? Spring of 88?'

Pascual closes his eyes. 'The plane that went into the North Sea just after taking off from Schiphol. A bomb in the luggage compartment. I remember.'

'That's right. My daughter was one of the three hundred and sixteen victims. She had done a year abroad at a university there and she was on her way home. She was sitting right above where the bomb went off. My wife and I flew over there and got her effects, but they were never able to come up with much of a body for us.'

'I'm very sorry.' Pascual can hardly get the words out.

'They think, or rather they *know*, that Ilmeddin was behind that. They say he was aiming for the army colonel who was on the flight and had been involved in a hostage rescue attempt in Lebanon. The men who actually built and placed the bomb were caught in 91, as you may recall, and are serving a life sentence in the Netherlands. They've been fairly tight-lipped, but there's evidence Ilmeddin was actively involved in the planning of the operation, at the very time the BKA missed him in Frankfurt. Somebody tipped him off and he tipped off the bomb-makers. And the operation went ahead a few weeks later. If he hadn't been tipped off, then or any number of other times, my daughter would still be alive. She'd be thirty-five years old, with a husband and kids probably and I could talk to her on the phone every day like I'm talking to you instead of crying over old snapshots late at night. Can you see why I got interested?'

Pascual can see much more than that, and it is making him ill. 'I can,' he says.

'As far as helping you out is concerned, one of my best sources when I was working on the book was a guy in London who'd been tracking Ilmeddin for a long time. Name of Hampton, Graham Hampton. He runs his own security firm now, but he's a former MI6 officer and he was all over Ilmeddin in the early eighties. He gave me a lot of good stuff and he'll probably talk to you. I don't have his number on me, but the name of his company is Global Consulting, in London. You can probably look it up.'

'I'm sure I can. Thank you.'

'I wish you better luck than I had,' says Prentice. 'Ilmeddin may be dead, but the folks who protected him are still there. And if they can't be prosecuted, they can at least be embarrassed all to hell. Find out who they are and tell the whole world about them.'

'I'll do my best,' says Pascual, just above a whisper.

14

Pascual has Campos drop him at the head of the Ramblas. Campos puts a hand on his arm as he opens the door. 'What's the matter with you? What did Prentice tell you?'

Pascual shrugs him off. 'Just what I told you, nothing more. I'm tired, that's all. Tell your wife thanks for the supper.'

'Tomorrow then?'

'*Vale*. I'll ring you.' Pascual leaps out and makes tracks before Campos can badger him further. There is always foot traffic on the Ramblas, but at this hour it is sparse and it should be an easy matter to watch for predators. Pascual, however, shambles along unseeing.

Pascual has carried the virus of guilt inside him for years, functioning numbly for long stretches of time, medicating occasional flare-ups with alcohol and waiting for time to turn it all to ash. He has long thought he knew the dimensions of his guilt, but Prentice's voice in his ear has knocked out a wall.

I did that, he thinks, seeing Prentice's daughter falling through the mist into the grey North Sea waters. He remembers the press photos, debris and bodies tossing on the waves. I sheltered the men who made the bomb, I banked the money that paid for it, I ate and drank with the man who planned it. I cultivated a wilful ignorance that does nothing but increase my guilt.

On the Rambla dels Estudis he brushes past a pair of wastrels who approach him for money. Father Costa has talked him through other times like this one, but if the old priest is still alive tonight he will be inaccessible, lying in pain in a darkened hospital room. The old church of Santa Maria del Mar, where he can usually find a tenuous peace, will be shut and locked for the night.

I want Sara, Pascual thinks. He walks, knowing where his steps are taking him but sure that it will end in disaster. I want Sara to hold me, love me, absolve me. She's all I have and I am losing her. At Ferran he cuts across the traffic lane and heads uphill.

By the time he reaches the Via Laietana it is past midnight. He is footsore and exhausted and he knows he is on a fool's errand. He cannot go and lean on her doorbell; he could not stand Pilar's gaze even if Sara would let him in. The best he can do is the bar, if it is open. Let them shoot him like a dog if they are lying in wait. At least he will die in surroundings where he was almost happy once. He veers off into the canyons of the Ribera, his steps echoing off high walls.

The bar is open; he can see the lit-up windows as he turns into the street. He listens for music but there is none. As he draws near Pascual can see that the place is nearly empty, nobody at the corner table and only a couple of desolate figures hunched over the bar. Tonight the Tavern del Born looks like the end of the line. Pascual pushes the door, hoping to find Enric perhaps, willing to pour him a drink and lend an ear. He comes face to face with Sara, alone behind the bar.

He stands still for a moment just looking at her. She has frozen too, and Pascual cannot tell if the frightened look on her face is because she fears him or fears for him. As a head turns drunkenly to see what the cat has dragged in, Pascual rouses himself and moves to the far end of the bar. He straddles a stool and watches Sara come down to meet him. 'What are you doing here?' she breathes. Her eyes flick to a corner of the room, over Pascual's shoulder. 'It's not safe.'

'I know.' Pascual wants to reach for her but is afraid of what may happen. 'What about you? I can't believe Enric would stick you back here so soon.'

Sara shrugs, a toss of the head. 'I have to work.'

'I need you.'

She stands a scant half-metre from him, arms clasped, rigid with tension. 'Please go.'

'I'm sorry for everything.'

'Please. For your sake, go away from here.'

Pascual shakes his head. 'I have things to tell you.'

'Not here.'

He sighs. 'Give me a *coñac*, then.' He will sit here until closing if he has to.

Moving with great reluctance, Sara fetches a bottle and a *copa* and pours. She shoves the drink towards him and says coldly, 'On the house. I'm sure Enric won't begrudge you one.' Then she turns on her heel and goes.

Pascual is staring into the bottom of the snifter when he hears the scrape of a chair and footsteps behind him. He was vaguely aware as he entered of a figure in the corner but paid it no attention, his eyes on Sara. Now a hand is clapped on his shoulder and a voice he knows says, '*Por fin*. You don't know how long I've been waiting for you.' Pascual turns and looks into the face he last saw under the brim of a panama hat. It takes him a second to place it because the hat is gone, but the moustache, the flat brigand's face and the pitiless eyes are the same. The eyes flick to Sara. 'Though it's been a pleasure to sit and watch her work. I had no idea I'd find such a celebrity behind the bar. Maybe she can join us. Come and sit with me.' He snaps his fingers at Sara. 'Another rum, *guapa*.'

Pascual rallies and says, 'Slow down. You owe me some explanations.'

'That's what I'm here for. Bring your drink.'

'You can start with the shot to the face, *cabrón*.'

A grin shows crooked teeth. 'Nothing personal, friend. Just thinking fast in a crisis. If I'd known who you were, it wouldn't have happened.'

'What do you mean? Who am I?'

The man's eyes sweep the room. '*Tranquilo*. Let's have a seat and talk about Giometti.'

'Who?'

The grin widens. 'Ah, it's too late for that.'

Sara arrives with the bottle and a wary look on her face. 'You know him?' she says. 'He's been here for hours.'

Pascual hesitates, and perhaps because of the odious grin on the other man's face or perhaps simply because he is sick unto death of lying, he says, 'This is the man who kidnapped Lola.'

Everything stops for a moment; Sara and the brigand lock eyes over the bar and Pascual sees the grin vanish like the flame of a match blown out. 'I didn't do a fucking thing to her,' says the man urgently, levelling a finger at Sara. 'If anybody got her killed, it was this bastard here.'

Pascual sees what is happening in Sara's face, and he has just begun to reach for her when the word *asesino* comes from deep in her throat. He is not quick enough to stop her from cocking her arm and the only reason the rum bottle does not shatter on the brigand's head is because he too has seen it coming and ducked. It smashes on the wall instead, sending a shower of rum and splinters of glass flying, jarring sleepy drunks upright. Somebody bellows an oath. The brigand is scuttling backward, stumbling into a table, and Sara is clawing at the shelves behind her.

'*¡Asesino!*' Pascual flops across the bar trying to grab her, but she is just out of reach and he watches helplessly as she flings bottle after bottle at the man as he dashes for the door. Fundador, Bacardi, Tío Pepe, Dewar's – a barrage of lethal liquor-bearing missiles chases him down the room, strewing havoc in his wake. Sara is screaming, drinkers are ducking for cover, Pascual is climbing over the bar.

The brigand catches the doorjamb just as Pascual catches Sara's arm. He points at Pascual now, growls, 'We'll talk, you and me,' and disappears into the night.

Sara is fighting to tear free of Pascual. 'I'll kill you!' she shrieks towards the door.

Pascual jerks her up short by both arms. 'What the hell are you doing? He could have a weapon!'

He hardly recognizes the Sara who finally focuses on him. Her hair has fallen into her face and her mouth is drawn back in a snarl, and what is blazing in her eyes makes it easy to believe everything he has ever heard about gypsy savagery. He calls her name, giving her a final shake.

Sara sags away from him, hands to her face. 'Police,' she says.

'He'll be long gone,' says Pascual. 'You should have let me talk to him.'

A face appears above the bar, bleary eyes wide with amazement, and somebody laughs, a nervous giggle. A footstep crunches on broken glass. 'We're closed,' says Pascual to a dazed clientele. '*Tancat, cerrado.* Go home.'

There is some grumbling, but in a minute the bar is cleared, the shutter pulled down nearly to the ground. Pascual surveys the wreckage. Sara is staring at nothing, arms folded tightly. 'Are you all right?' Pascual says.

She focuses on him. 'I don't know what happened to me. I just wanted to kill him. Is that really the man?'

'That's him. What the hell was he doing here?'

'He came in early in the evening and asked for you. I told him I didn't know you, but he stayed. He just sat in the corner and drank.'

Pascual fetches the broom from its corner. He shoves glass this way and that, puts a few chairs up on the tables. 'God, what have I done?' says Sara, stirring. 'Enric's going to kill me.' She comes out from behind the bar. 'Give me that.'

'I'll sweep. You get a rag and start sopping up liquor.'

They work in silence. Pascual is grateful to have something to absorb him, grateful to be working close to Sara, grateful for the illusion that nothing has changed. In half an hour they have restored order, though the place smells like a distillery. They are both behind the bar, Pascual sucking at a finger where he has just pulled out a splinter of glass and Sara wiping out the sink. 'How many thousands of pesetas did I smash?' says Sara, wringing out the rag.

'Nothing Enric can't afford.' Pascual reaches to switch off the ceiling lights, leaving only the single light above the cash register on. In the gloom he looks at Sara, drying her hands. 'If that bastard hadn't been here waiting for me, would you have still told me to go?'

Sara does not answer. When it becomes clear that Pascual is blocking her way and expects an answer, she finally looks at him. 'I don't know,' she says. 'I'm still in shock. About everything.'

Pascual nods. 'I came here tonight to tell you more stories about myself.'

She shakes her head. 'Don't start.'

'You don't know the half of it. I killed people, Sara.'

'I don't care.'

'You want details? I talked with the father of one of my victims tonight.'

'Pascual, stop it.'

'I lied to you. I'm not the man I let you believe I was. And if you tell me to go to hell it would only be what I deserve.'

'Is that what you want me to do?'

Pascual has to think about that. Miserably, he says, 'I want you to tell me it doesn't matter. But I know that's asking too much. Maybe I want you to tell me what I can do to earn your respect back.'

Sara gives him a long look that he cannot read: is this pity, regret, exasperation? The one thing he cannot find is the old tenderness. 'You don't have to earn my respect,' she says.

Then reach for me, he thinks. Don't stand there with your arms at your sides. She has just parted her lips to say something when a loud rapping on the metal shutter startles them both.

'Sarita, are you there?' This is a voice Pascual knows.

'*Momento.*' She brushes past him, trailing a hand across his cheek. She crosses the bar, opens the door, stoops to grasp the handle and raises the heavy shutter with an effort. Fernando ducks under it and steps inside.

He fixes on Pascual, still standing dazed behind the bar, and nods. '*¿Qué tal, primo?* Aren't you taking a chance?'

Pascual produces a shrug. 'Maybe.'

'I tried to tell him,' says Sara.

Fernando takes things in at a glance. 'You want me to wait outside?' he says to Sara.

'For a minute, if you don't mind.'

'Take your time.' Fernando gives Pascual a wink and retreats into the street.

Sara walks slowly towards the bar. The penny is just dropping for Pascual and he is stunned at the realization that this is a tryst. 'Don't let your imagination run away with you,' says Sara. 'Fernando's been escorting me home at night. You're not the only one who could be in danger, you said so yourself.'

Pascual nods, numbly. 'I'll shove off then.' He can hear Fernando's *Sarita* ringing in his ears. He shambles out from behind the bar.

She reaches for him then, and holds him very tightly and all too briefly. 'I have many things to say to you,' she whispers and then releases him. 'Soon. Very soon.'

'I'll phone.' Pascual heads for the door.

Outside, Fernando is smoking a cigarette. He peers at Pascual in the dim light from the streetlamps. 'You're walking alone?' he says.

'No, I've got a regiment of infantry waiting just round the corner. Don't worry about me.'

Fernando blows smoke at him. 'Watch yourself. I'll see Sara home safe.'

'I don't doubt it,' says Pascual. 'Many thanks.'

'Vicente Torres Moreno, we think. Known by his trademark panama hat. Quite an accomplished man in his field. Thief, procurer, fence, breaker of bones and trafficker in drugs. He's done a little of everything and we've known him for a long time. For the past few years he's been up to his eyes in the heroin trade, part of Ilmeddin's organization we think, but we haven't made anything stick.' At the other end of the telephone line, Serrano sounds like a man reminiscing about old school mates.

'He's lost the hat.' Across the foyer of the *pensión* Pascual can see Senyora Prat straining to mop without making a noise so that she can eavesdrop.

Serrano says, 'He's probably got a dozen in the wardrobe, but he's smart enough not to wear them when he's lying low. We started looking for him the moment you mentioned the hat, but he's gone to earth. What did he want?'

'He wanted to discuss business, he said. That's when he lost me.'

'He probably thinks you're an associate of Ilmeddin's, or at least a potential partner. We don't exactly have the *organigramae* sketched out, but Ilmeddin certainly still had a hand in the business, and his death will no doubt set off a power struggle. Torres would be looking for allies, wanting to move up the ladder.'

'Maybe. He mentioned a name, nobody I'd ever heard of, as if it should mean something to me. An Italian name, Giacometti, something like that. No, that's not it. Let me think.' Pascual cannot quite hear it, though he can see Torres saying it. 'Giacomo, Giono, Giovanni, something like that.'

'Beginning with G?'

'Yes. Christ, I hadn't thought of that. Yes, G.'

130

'But you can't remember the name?'

'I'll come up with it. It'll come to me.'

'Why didn't you report it immediately? The man's an urgently sought fugitive.'

After a few seconds Pascual says, 'I was distracted.'

'That seems to be a weakness of yours.'

'I've got a lot on my mind. Is there any news from Madrid?'

'For you? Not that I'm aware.'

'All right, I'm only a material witness, maybe a suspect still. But you've practically ordered me to solve this thing myself, and I'm just wondering if anyone's come up with anything that might help.'

'All anyone's told me is to have you ready at a moment's notice when the great man decides he wants to talk to you. He's read your statement, he's seen Weiss's notes, and presumably he's aware of the outline of things as you see it. But when somebody like Ilmeddin dies, there's no shortage of suspects, and the judge has a fairly thick folder of his own notes. I imagine he's finding a lot to occupy him in Marbella. That's where Ilmeddin lived, that's where the first attack took place, and that's where any investigation's going to start. You just keep yourself available. Can I reach you at your *pensión*?'

'I check for messages every day.'

'*Perfecto*. You will phone me if you think of the name of this person Torres wanted to speak to you about, won't you?'

'You can count on it.'

'Giometti.' Pascual says the name out loud, startling an elderly widow in black just ahead of him on the pavement. She halts to see who is spouting incantations behind her and Pascual, intent now on finding a phone, jostles her as he passes. He leaves her muttering in his wake.

'Giometti,' Pascual says when Campos comes through the ether from his mobile phone. 'What does the name Giometti mean to you?'

'Not a thing. What's going on?'

'I had a visit from Ilmeddin's errand boy last night, a fellow named Torres, I'm informed. He wanted to talk about somebody named Giometti, but we were interrupted.'

'Two *t*'s?'

'I imagine. Torres didn't spell it out.'

'Sounds Italian.'

'Well, why not? We've got everybody else involved. What's interesting is the initial.'

'Yes, of course. And why did he want to talk to you about this fellow?'

'How should I know? I never heard of the man. And Torres was chased off before he got a chance to explain. Look, I've got to give this to Serrano, too. You can match wits with him. We'll see who gets to Giometti first.'

'*Hostia*. I don't know when I'll get to it. They've got me chasing down relatives of that woman who got run over on the Diagonal the other day. What are your plans?'

Pascual plugs his ear as a lorry roars by on the street. 'Beyond not getting shot? I hadn't really made any.'

'You've got your assignment, remember?'

'I remember. Figure out what I know.'

'You and nobody else,' says Campos. '*Ciao*.'

15

'What I know', says Pascual, 'is how devious minds work. I know how agreements are made and enforced in a world where nobody would respect the law even if there were any laws. I know about blackmail, extortion, intimidation and terror. I know there is no honour among thieves or political gangsters. This is my area of expertise.' From the window of Father Costa's room Pascual can see the park that stretches along the front of the Clinical Hospital. Children play in the dust, old men in *boinas* and grey suits vegetate on benches. Pascual is watching for familiar figures, idlers who are not quite idle enough, anybody who might be waiting for him. He took elaborate precautions to ensure that his back was clear on his way here, but there are never any guarantees.

By now he knows better than to assume Father Costa is asleep. Physical energy is so precious to the dying priest that it must be hoarded; even the effort of keeping one's eyes open or making polite noises of response is wasteful. Pascual looks across the room to the other bed, occupied again, and wonders if the new patient is also more conscious than he looks and hanging on every word. He decides that it makes little difference; this ward is for the dying and nothing is going to leave this room except what he takes out.

The priest's lips work briefly and his eyes open. In a hollow voice, articulating carefully, he says, 'In the light of all that, it seems to me that you have not given enough thought to G.'

Pascual nods, watching a pretty med student with flowing auburn hair and a long white coat as she crosses the park. 'You're right. I've been trying to put my finger on it all morning.'

The eyes close again and the brow furrows. 'You've been

assuming G must be an ally of your reporter, meaning he's in a camp opposed to both Ilmeddin and M. A disinterested party wanting only to expose scandal. But think about the effect of his accusation. Who loses if it is proven?'

Pascual begins to nod, seeing it. 'M. Only M. Ilmeddin had nothing to lose anyway. His misdeeds have been more or less public knowledge for years. His only concern was to keep them from being proven in a legal sense.'

'Or, from what you've told me, simply to avoid being extradited to a country willing to prosecute him.'

'Yes, of course.'

'And how did he prevent that?'

'Blackmail.'

'Mm.' The priest is running out of energy for speech.

'And a threat to expose M could be an attempt to prevent extradition.'

'Ergo . . .'

'Ergo the threat came from Ilmeddin himself. G is an ally of Ilmeddin.' Father Costa's lips stretch infinitesimally in a phantom smile. 'And further,' says Pascual, 'the place to look for M is in countries trying to extradite Ilmeddin.'

'Bravo,' comes one last word in a whisper.

Pascual learned his English in a high school in Brooklyn, New York, and he has retained the Yank reflex of instant inferiority complex when confronted by plummy upper-class British diction. The fact that the person who answers the telephone at Global Consulting in far-off London is a woman with a husky insinuating purr only compounds Pascual's confusion. 'Mr Hampton, please,' he manages. 'Tell him Stanley Prentice gave me his name.'

Pascual expects to have to jump through the usual hoops, but perhaps because of the magic of Stanley Prentice's name or perhaps because he is once again impersonating Ernesto Campos of *El Mundo*, only a minute passes before a male version of the accent oozes on to the line. 'Hampton here. Campos, the name was?' The voice manages to coat profound scepticism in disarming courtesy.

'Yes. Stanley Prentice suggested I speak with you.'

'Prentice.'

'The American who wrote a book on Hussein Ilmeddin.'

A couple of seconds go by. 'Ah. The man who lost his daughter, I remember. Yes, I spoke to Mr Prentice at length, a number of years ago. He was writing a book, as I recall.'

'That's right, about Ilmeddin.'

'And suddenly Ilmeddin's in the news. I'm assuming that's what you want to talk about?'

'If you've got a few minutes.'

'If it's only a few. So you're delving into Ilmeddin's life and times at last, are you? Too bad it took his death to get people interested.'

'That was pretty much what Mr Prentice said. He also said you might be able to tell me more than he could about Ilmeddin's career.'

'At one time I was quite familiar with Ilmeddin's career. But that was a long time ago. I've been out of the business since 1992. When the Cold War ended I was demobbed, so to speak, and I've been in private business ever since. If you want a précis of his career up through the end of the eighties I can give you one. Whatever he did after that, I really can't say.'

'What I'm interested in is who tipped off Ilmeddin just before a BKA raid in Frankfurt in 1988.'

'Yes, Prentice went on about that at length, I recall. That's been fairly well raked over, actually, and I think the consensus is it was a mole in the BKA. The West German establishment was riddled with spies back then. Every week it seemed they turned up some new fellow who'd seduced a secretary in the Chancellor's office or smuggled out copies of NATO's order of battle or something like that. The BKA wouldn't have been immune, and Ilmeddin was the type of fellow the Soviets might well have protected, at several removes, of course. Ultimately he was serving their interests.'

'Could there be an alternative explanation? An American author named Weiss believed that Ilmeddin had been, what's the term, "flipped" by somebody in the West and used to run stings on the terror groups. Could he have been protected by whoever flipped him, not wanting the BKA to break up whatever they had going?'

After a pause Hampton says, 'Weiss. Would that be the fellow who wrote an exposé of the Iran-Contra thing a few years back?'

'Yes. He was working on Ilmeddin when he died.'

'He's dead?'

'He was shot, actually, here in Barcelona. Shortly before Ilmeddin was killed. You can see why I'm interested.'

'Heavens, yes. Do they know who did it?'

'Nobody's been arrested. But it's believed the two killings are related, along with a third.'

'Good God, somebody's been busy. Who was the third?'

'A fellow who appears to have been an innocent bystander. The theory at the moment is that Weiss was on the track of whoever protected Ilmeddin and that person is trying to cover up.'

'Well, I can't speak to that, I'm afraid.'

'Could I ask you to speculate for a moment? Prentice said that there had been an attempt recently to extradite Ilmeddin to the US, but that it had been dropped. I'm wondering if that might have been because someone over there didn't want certain things to come to light.'

'The Yanks? I suppose it's possible. They did rather a lot of foolish things back in those days, didn't they? Sending missiles off to Iran and so on. And using Ilmeddin would have been damned foolish. The man was a swindler, a professional liar. Not a good risk for an intelligence agent, and it would have been bloody irresponsible to bring a known trafficker in drugs on to the payroll.'

Pascual has personal knowledge of intelligence operations for which 'bloody irresponsible' would be a mild term, but he is willing to make allowances for Hampton's sense of professionalism. 'You wouldn't say it's impossible, though?'

'Certainly it's possible, but then a lot of things are possible. You asked me to speculate and I'm speculating.'

'Could you possibly point me to anyone who might know more?'

'About what the Americans got up to in the eighties? I don't know really – I've got some contacts over there, but I'm not sure anyone I know would be able and willing to talk to you. They're all still active intelligence officers, and like it or not, intelligence still involves keeping secrets. If I were you I'd go back to old

136

Prentice. He did quite a bit of delving on his project, and he'll have the contacts.'

'Yes, I see.' Pascual senses he is bumping up against the limits of Hampton's patience. 'I appreciate your time, Mr Hampton.'

'Not at all. Say hello to Mr Prentice for me, will you? I always felt sorry for the chap. He used to carry a picture of his daughter about, which he'd haul out at odd moments to show people. A real pity.'

When the telephone rings Pascual nearly falls off the chair; he has dozed off under the benign effects of another dose of Father Costa's brandy. He recovers and gropes for the receiver. 'Yes?'

'Mr Campos?' Stanley Prentice's voice crackles in his ear.

'Yes, Mr Prentice. Thanks for getting back to me.'

'Sorry to keep you waiting. I was busy explaining to a client how to keep the government from getting its mitts on the greater part of his estate and these things take time.'

'I understand. I know you must be very busy.'

'So how can I help you today?'

'A couple more questions if I could.' Pascual is trying dizzily to pull together his thoughts. 'You mentioned the last time we spoke that there had been some talk in the States about going after Ilmeddin for his drug-running.'

'That's right. Two or three months ago, I think it was. And then suddenly nothing happened, as they say.'

'Yes. Well, I was wondering if there was some way I might be able to find out what happened, or didn't happen. I mean, why it was that nothing was done.'

'I don't know. It was just bureaucratic business as usual, probably, somebody's bright idea getting vetoed because somebody else higher up says, no, we're not going after heroin dealers this month. Happens all the time. Like I say, they've only got so many bullets in the gun, even at the federal level, and everybody wants a shot.'

'I'm wondering if it might not be because somebody had an interest in keeping it quiet.'

'What do you mean?'

'I mean somebody on your side protected Ilmeddin and tipped him off ahead of the raid.'

'Why the hell would they do that?'

'Because they were using Ilmeddin to run a sting operation involving his terrorist connections and they didn't want that to be disrupted.'

Prentice makes a contemplative grunt. 'Who was it who suggested this to you?'

'It's my own idea, Mr Prentice. Weiss was American and specialized in American scandals, and the logic of it seems to fit. That's all.'

'Well, I can't say it's impossible. I'm not sure how I'd go about proving it.'

'That's why I thought it might be interesting to find out just why the recent attempt to go after Ilmeddin went nowhere.'

'The suggestion would be that the person who protected Ilmeddin back then is in a position to smother a Justice Department investigation now, to keep this from coming to light?'

'Well, if you were a CIA officer who had kept the German police from reeling in one of Europe's biggest dope dealers because you were running an operation of your own, and a few weeks later an operation financed by the dealer killed three hundred and some people, wouldn't you want to keep that quiet?'

Pascual hears nothing but transatlantic ethereal hum for a long moment. 'Mr Campos, you're stirring up things I was hoping I could finally forget about.'

'I'm sorry. People are getting killed over here and I think it's because somebody's still trying to screw the lid down tight.'

'After all these years?'

'Something set things off. Weiss indicated it was because somebody was about to move into a position of power.'

When Prentice speaks again his voice has changed subtly; there is a new note of weariness, almost despondency. 'All right, Mr Campos. I'll tell you what I can do. I can make a few phone calls. We've got a Congressman in this district who's been very helpful to me through the years and I've got a few contacts left from my research. Give me a day or two. You're making me dig into old scar tissue over here and it's not going to be much fun.'

★

138

Pascual is not having much fun either; one aspect of life as a hunted man which he had forgotten is the sheer tedium. Robbed of his livelihood and shut off from his closest friends, he must make the day pass somehow, and after a while he has exhausted even the pleasure of an unmolested nap on Father Costa's sofa.

He hits the street, needing companionship but not knowing where to find it. On the street he has exchanged tedium for stress: constant vigilance, detours and double-backs to make sure he is clean, the need to avoid precisely those few places where he can feel comfortable – Pascual is reliving the worst days of his life.

Or perhaps these are the worst, he reflects as he ducks off the Ronda de Sant Pau into the narrow lanes of the Raval. If he loses Sara everything else will be meaningless. For all Pascual cares, CIA grandees may go on running the world as they please and mercenaries earning an honest living with their marksmanship. Without Sara nothing will matter.

He has a late supper in an old haunt in Carrer del Carme, a long tenebrous room last redecorated about the time Primo de Rivera was trying on his first brown shirt. Hams dangle menacingly from the ceiling and something, maybe bullets, has taken chips out of the *azulejos* tiling the walls. Pascual has been living on sandwiches and coffee, and his lamb stew absorbs him almost to the point of forgetfulness. A liberal dosing of *tinto* on top of it does not hurt.

The worst of his depression dulled, Pascual moves on, tending vaguely in the direction of his *pensión* through the narrow empty streets. He is aware of the risks but thinks the most likely candidate to be lying in wait is Torres, and he would not mind a chance to finish their conversation.

Pascual turns into the Carrer Nou and pauses to light a cigarette, watching. There are no obvious signs of ambush, just a few lighted doorways beneath bar signs and isolated pedestrians. Pascual throws the match into a gutter and makes for his *pensión*. His way is clear until thirty metres shy of his door, when a bar door opens in front of him and a bad dream or a very bad joke spills into the street in the person of four *cabezas rapadas*, two of whom Pascual knows.

Recognition is instant and mutual, and the eyes of the first skin light up before Pascual has time to weigh options. '*Miráaaa . . .*

You I know, *hijo 'e puta*. Look who's here, *chavales*. And no big stick this time.' His hand is on Pascual's collar and the light of alcoholic dementia is in his eyes. Shaved heads, leather jackets, tattoos and all, the entire skinhead nation is suddenly focused on Pascual, radiating instant bloodlust.

He flips his cigarette into the cadaverous face, knocks the hand off his collar and takes to his heels, knowing the odds are slim he can outrun four younger men well conditioned for this kind of sport. His best hope is to make it to a friendly bar, but he has gone only ten metres before he is hauled down from behind, wrestled to the ground like a stag caught by hounds. Now it is a matter of survival; thoughts of inflicting damage simply do not enter the calculation. Foetal position, thinks Pascual as the first kick to the ribs jars him. That is easier said than done in the maelstrom of booted feet and with his jacket torn half off him, restricting the movement of his arms. A blow to his face stuns him and from then on there is only a cruel, sick Calvary of mounting damage to flesh and bone, sensed all too vividly through the black fog that is descending. Even through the catastrophic noises of facial bones breaking he can hear the grunts of the skins as they deliver the blows, men concentrating on their work. Somewhere someone is screaming.

It is only a groan now and Pascual knows he is conscious again when he realizes that it is his groan. There is a liquid element to the sound which tells him, along with the rich salt taste of blood in his mouth, that he is bleeding on to the cobbles. The pain in his face is distributed in an alarming way that hints at features out of place and there are teeth where no teeth should be; his tongue can no longer make sense of his mouth. The agony in his torso goes all the way to the core.

He becomes aware of feet, shuffling near his face; he can hear voices now, hushed and appalled. Someone is calling his name. He groans louder in response. Hands cradle his head, roll him gently on to his back. 'Pascual.'

She is crying, he sees as he focuses with eyes that are rapidly swelling shut, crying for him, crying at the sight of what they have done to him and Pascual wants to comfort her, to tell her that he has survived, that nothing they can do to him is worth these bitter tears. He tries to reach for her, but there is nothing he can do that does not bring pain, and through the pain Pascual begins to feel a great joy, because only now is he realizing how extraordinary it is to see Lola here, back from the dead, weeping over him.

16

'How long have I been here?' says Pascual, articulating carefully with swollen lips.

'Two days,' says Sara, tenderly brushing hair from his forehead. He can see her with his good eye, grave and pale, brows contracted slightly in a frown of concentration, hair drawn back to reveal the long clean lines of her face. His recollection is fogged by painkillers, but he thinks she has been here through the worst of it. Around him in this crowded ward lie other casualties of urban life, accident victims, survivors of falls, losers of bar fights.

'I have to get out of here,' he says.

'Soon. You'll come to stay with us until you're better.'

Suddenly Pascual remembers his vision. 'I saw Lola. She's back, isn't she?' The look of dismay on Sara's face is all the answer Pascual needs. His spirits, briefly revived, plummet anew. 'I thought I saw her. She was there. Just after it happened. She was crying.'

'We'll talk about all that later.' He can tell she does not believe him and now he doubts: was it only a peculiar effect of concussion, the confounding of Lola's shaved head with those of his assailants? None of what has happened since the skinheads tore into him is clear enough to swear to. Sara squeezes his hand and says, 'Can you tolerate another visitor?'

'Who?'

'Your minder,' says Serrano, moving into view, 'who hasn't been doing a very good job, apparently.' Scowling down at him, hands in his trouser pockets, the inspector looks like a man whose dog has disappointed him. 'Feel up to a chat?'

'There was a policeman here yesterday, I think. I made a report, if I remember rightly.'

'Yes, and the papers are playing it as skins on a spree. I'm wondering if you want to say anything different now that I'm here.'

'No, that's what it was. Just boys having fun.'

Serrano makes a noise of contempt. 'Why you?'

'We'd crossed paths before. The Old City's a small town, really. I was bound to run into them again eventually.'

'Random violence, eh? Nothing to do with dead Arabs or American reporters?'

'Nothing at all. Did my name appear in the paper?'

'Only the first name and an initial. And there must be several thousand men named Pascual in this city. If anyone's on the lookout for you, I don't think they've been tipped to lie in wait outside the hospital.'

'You should have kept the tail on me,' Pascual says.

'The thought has occurred to me. Not that it would have saved you the beating, necessarily.'

'Very funny.'

'When you're up to it,' says Serrano, 'I'd like you to come in and look at some pictures.'

'You've got all our local skins on file, have you?'

'I don't mean pictures of skins. I want you to look at some pictures we've been sent by Interpol.'

Pascual waits out a few heartbeats and says, 'Who?'

'Very possibly, the men who killed Morris Weiss and Gabriel Heredia.'

Pascual walks down the steps of the Clinical Hospital like an eighty-year-old man. An oral surgeon has saved his teeth, though one chipped incisor is now permanently jagged against his tongue; other doctors have rerouted his nose, which is functional again but looks something like a topographical model of the Guadarrama; a broad elastic band around his chest holds his mending ribs in place, constricting his breathing; he walks with care to avoid jarring his bruised kidney. In his pocket is a vial full of pills which are to get him through the next few days and nights. He can see out of both eyes now and is grateful for it; after the

143

gloom of the ward the bright May sunshine is making a paradise of the dusty park in front of the hospital. A child flees crying to his mother's skirts at the sight of him.

He can still hear the hurt in Sara's voice on the telephone, trying to persuade him to wait for Joselito to arrive with the car. There is nothing he would like better than to spend his convalescence in the flat in Carrer Princesa, letting Sara nurse him slowly back to health, but he has one principle to guide him: as long as ruthless people are looking for him, knowledge of his whereabouts is dangerous to anyone who possesses it. He rounds a corner and makes for the Metro station.

On the platform, people give him a wide berth; on the train the crowd makes way like the Red Sea parting before Moses. Pascual wonders why signs of grievous injury should be taken as threatening, but he is happy to have a seat.

The desk sergeant at the side entrance to the Jefatura is not at all sure he should admit this walking corpse, but a phone call upstairs confirms that he has been summoned by Serrano, and Pascual labours up the stairs, escorted by Delgado, who looks as if he is enjoying the pitiful sight. 'Back from the dead, I see,' says Serrano cheerfully from behind his desk.

'I suppose I must be. A dead man couldn't possibly feel this bad.' Pascual eases his battered carcass on to a chair. 'You said you had some pictures.'

'Yes. We've had a little luck and Interpol's been very helpful and we think we may have some suspects.' He pulls a folder out of a drawer. 'The photos are not very recent and they're only faxes, of course, but you never know. Have a look and tell me if anyone looks familiar.'

Pascual opens the folder to see what appears to be a fax of a police record sheet with the usual mug shots and fingerprints and other particulars. The top sheet is headed *Police nationale – DCPJ* and shows a moustachioed man on the down side of forty, looking into the camera with a sullen glare because a big hulking copper has ordered him to. Pascual's first reaction is to say that he has never seen this man in his life; his second reaction is that he has seen a million men who look just like this. The face could be Latin; it could be Arab; it could be Serbian or Turkish. It is a generic southern Caucasian face, made to pass unnoticed in

144

crowds from Buenos Aires to Baku. Pascual looks at the name: *Gómez, Esteban*. 'Arrested in France but with a Spanish name. What is he?'

'Cuban.'

'Cuban? Not many of those about.'

'No. This one apparently floated ashore in Florida when Castro emptied his jails back in 1980 or so. He'd fought in Angola and then got in trouble back home and decided to take his chances with the sharks when given the chance. How he got to France nobody knows, but he was arrested in Paris three years ago and charged with murder for hire. He was acquitted when the key witness changed his mind about testifying.'

'I see.' Pascual is getting a tickle at the back of his mind, but when he chases it it vanishes. If he has seen this man before, he will be lucky to remember where. He goes to the second sheet.

This one he knows. *Fuck you, mate*, he can hear him saying. He can see the old man's beret on his head and the dispassionate look in the light-coloured eyes as he raises the automatic towards Gabriel at point-blank range. 'That's him,' Pascual says. 'That's the man who shot Gabriel.'

Serrano is leaning towards him, intent. 'You're sure, are you?'

'Absolutely. His hair was a little longer, but it's the same man. I'd swear to it before any judge you want.' Pascual drops the paper on the desktop, light-headed.

'Are you all right?'

Pascual steadies. He reads a name at the bottom of the sheet. *Coetzee, Adrian.* 'I'm fine. So who's this one?'

'This one's a South African. Also fought in Angola, strangely enough. Since then he's been arrested once for assault, in London, and that's all that's known about him.'

'How did you get on to these fellows?'

Serrano stows the folder and leans slowly back on his chair. 'As I said, we needed a bit of luck. Two days after Weiss was killed we got a call from somebody at the Hotel Colón. It seems a chambermaid there had reported something that bothered her. Shortly after Weiss got there she was doing his room when another guest came in and started speaking to her in some language she didn't know, making signs demanding that she

145

come with him. She went with him to his room, which was just down the hall, and found he'd broken a glass in the bathroom. She went to fetch a brush to clean it up, which meant going back to her cart just outside Weiss's room, and she heard a noise in the room, took a look and found a man in there. She'd never seen Weiss, so she didn't know if this was the guest who belonged there or not, but what was curious was that he seemed to have been fiddling with the telephone. He made some excuse and left, and she went about her work and didn't think much more about it until Weiss turned up dead. Then she reported it.'

It takes Pascual a moment to see it. 'They bugged his phone.'

'Yes. As soon as we heard the chambermaid's tale we sent the forensic team over there. Unfortunately we just missed these two – they'd just checked out, together, though they'd had separate rooms. This was the morning after Heredia was killed. But, sure enough, they'd put a bug in the receiver of Weiss's phone. And, more to the point, not worn gloves while doing it.'

'Fingerprints. Brilliant.'

'That's right. Weiss had used the phone for a week after that, but fortunately the bits you handle to install a bug are different from the bits you touch to make a call, so the technicians could distinguish Weiss's prints, which they got off his body, from the ones they wanted. And we were lucky again in that the maids hadn't got around to cleaning the rooms the two had vacated, and we took prints from them as well. Those in one room matched up with those on the bugged phone. We got just enough clear prints to send off to Interpol and their omnipotent computer. And the final bit of luck, of course, was that these two specimens had been arrested and fingerprinted before. It took a while, but they came up with possible match-ups yesterday.'

'Unbelievable.'

'The march of progress, my son.'

'No doubt they were registered under false names?'

'No, actually, the names seem to be real. Interpol was able to trace one of them. The man was most surprised to find out that he had spent a week at the Colón recently, as he was not aware of having budged from Manchester. He'll be even more surprised when he gets the bill.'

'They stole his credit card?'

146

'Not the card, just his identity, apparently, to obtain their own card in his name. It's getting easier all the time. Nick a pre-approved credit-card application out of someone's rubbish bin and correct the address, send it in and there you go, you've got a new life, at least until the real owner of the name starts getting billed for things he didn't buy. Just make sure you can't be traced through the address you had the card delivered to. Or they may have used any of a hundred other stratagems. If you're only interested in the short term, something quick and disposable, it's easy to set up a false identity.'

'So where are they now?'

'Unfortunately we don't know that. But we were able to find out that they flew out of Barcelona that same day, for Frankfurt. God knows where they went from there.'

'They're gone?'

'That's right. Which means . . .'

'Which means they never realized they hit the wrong man.'

Serrano nods. 'Not unless someone's tipped them off since. And I don't think Heredia's death would have made the papers outside Spain.'

Suddenly Pascual is dizzy with relief. 'All that sneaking about, all the precautions.'

'The assault on a police officer.'

'Yes, that too. It was all for nothing. I was looking for professional *sicarios* and all the time it was the local *gamberros* I had to worry about.'

Serrano cocks his head to one side. 'Maybe. But their departure means something else, too.'

'What?'

'It means they didn't kill Ilmeddin.'

Pascual can only stare, swollen lips parted. 'So there was another team.'

'Apparently. The same one that tried it in Marbella, perhaps. We don't know. It would be interesting to know how they traced him here.'

'But since they got him the second time, they're probably long gone as well.'

'Could be.'

Pascual senses that he will need to devote a little thought to this

147

some time when painkillers are not slowing his mental processes. 'Did you ever find out who this Giometti might be?'

Serrano shrugs. 'It's not an uncommon name in Italy. There is a family of that name associated with the N'Drangheta in the south, for what that's worth. And there could be a connection with Ilmeddin, since the Italian crime families are up to their eyes in the heroin trade. It's possible there was some negotiation in the works and Torres took you for an emissary, given that Ilmeddin wanted to see you so badly. But I'm just guessing. Until we can find Torres and sweat it out of him that's all I can do.' Serrano gives Pascual a contemplative look. 'Feeling better?'

Pascual assesses his physical and psychic condition. 'Starting to. Just starting.'

Senyora Prat blanches at the sight of him, delivers a long harangue on the disgraceful lack of security in the quarter and finally leaves him alone. Pascual lies on his bed and looks at the cracked ceiling until he drifts off to sleep with late afternoon commotion drifting up from the street.

His dreams are turbulent and perverse and he awakes in the dark feeling feverish and unrested. His mouth is dry and his painkillers have worn off and certain things have become clear to him. He lies in his sweat-damp clothes for a while, wondering at the obscure workings of the mind, before rising slowly and with great effort to hobble down the hall to the WC. Back in his room he pops more pills and stands at the window looking down into the narrow street. The evening is tolerably warm and the pavements are crowded. He is bemused by his new knowledge. It amazes him that he could have lain for days in confusion. What he so easily took for a hallucination was, he knows now, nothing of the sort. He knows without doubt that Lola is alive and held his head in her hands on the night he was beaten. From where he stands he can see the spot in the street where he lay.

Pascual goes down the hall to the telephone and punches in the number for the bar. Enric answers. 'They've hauled you back from death's door, have they?' he says. 'I don't suppose you'd like to come back and work? They're running me off my feet.'

'Sara's not there?'

'It's her night off. I've stuck Nuria behind the bar, but she's about as useful as a three-legged donkey.'

'Where's Sara?'

'Sorry, it's not my day to mind her. You just missed Joselito, though. He was here not five minutes ago, looking for you. He said to ring him or come by the house, very urgent. Hang on, he left his number here somewhere.'

Pascual rings off without ceremony and dials Joselito's number. At the other end, Joselito's voice is crackling with urgency. 'Be waiting in front of your door in ten minutes. I'm coming to get you.'

'Why? What's going on?'

'Pilar needs us.'

'Pilar? What happened?'

'Her father's back.'

17

Joselito throws the old SEAT into gear while Pascual still has a foot trailing out of the passenger door. Pascual swears and pulls the door shut just before it knocks down a pensioner tottering along in the gutter. 'Explain,' he says brusquely. 'What's Pilar's father got to do with me?'

'The brother's with him. I can't do it alone.'

'Do what for Christ's sake?'

'Get her out of their clutches.'

Pascual goggles at the little man hunched over the wheel. 'What, you mean they've kidnapped her?'

'Not as you might say kidnapped. She walked out with the old bastard of her own free will. But he's taken her to some other relative's house, in the Barceloneta. She phoned an hour ago and said could I come and get her and be prepared for some resistance. Then the brother cut in and told me to fuck off and hung up. Don't you see? They want the flat back and they're going to wear her down until she agrees to give it up.'

Pascual has to close his eyes for a moment. 'Joselito, it's not my fight.'

'It is now. We're going to go and get her out of there. She gave me the address. Those two, they're capable of putting up a fight out of sheer bloody-mindedness. That's why I need you.'

'You want me to come and start a brawl with people I don't even know? The shape I'm in, I'm as much good in a fight as your grandmother.'

'You never knew my grandmother, *chico*. She decked a few men in her time, believe me. Look, all you have to do is stand there and be ready. The way you look, they'll believe you're fearless.'

'They'll believe I'm an easy target. Joselito, this is absurd. They can't hold her against her will. What the hell are they going to do to her?'

Joselito is the least imposing of men, but right now the look in his eyes would clear a dockside bar-room. 'Who knows? But I saw how that fucking villain treated his wife. I'm not going to let him do that to his daughter as well.' He pulls on to the Ramblas with a screech of tyres. 'He used to hit his wife in the stomach so her face wouldn't be marked. She'd come down the stairs like an old woman, bent over from the pain. And then give you a cheery hello as if nothing in the world was wrong. A saint, she was, that's where Pilar got it. The brother, he turned out like the old man. I nearly hit him once, the little shit. Maybe I'll get a chance tonight.'

'If you go looking for it, it's going to happen. And I don't have the stomach for a fight, I'm telling you.'

'*Tranquilo*. I'm not going to start anything.'

Joselito drives like a ferret scattering chickens, pushing the old coughing SEAT to its limit. Pascual waits until the car settles back on to four wheels after screeching around the base of the Columbus monument and says casually, 'Where's Sara tonight?'

'I don't know. At the bar probably.'

'She's not. I tried to phone her there. Is she with Lola?'

'With Lola? What gave you that idea?'

'Lola's alive, isn't she?'

Joselito veers across two lanes before answering. 'Of course she's alive. I told you so.'

'I mean you've known it all along. You've been hiding her.'

'Not me. I haven't seen her.'

'What's going on with those girls, Joselito?'

'Right now what's going on is that Pilar needs us. Let's get her home and then we'll worry about Lola.'

The Barceloneta is the crotch of the thumb on the giant hand that encloses the port of Barcelona, a perfectly regular grid of high cramped houses on narrow straight streets, all that is left of the old fisherman's city and a roistering working-class haven. The ruthless Olympic makeover leached out some of its roguish

151

charm but left it with a long stretch of pleasant palm-lined beach on the side away from the harbour. Joselito careens along the Passeig Joan de Borbó and wheels abruptly into a cross street that takes them into the heart of the district. Startled pedestrians leap out of his way. 'Not too far now,' he mutters. 'Look at this imbecile, walking in the street.' He has located the brake and rolls slowly through the narrow lanes, muttering street names under his breath.

'What are we looking for?' says Pascual.

'This, I think,' says Joselito, slowing. A plaza opens on their left, a narrow tree-lined strip with traffic lanes on either side. Joselito turns down the long side of the square. A few people, mostly children, are milling listlessly in the middle of the plaza or in dimly lit entrances to the buildings. The edges of the square are packed tightly with parked cars and motorcycles. 'What's that number? Can you see?'

'What number? I can't see a fucking thing.' Joselito makes a slow circuit of the plaza, turning at the end to come up the other side. Pascual spots a number and reads it.

'No, we want 25. Must be further on.'

'We've seen the whole place. Let me ask someone.'

'Hang on, let's try the other side again.' He rounds the end and begins a second lap.

Pascual has lost patience. 'Look, let me get out and ask this woman. I believe they speak some known language here.'

'*Momento.*' Joselito accelerates slightly and swerves over a few metres on. 'I think it's here. Pilar said look for a *peluquería*. Go and see if you can find the number.'

Pascual heaves a sigh and gets out. He has begun to close the door when Joselito says, 'Pascual.'

'What?'

'Take this.' Joselito reaches across the seat and hands Pascual a plastic bag he has pulled from his jacket pocket.

'What's this?' The bag swings against the door with a clunk.

'Something you'll need. Look inside.' Abruptly Joselito hits the gas and the car lurches away, the door swinging partially shut. Pascual stares after the car in astonishment for two seconds and then a slow freeze begins to rise from his entrails. He reaches into the bag as he becomes aware simultaneously of two things: a figure running across the plaza near the far end, which he recognizes instantly and beyond doubt as Pilar, and the noise of a car pulling away from the kerb twenty metres behind him.

'Pascual.' He is still gawking at Pilar, watching her run as Joselito tears up the street towards her, and it is not until he hears someone behind him call his name that his hand closes on the object in the bottom of the bag. There is not much time left now, as the car has drawn nearly even, and Pascual spins to see the man in the passenger seat of the maroon Peugeot extending his arm for a one-handed shot that cannot miss at a range of a metre and a half from a slowly rolling car.

Pascual fires through the bag with Joselito's undersized automatic. It makes an absurd crack-crack noise and Pascual compensates for its small calibre by squeezing the trigger repeatedly as fast as he can, peppering the man in the Peugeot with five, maybe six shots as he rolls by, with no visible effect but for the sudden expression of distress on the man's face and the absence of any return fire. The Peugeot accelerates suddenly with a squeal of tyres and leaves Pascual reeling against a parked car at his back.

It is a fine vantage point to watch the sequel. The Peugeot is still accelerating, starting to overtake Joselito's old battered SEAT, when Joselito goes into a sudden skid, slewing sideways with an agonizing screech of brakes, blocking the way. The Peugeot brakes as well, but too late; the crash resounds across the square as it broadsides Joselito's car and rams it into a parked car before coming to rest. The driver's side door of the Peugeot opens and a man stumbles out and begins to run, across the square. The world is starting to turn again, voices beginning to break the shocked silence. Pascual begins to run towards the wrecked cars. Every jarring step hurts but he barely notices.

Joselito sits motionless, his head lolling against the seat back, eyes closed and mouth open, not a mark on him. On the passenger seat of the Peugeot a man has been thrown forward against the dashboard by the force of the crash and his face is hidden; he is as still as Joselito. Others have got there before Pascual and are staring with blank faces. Pascual is still clutching the gun, the shredded plastic bag still masking it. He moves slowly away, dazed but starting to think. Nobody is looking at him and he shakes off the plastic bag and stuffs the gun in his pocket. On the far side of the square a van is rolling; it halts just long enough to allow the running man to leap into the passenger seat and then it tears away. Pascual is looking for Pilar but she is gone.

The *serenos* with their long blue coats and staves of authority are long gone from the night-time streets of Barcelona, banished by progress. Pascual can remember when the *serenos* ruled the night; once the street entrance was locked at midnight, the only way to gain entrance to one's own building was to appeal to the *sereno* with his jangling ring of keys. Pascual remembers his mother standing in the street and clapping imperiously, summoning the *sereno* from around the corner or down the block. By the time he was a teenager and old enough to defy his mother's curfew, it was the dread of an interrogation from old Ferrer that brought him hustling through the streets desperate to arrive before the witching hour.

Pascual has wound up here in the Eixample in the same way that a wounded animal finds its way back to home turf. He has come all the way from the Barceloneta trying to get his mind around what is happening.

He does not blame Joselito; he can work out what crushing pressures must have been in operation and it is after all Joselito's gift that saved him. Joselito made the choice Pascual would have expected him to make.

Now shelter is his first concern. He has been through the options and rejected them all. His *pensión* is out; at this point the Raval as a whole must be considered too much of a risk. There must be someone who would lend him a sofa on the strength of a phone call, but he has let too many friendships erode. In the Eixample he has relatives, but these are neither the time nor the circumstances for a family reconciliation.

Which leaves old Ferrer. On one of his wistful rambles through the Eixample, Pascual discovered the old *sereno* propped at the bar of a *bodega* in Carrer Mallorca, whiling away the long nights of his retirement. Recognition was quicker on Pascual's side than on the old man's, but a casual friendship ensued. When a certain mood strikes him, often late at night, Pascual can reliably find Ferrer in the *bodega* and soothe his ache for a vanished past by feeding the old man drinks and listening to his reminiscences.

Tonight Ferrer is nursing a *fino* at a table in the rear of the *bodega*, hands resting on the head of his cane, muffled in overcoat and scarf. The *bodega* is dark and gloomy, with black casks of wine perched threateningly on racks above the heads of the men hunched over the bar. Women do not enter here, nor do men below a certain age tread lightly. As Pascual steps down the room, heads turn. 'What happened to you?' says Ferrer, eyes glinting through thick spectacles, as Pascual approaches.

'I had a little disagreement with some neighbours.' Pascual's legs give out just as he reaches a chair.

'You need to move to a better neighbourhood,' says Ferrer. 'I've been expecting you, you know.'

'Eh?'

'For days I've been saying it was about time for you to straggle in again. I was talking to your cousin Pere the other day. He was astonished to find you're still about.'

'Ah yes, Pere. Does he still live around here?'

'He's got your grandmother's flat. Three children he's got now. Didn't you know?'

Pascual shrugs. 'Probably. I don't keep in very close touch.'

'So I understand. "I'm surprised he's not in prison, that one," Pere said.' A corner of Ferrer's mouth twists in amusement.

'He's always had sharp judgement, Pere has. Can I buy you another sherry?'

The ritual accomplished, Ferrer raises a fresh drink and says, 'So. What really happened? Money troubles? Women troubles?'

'Both. You must be psychic.'

'Just old. Seen it all, I have. At least twice. And usually in the wee hours, when people are most likely to pour out their hearts.'

'Then you won't be too shocked to hear my tale.' Pascual gives it a second or two and says, 'She's thrown me out on the street. The beating's courtesy of her brothers.'

Ferrer smiles again. 'And what did you do to her? You didn't hit her, did you?'

'Never. Just strayed a little, that's all. Too many pretty women about. A little too much to drink, a little kiss, things got out of hand. She's a jealous woman.'

'Ah, that's a tough one.' Ferrer shakes his hairless pink head in sympathy. 'Literally out on the street?'

155

'Without enough money for a place to lay my head.'

'Then perhaps it's me who should be buying. What are you going to do?'

Pascual shrugs and empties his glass. 'I was hoping actually you might be able to help. Somebody with a spare room, a place I could sleep for a couple of nights until I touch some money that's owed me.'

He can see Ferrer sizing him up, an ironic light in his eyes, suddenly thirty years younger and in full regalia, looming over a quivering adolescent who has stayed out too late. 'I'm not sure I could inflict you on any of the good ladies who rent out rooms hereabouts, but I may be able to help.' Ferrer taps a finger on the head of his cane. 'You always were a trial to your mother, that I recall.'

Pascual has dossed down in worse places; this dank windowless cell at least has an intact roof and is free of smells associated with vermin. 'Nobody's ever taken the trouble to change the lock,' says Ferrer in a hushed voice, aware of the six storeys of sleeping families above their heads. 'I'm not sure the current owner of the building even knows it's here. These old cellars go on for ever, real labyrinths. This was on old Roca's beat. He bequeathed me the key when they put him out to pasture, poor man. It was always nice to have a place to duck in out of the cold for a few minutes on winter nights, even though one couldn't tarry, of course. He kept a little electric stove in here and he'd invite you down for a quick nip of something hot.'

'I'm most grateful,' says Pascual, looking about in the weak light of the single dusty bulb high on the wall. He sees pitted masonry walls, a chair, a moth-eaten blanket on a crude wooden cot. 'I only hope I can find my way out again.'

'Down the passage, right, left again, up the steps and out through the garage. Just don't make a lot of noise and remember to lock the door when you leave.' Ferrer holds out the key and fixes him with a look. 'I'm trusting you,' he says.

Pascual takes the key and avoids the old man's eyes. 'Nobody will know I'm here.'

Ferrer nods once in approval. 'That would be best.'

★

156

The barman gives Pascual the eye as he slouches along the bar towards the telephone; Pascual would stop and order a coffee to establish his bona fides, but he is a driven man this morning.

There is no answer at the flat; Pascual lets it ring long after even the soundest sleeper would have torn the receiver off the hook and snarled into it. Relieved, he hangs up and dials his *pensión*. This time it is the stolid Prat, his landlord, who answers. Pascual has some difficulty in establishing his identity, as Prat seems unable to grasp that he is not just down the hall in his bed. Pascual finally manages to extract the information that someone named Sara has left a message for him. 'One moment, I've got it written down here.' An eternity of muffled noises follows, and then old Prat says, 'I'm just reading you what it says here, as far as I can make it out. The wife's not got the easiest hand to read.'

'*Vale, vale*. What's it say?'

'It says, "Sara's with Fernando, in La Mina. Will call you." Does that sound right? I'd swear it says La Mina. I'll go and ask the wife if you want.'

Dully, Pascual says, 'No, no. I'm sure that's it.'

'*Mare de Déu*, La Mina. That's a neighbourhood you want to steer clear of. Full of gypsies, La Mina is. You want to warn your friend.'

Pascual rings off in his ear.

'Why did you run away?' Serrano looks as if he has wearied of this game. 'Why did you wait until this morning to come in? I should think you might consider shooting a man to death the type of thing that might require a word with the authorities. There's a *comisaría* in the heart of the Barceloneta, not two hundred metres from where you were. If I'm not mistaken, they were open for business last night.'

Pascual is as sick of the whole process as anyone. 'The shooters were still in the neighbourhood. You really expect me to stand there calling loudly for the police? I made tracks like a fucking rabbit.'

Serrano nods. 'Perfectly reasonable. And, of course, you'd just killed a man.'

On top of his other ailments Pascual is suddenly experiencing a nasty queasiness. 'I had no idea I'd hit him. I fired in sheer panic, if you want the truth.'

'You only hit him once, but you hit him where it counted. He bled to death from a wound in his throat.'

'It was self-defence. You must have found his gun.'

Serrano gives his partner an enquiring look. 'Did we find a gun?'

Delgado shrugs. 'I didn't.'

'Ah, stuff it,' says Pascual. 'He had a great fucking automatic he pointed at me. What would you have done?'

Serrano shrugs. 'Probably about what you did. But I'd have gone straight to the *comisaría* and turned myself in, if it truly was self-defence. And I'd certainly have reported the attack on my friend. Weren't you concerned about her?'

'I ran after her, but she'd disappeared. There were plenty of people about, so I thought she'd probably find help. Then I thought I saw the van again, coming along the street, so I ran. I wound up on the beach and I just lay there for a long time, watching for pursuit, right at the water's edge. When I thought it was safe I walked up into the Eixample.'

'In your condition? Quite a feat. Where's the gun?'

'I threw it into the sea.'

'Why? Weren't you afraid you'd need it again? Since the shooters were still about, I mean.'

'It was empty. I could possibly show you the spot if you want to drag the sea bed.'

'Mm. Where'd you spend the night?'

'With friends.'

'You've got a few left, have you? I should think most of them would have learned to run the other way when they see you coming.'

Pascual has had enough. 'You think I'm enjoying this? *You think I've got no bloody feelings?*' With Delgado's firm hand on his shoulder he subsides on to the chair. His head hurts, his ribs hurt, his ears are ringing. 'All right. I panicked. All I could think of was finding a place to hide. Look, I'm here this morning. What more do you want?'

Serrano gives him a long dispassionate look, hands clasped on his belly, rotating very slightly back and forth on his swivel chair.

'At this point, I'm afraid it's not so much what I want as what the magistrate who got called out to the Barceloneta last night wants. *Dios mío*, you're going to be acquainted with the entire Audiencia before long if you keep this up.'

As with so many other things in his life, Pascual has found the dreaded *calabozo* in the cellars beneath the Jefatura less than it's cracked up to be. There are no signs of torture or extrajudicial executions, only the utterances of losers of all stripes, scrawled, scratched or burned into the less-than-virginal white paint. *Curro 24/8/88 que se jodan* he reads, for the hundredth time. They have put him in a cell all his own, with bars over a small window in the door. A shelf of concrete and a cracked and seatless bowl of porcelain constitute the only furniture; at night they will give him a mattress, if he is here that long. He can hear murmurs in nearby cells and has begun to long for companionship, even of thugs or drunks; the solitude is killing him. He spoke with the *juez de instrucción* for fifteen minutes several hours ago and has been left to rot here since.

A key rattles in the lock and the door swings open. 'Eh, stuff it back in your pants and make yourself decent. You're wanted upstairs.' The mocking eyes of the duty officer appear in the doorway. It has not taken long for Pascual to begin to hate him. He grins as Pascual shambles past him into the corridor. 'Your lucky day, *chaval*. You missed the bus to the Modelo.'

Upstairs, Serrano comes out of the interview room when he catches sight of Pascual and waves him to a chair. Pascual sinks on to it and stares through the glass at Pilar, sitting rigid and straight, her lips barely moving. Delgado sits at a desk taking notes.

'How is she?' says Pascual.

Serrano fills a glass with water from a plastic bottle and shoves it towards him. 'She's all right. They kept her overnight at the hospital but she's not hurt.'

'And Joselito?'

'He's got concussion and some broken bones but he'll live. It will take more than an auto wreck to kill that one.'

'He saved my life. Pilar's too. He knew they didn't intend to leave anyone alive.'

'No, probably not.' Serrano's harsh manner of earlier in the day has faded and he looks weary. 'You and your friend seem to have collaborated perfectly in this matter. He'll get no worse than a fine for the illegal weapon, and you'll be found to have acted in *defensa propia*, provided the judge decides everybody's telling the truth.'

'Is that in doubt?'

'It's always in doubt. For what it's worth, the accounts of both your friends confirm that there was an attempt to kill you.'

'What happened, exactly?'

'What happened was, somebody knew who your friends were. Two men turned up at the building in Calle Princesa, yesterday afternoon. They knocked up Joselito and told him they had Pilar. They'd shoved her into a car in the Passeig del Born half an hour earlier, when she was heading home after a quick coffee at the bar.'

'They've been watching the place. For days, maybe weeks.'

'No doubt. They needed two hostages, of course, to get to you. They told Joselito to produce you or the girl would face the consequences. He didn't feel he had much of a choice.'

'I'm not going to hold it against him. You should give him a medal instead of a fine.'

'I don't make the weapons laws. But you're right about his saving your lives. He played it as well as it could be played. According to him, they wanted him to park the car and walk away, but he insisted he wasn't stopping until he saw the girl freed. "I don't see her running, I'm not stopping," he says he told them. He knew what he had to do.'

Pascual shakes his head in wonder. 'So who did I shoot?'

A thin smile narrows Serrano's eyes. 'If the Sandinistas had had a few more like you, they'd still be running Nicaragua.'

'What are you talking about?'

'You potted yourself a Contra, friend. At least, that's what the speculation is. He had a Mexican passport but a tattoo on his arm that says *Patria y libertad* above the initials *ARDE*.'

Dazed, Pascual says, 'Did you get any of the others?'

'How many others did you see?'

'Only the one who ran from the car, but there must have been at least two more in the van.'

'Yes, the van. Could you identify it, do you think?'

'I don't know. It was white, I think, with something written on the side in red. There was a lot happening suddenly and the circumstances weren't ideal for observing details.'

'Well, fortunately your friend Joselito had had the leisure to note a few things. He was able to give us a number-plate and the name of the company it belonged to. It had been stolen from a courier service out near the airport that morning. Unfortunately they hadn't noticed it was missing until late afternoon. By the time they reported it stolen the whole thing was almost over.'

'Car thieves and Contras. What next? We haven't seen any Chinese yet.'

'Yes, there haven't been so many foreign villains in Spain since Napoleon came over the Pyrenees. And it's all because of you.'

Pascual throws up his hands. 'I've told you everything I can think of. What more can I do?'

Serrano gives him a pitiless stare. 'You can tell me why the killers came back. Who told them they'd hit the wrong man?'

'I don't know. Maybe someone read the papers.'

'Who? Who's their local correspondent?'

'I don't know.'

'You might wish to give it some thought. When you get back from the Juzgados.'

'I'm up for trial? Already?'

'No, actually I think you'll probably be released. Right now, however, your presence is required by our friend Espinoza, who's received a *mandamiento* from on high.'

'Meaning Madrid?'

'That's right. Pinzón has decided it's time to find out what you know.'

18

Els Jutjats, seat of the Audiencia, the principal criminal court of Barcelona, stands just across from the Zoological Museum at a corner of the Ciutadella park, an ugly building on a pretty tree-lined street. The hoosegow, thinks Pascual with foreboding, his mind lighting on the Yanqui slang derived from *juzgado*, the Castilian form. 'So what's going to happen?' he says to Serrano as they clear the security barrier inside the entrance.

'Whatever His Eminence in Madrid has told Espinoza he should make happen,' Serrano tosses over his shoulder. 'A *mandamiento* is an order from a superior judge to a subordinate to carry out whatever he wants done. I imagine Espinoza will take you through everything and have you sign a statement.'

The building is entirely decorated in grey, floor to ceiling. Espinoza occupies an office on the first floor, where functionaries mill in an anteroom. Pascual sits and tries to find colour to look at while Serrano murmurs importantly to his colleagues. Time grinds to a halt and Pascual dozes.

He comes awake with a jerk when Serrano nudges him. Still not entirely focused, he allows himself to be led into the inner office, where Espinoza sits behind a large desk. Serrano steers him to a chair and takes a seat at the side of the room.

Espinoza has traded the blazer for a more sober dark grey suit today, a pair of reading glasses perched on his nose. 'What happened to you?' he says, peering at Pascual over the top of the lenses.

'I was attacked by some wild animals.'

The judge's eyes flick to Serrano. 'This is the business that happened last night?'

'No. This was something else. He seems to have a lot of enemies.'

Espinoza appears to mull this over for a long moment before turning to Pascual and saying, 'So you're the man everyone wants dead.'

'So it seems.'

'Do you know why?'

'I only know what I've been told. The American was the one who thought he knew what was going on.'

'Mr Weiss. Yes, he thought he knew. Was he right?'

'I don't know. All I can tell you is what I did and what I saw in 1988.'

'Your collaboration with the late Mr Ilmeddin.'

'Yes.'

'And you can identify the man who protected him?'

'If you can find out who he is and if he hasn't changed too much, maybe.'

'Oh, we know who Weiss thought it was.'

Pascual gapes. 'You know?'

'Oh, yes. The police in New York sent Madrid a full set of Weiss's notes. It's all there.'

'You have a name?'

'Of course. Weiss had the whole story. He only needed to prove it.'

'And you know who his source was?'

'Oh, yes. Apparently Ilmeddin planted the story himself, as a way to pressure our man to call off the dogs. There was an effort to extradite him in Washington, which seems mysteriously to have come to naught. The source appears to have been an associate of Ilmeddin's from Marbella, an Iranian named Ghafarzadeh, who flew to New York in December to meet Weiss and give him the story. Unfortunately Ghafarzadeh does not have a reputation for credibility with the American authorities and it's very unlikely his testimony would be worth anything. And it's only hearsay in the first place. That leaves you as the only one who can put our man in the right place at the right time.'

Pascual is still racing to catch up. 'You've known all along.'

'Me? You flatter me. My colleague in Madrid has known since he got access to Weiss's papers. He left a very clear account of the whole thing. A good thing to do if you think you're getting into murky waters. It's only too bad he didn't publicize it more.'

Pascual looks at Serrano, who is wearing a bored expression again, and back at the judge. 'So why am I here?' he says.

The judge's eyebrows rise. 'To identify the man who's most likely behind these killings. I've got some photos for you to look at.'

'And you'll want me to go into a courtroom and swear that's the man?'

'If it comes to that, though it probably won't. If we ever get him to a Spanish courtroom it'll be for these killings, and your identification isn't, strictly speaking, evidence of his involvement in that. What you can finger him for is what he did in Germany twelve years ago. The only way we'll link him to these killings is by getting the ones pulling the trigger and getting them to talk, all the way back up the chain.'

Pascual reflects for a moment. 'But you've already got what evidence I can give for that.'

Espinoza blinks at him for a longish moment before saying, 'Yes. But now we need you to prove Weiss's original allegation.'

Eyes narrowed, Pascual says, 'Why?'

'Why?' The judge spreads his hands as if the answer is obvious. 'Because this man was intimately involved in one of the great terrorist crimes of the nineteen-eighties. He protected the men who brought down KLM 640.'

Pascual blinks into the judge's glare and finally says, 'I didn't realize the jurisdiction of the Audiencia Nacional extended to the Netherlands.'

The judge freezes for a moment and then frowns. 'You misunderstand me. What we wish to do is merely to cast light on the matter. In support of ongoing efforts to bring the perpetrators of the crime to justice.'

'Ilmeddin is dead. The men who actually placed the bomb are in jail. Who's left? Are the Dutch trying to extradite this man? Is there evidence he knew the crime was being plotted?'

Espinoza is beginning to look annoyed. 'That's not the point. Let me tell you something about the man we're concerned with.

In the eighties the US intelligence apparatus was out of control, running rogue operations, concealing its actions from the Congress and the President himself. Our man was in the thick of that, very close to the Vice-President, who you may recall had been the director of the CIA. Then, when the Vice-President succeeded to the top job, his protégé left the Agency and took a very influential post as adviser to the Intelligence Committee of the Senate. Now, as you're no doubt aware, that President's son is running for his father's old job. And our man's in his inner circle, poised to take an extremely sensitive position, possibly National Security Adviser, if the son wins the election. A man who protected Hussein Ilmeddin from arrest and allowed him to go on funding terror attacks and channelling secrets to the Soviet Union. A man who no doubt wants to put the CIA back at the forefront of American foreign policy. And your ability to identify him is one more lever we can use. If we can't prosecute him we can at least tear off his mask. We can assure that he never reaches a position of power. Don't you consider that a worthy goal?'

'I don't consider that *my* goal,' Pascual says. 'I'm not sure why it should be the goal of a Spanish magistrate, for that matter. It seems to me it's a matter for the Americans to decide. If they bring someone to trial and want me to come and testify I suppose I'll have to. But I'm still not sure what I'm doing here.'

Espinoza has reached the end of his patience. With a look of exasperation masterfully controlled he says, 'Very well. I am merely executing a *mandamiento* here. I have been asked to show you some photographs for the purposes of identification. If you refuse to co-operate, you'll be charged with obstruction.'

Pascual gives the judge a long melancholy stare. 'All right then. Who are we talking about?'

The judge sits back with a satisfied look. He reaches for a folder. 'I'm not going to tell you his name. We're going to do this in proper form, like a line-up. You're going to look at pictures of three different men and tell me if you see anyone you know.' He slides three sheets of paper across the desk. Each one bears four photographs of a man's head and shoulders, taken from various angles. The men are all in late middle age, balding and with facial whiskers, two fully bearded and one with a goatee and moustache.

The photos show them in suits and in casual wear, outdoors and in, with varying degrees of sharpness.

Pascual needs about three seconds to identify the man on the left-hand sheet of paper as the man who drove him and Ilmeddin from Frankfurt to Strasbourg twelve years ago. He has aged and trimmed the beard down to a goatee, but the distinctive eyebrows catalyse Pascual's recognition instantly. Pascual purses his lips and very deliberately looks over the other two sheets, taking his time. Finally he nods. 'It's been a long time,' he says.

'Don't guess,' says the judge. 'Make sure.'

Pascual stops nodding. He shoves the papers away and sits back. 'It could be any of them,' he says, looking the judge in the eye. 'They're all of a type. The beards, the bald heads. I just don't remember the face clearly enough. I couldn't possibly tell you which man it was.'

Pascual is starting to wonder how long a man can remain totally immobile when the judge finally blinks. 'Take another look.'

'I don't have to. It's not going to get any clearer. That was twelve years ago. I spent an evening with the man, a lot of it in a darkened car. There's no way I can possibly be sure.'

'You'd recognize him if you saw him in person. On video even.'

Pascual shrugs. 'Who can say? None of these photos triggers a reaction of certainty, that's all I can tell you.'

Very slowly, the judge leans forward to gather up the photographs and replace them in the folder. He shuts it and gives Serrano an icy look. 'Well, Inspector. It seems your witness is not as useful as we thought.'

Serrano shrugs, an old district policeman unused to the rarefied atmosphere of international intelligence scandals. 'Personally, I've never considered him particularly reliable.'

Pascual follows Serrano towards the door of the Jutjats like a dog at heel, hands in his pockets and head drooping. 'Where are we going now?' he says as Serrano pushes through the door.

'Me, I'm going back to the Jefatura,' Serrano says. 'I've got work to do. I don't care where you go.'

'I'm free to go?'

Serrano halts and turns. 'You've been cleared of all charges in the shooting last night and we've taken statements from you on all matters relevant to these killings. You're bloody useless as a witness, apparently. As far as I'm concerned we're finished with you.'

Quite irrationally Pascual feels he has let Serrano down. He looks into the old policeman's withering gaze and says, 'You know he doesn't need me to sort out this story. Pinzón's playing for international headlines and he's got Weiss's source to help him with that.'

'I'm not arguing with you. I'm just wondering how long you can go on trying to dodge the consequences of your behaviour.'

'Who says I'm trying to dodge them?'

Serrano makes a noise of dismissal. 'Your whole life is a dodge.'

Pascual moves a step closer to him, into head-knocking range. 'What do you need, right now? What would make your case?'

'Names. A chain of command. Who gave the orders to whom. Proof.'

'I'll get all that for you. I'll hand it to you in a package with a ribbon on it.'

Serrano's face freezes in a look of incredulity and then a smile slowly stretches the seams and hollows. 'On past form you'll just get somebody else killed,' he says. 'Maybe yourself, this time.'

'I'll try not to give you that satisfaction,' says Pascual, turning to trot down the steps.

In the Passeig de Picasso a car slews to the kerb and beeps at him. Pascual sees Campos at the wheel and with some reluctance climbs in. 'Can I give you a lift somewhere?' says Campos.

'Just drive for a while,' says Pascual. 'How did you know where I was?'

'Sources, my friend. Christ, you were in there a long time.'

Pascual makes rapid calculations. 'And all for nothing.'

'Nothing? What do you mean?'

'I mean he knows the whole story. Weiss wrote it all down. I'm completely irrelevant. They can break the thing wide open without me. And to top it all off, I didn't even recognize the fellow they say is behind it.'

'You couldn't identify him?'

'It's been a long time. I couldn't pick him out.'

167

Campos drives in silence for a while. 'But it's not what you can do that counts, it's what people think you can do.'

'Precisely. Bad luck for me. And everyone else involved. Weiss and Gabriel got themselves killed, stupidly, because somebody thought I could finger a man I met once, twelve years ago.'

'So who is it? Did you get a name?'

'The judge wouldn't give it to me.'

Campos scowls out of the windscreen. 'Well, in the meantime things are getting interesting on other fronts. Interesting and a little odd.'

'What happened?'

'I got an anonymous tip on the phone this morning, at the office. Very cinematic. A man's voice, good Castilian but a foreigner. He said he could tell me some very interesting things about you.'

'About me? He mentioned me by name?'

'Yes. He said, "I can tell you all about this fellow Pascual who's been dodging bullets."'

After a long moment Pascual says, 'And did he?'

'Well, no. He said he wouldn't talk over the phone. He told me to meet him at the Bar Estudiantil, across from the university, at one o'clock. He said sit at the end of the bar with a copy of *El Mundo* and he'd find me. It was a bit of a struggle to fit it in around all the other things I was supposed to do today, but I showed up on time. I waited for half an hour, but no one approached me. What do you suppose that means?'

Pascual has had too many surprises; he knows it means something but he is having trouble processing things. 'Why you?' he says finally.

'What do you mean?'

'I mean why you, out of all the reporters in the city?'

'Because I'm interested in you, I suppose.'

'But how did he know that? Have you published anything on me yet?'

The chilled silence that follows brings them to the stoplight across from the long arcades of the Estació de França. 'He just wanted to spot you,' says Pascual as Campos coasts gently to a halt behind an Opel. 'Which means . . .' The sound of the trailing motorbike finally pierces Pascual's awareness just as he realizes

168

what this means; Campos is only a split second behind, and the reporter has opened his mouth to speak when Pascual sees the whole thing clearly: they are immobilized, hemmed in front and back, and the motorbike is creeping up between the files of cars halted at the light. Twisting to look over his shoulder, Pascual has no time to weigh probabilities; in the world he has inhabited for the past few days this helmeted figure is as likely to be lethal as not. The motorbike has nearly reached the rear of the car, on the passenger side, the helmet obscuring the rider's face, the hand in the dispatch bag at his side. With an eerie precision of motion, time slowed in the crystalline clarity of an adrenaline surge, Pascual finds the handle of the door on his side and waits, knowing his life depends on perfect timing, hoping the man in the helmet will do the obvious and wait to draw even to make sure of his shot. Pascual rams the door open as the front wheel of the motorbike passes the door, putting his shoulder into it and knocking the man on the bike off-balance and against the car in the neighbouring lane. Momentum carries the bike just far enough beyond him before it spills for him to scramble out on to the pavement. He is praying that Campos has the sense to get out as well as he begins to run, hearing metal scraping on metal, expecting a shot in the back. The rider has become tangled in his bike and that is what saves Pascual; he can hear curses as he runs.

He ducks behind a car, keeping low, and cuts across several lanes of traffic amid screeching brakes and blaring klaxons, leaving Campos to fend for himself. He has heard no shots by the time he limps through a gate into the Ciutadella park. Assuming he has not just toppled an innocent man on to the pavement in a fit of paranoia, he is not yet in the clear; there will be a team, another bike or a vehicle in the vicinity. Having seen him run they will be coming after him. As long as he is in the park they can only follow him on foot; he has seen no signs of pursuit but knows he has limited time to work his way across the park, past the zoo and the parliament building to the far side, where a block or two away he believes he can duck into the Metro.

Pascual hoofs it, grateful for the camouflage of a better-than-average crowd milling about the entrance to the zoo, and makes it unassaulted to the far side of the park, where he halts in the shade of a plane tree overlooking a busy street, scanning, trying to anticipate. He is half convinced he is clear until bells begin ringing loudly in his head for reasons it takes him a moment to pin down. He moves further into the shade as a white Renault Comerciales van comes cruising slowly up the street, the driver seeming to pay more attention to things in Pascual's vicinity than to the traffic ahead of him. The car has a logo and company name stencilled on the side that it takes him only a few seconds to place; it is identical to that on the stolen van he saw careening away from an accident scene in the heart of the Barceloneta the previous night.

19

Pascual has been wondering how long it will take for the administration of the Residencia de Estudiantes to smell a rat; the *conserje* raps on the glass as he slinks past and beckons him to the window above the counter. 'A word with you, *señor*.' The *conserje* is a stocky man with the no-nonsense look of a retired *sargento de infantería*. 'How is Father Costa?' he asks, giving Pascual a withering look.

'Much the same,' says Pascual with a pang of guilt; he has had no thought to spare for the old priest for days. 'Fighting courageously for his life. He won't go easily, that one.'

'*Dios lo guarde*. And how goes the research?'

'Slowly. Father Costa has been a working scholar for fifty years. There is a lot of material to collate.' Pascual has done his part by shoving paper into a pile to wipe up spilled brandy from the desktop.

The *conserje* nods gravely. 'There is a small matter of the telephone. Apparently you have made a number of calls outside the city. Outside the country in fact.'

The continent, if you must know, thinks Pascual. 'Ah, yes. The Father has colleagues abroad whom it has been necessary to consult about some of the material. I have made a few calls, yes.'

The *conserje* rises to his full height, the embodiment of bureaucratic rectitude. 'I'm afraid I must insist on written permission from Father Costa before you use the telephone again.'

Pascual makes a gesture of gracious assent. 'Of course, of course. I'll be seeing him later today and I will make sure to obtain it.'

'You're going up to work now, are you?'

'Yes, for an hour or two.'

'Very well.' The injunction is left unspoken, but the glower lingers. 'It costs money, you know. And who pays, eh?'

Pascual makes for the stairs. 'I'm sure Father Costa will have no objection.'

'The man we're looking for is a former CIA officer, later on the staff of the Senate Intelligence Committee and now closely associated with the Republican candidate for President, possibly in line for a job as National Security Adviser. What are the chances you can track him down with that much to go on?'

There is nothing but transatlantic hum on the wire for a long moment and Pascual is beginning to think he has lost Stanley Prentice when the old lawyer finally says, 'I'll be God-damned.'

'I beg your pardon?'

'That's real interesting.'

'I'm sorry, I missed something. What's interesting?'

A quarter of the way around the world, Stanley Prentice draws a deep lungful of tropical air and says, 'It so happens I talked to a man who fits that little profile to a T yesterday. I was referred to him by my Congressman friend. He'd made a few phone calls and said this was a man who could clarify matters for me. Instead all he did was give me the party line. I got a little lecture about the realities of the intelligence profession and the difficulties involved in prosecuting people like Ilmeddin. I figured I'd just run into a professional ass-coverer. But if you're right, I'd found the son of a bitch himself.'

Very calmly, Pascual says, 'Would his name begin with an M, by any chance?'

'You got it, Mr Campos. His name's Everett McDuff.'

'And he was with the CIA?'

'That's right and then with the Senate committee. For the past couple of years he's been on the staff of a think tank in Virginia called the Freedom Institute and now he's right at the top of the campaign brain trust. The word is he's got his sights set high if they win the election.'

'Is there any chance you could fax me a photo of him? We've got a man here who claims to be able to identify him.'

'A photo? That might be tough. I wouldn't know where to lay my hands on one right offhand. But the think tank probably has a website. You might find one there. Who's the man who can identify him?'

'Somebody who claims to have known him in Germany.'

'You've been busy, haven't you?'

'A little bit. Can you give me the number where you reached McDuff?'

'I can do that. But you're not going to get any farther than I did.'

'Maybe not. But I can try.' Pascual is staring intently out the window of Father Costa's room; on the football pitch below two teams are raising clouds of dust. 'Did you by any chance tell him about me?'

'No, I told him I had sources in Europe, that's all. He didn't push.'

'That's good. Mr Prentice, if I were you, I wouldn't do anything to give this McDuff the idea you weren't satisfied with what he told you.'

'You think it's that serious?'

'It's that serious here.'

Time goes by and Stanley Prentice says, 'Mr Campos, I'm too old to take any more disillusionment. I'm not going to rock any more boats in this life. Just keep me posted, will you?'

'I'll do that.'

There is a single precious computer in the library of the residence, down the hall from Father Costa's suite, and in the library there is the inevitable gangling pimply youth who in aid of Father Costa's fictional research project agrees to log Pascual on and show him how to search. Pascual has decided it is time to keep his thoughts very much to himself.

He feels a quickening of the pulse as the promised Hi-Res picture of Everett McDuff comes up on the computer screen next to his bio and credentials. *Analyst, Central Intelligence Agency, 1968 to 1992* leads off the curriculum vitae, the term 'analyst' being a bit of a euphemism in Pascual's estimation. The photo crystallizes and Pascual gazes at it. This is one of the three photos Pascual saw this morning at the Jutjats, the modern version with the neat goatee, making McDuff look distinctly sinister with the slight lift of the eyebrows despite the jovial smile he is wearing for the camera. Pascual clicks and the page vanishes.

Another few minutes of poking about in the electronic nowhere brings him to the home page of Global Consulting. He clicks hither and yon, following trails of links, admiring the worldwide empire of security, management consulting and human resource companies that an ex-MI6 man named Hampton has built. On the list of clients served by a human resources subsidiary of Global is a Spanish transport company with offices in Prat del Llobregat. Pascual logs off.

Back in the priest's room he sits staring at the phone for a long time. It would be easy to ring Serrano and tell him he has changed his mind, that he is willing to go before the cameras and tell his story, become a public figure and kiss his anonymous existence goodbye. If he could be sure that doing so would make his friends forever safe he would do it despite the cost to himself. He has a feeling that it is not that simple. Finally he lifts the phone.

He has two numbers to try and he is prepared to spend the night waiting for return calls if necessary, but apparently Prentice's Congressman wields enough clout even to get the number of a Washington capo's mobile telephone, and again Pascual is caught short, abruptly confronted with a man's voice in his ear before he has had a chance to rehearse. 'Yes?'

'Is this Mr Everett McDuff?'

'Who is this?'

'My name is Pascual.'

McDuff is driving, apparently, careening around the Beltway in some battleship of an American car, no doubt; Pascual can hear the telltale susurrations in the background. 'I don't know any Pascual.'

'I did you a great service today, Mr McDuff.'

A few seconds go by. 'And what would that be?'

'I failed to identify you.'

The answer comes more quickly this time. 'I have no idea what you're talking about.'

Pascual remembers watching his grandfather fish for trout far up in the Pyrenees, using a deft touch on the line. 'Do you want me to explain it over the air like this, or would you feel better talking on a more secure line?'

'I don't think we have a thing to talk about, but if you want you could leave me a number and I'll get back to you. I'm kind of busy right now trying not to get run off the road by a semi.'

Pascual has no doubt a man with McDuff's contacts could trace a phone number and have someone sitting outside in a parked car in a matter of hours. 'I think we'll do it the other way. You give me a number you're happy with and a good time to call and I'll get back to you.'

Perhaps the semi makes its move at that moment, for Pascual hears nothing but a swelling murmur in the background for long seconds. The background noises stabilize and McDuff says, 'Got a pencil? It'll take me about forty-five minutes to get there.'

'How did you get my number?' says McDuff. There are no background noises now; McDuff answered on the first ring and sounds as if he is in the next room. Armed with a brand-new phone card from a tobacconist in Urgell, Pascual has chosen this bank of phones in the vast complex of railway and Metro stations under the Plaça Catalunya to make his call. If the CIA can trace this call, they are welcome to it.

'I looked in the Yellow Pages under ex-spies. Look, I want to make sure you understand what happened this afternoon.'

'So talk. What happened?'

'An investigating magistrate here in Spain showed me some pictures. He asked me if I recognized any of them. I said no, nobody looked familiar. Then I was released. You understand what I'm saying, don't you?'

After a long pause McDuff says, 'What do you want?'

Pascual takes a deep breath. 'I want the killers.'

'I don't know what you're talking about.'

'Then why are you talking to me?'

The brevity of the succeeding pause is a sure mark of McDuff's professionalism. 'You're not making yourself clear.'

'All right, here's the deal. This is good old-fashioned blackmail. I could always recover my memory. I could go back to that judge tomorrow and say, "I've managed to place that face." And that could cause you a lot of trouble.'

'I don't think so. There have been some preposterous accusations made, but I'm used to that. I've been accused of everything from drug-running to harvesting kidneys from orphans. Nobody's going to bat an eye over one more.'

'Then hang up the phone and take your chances. I can have a detailed account of your dealings with Hussein Ilmeddin and the sequel to those dealings faxed to every major paper in the US in about an hour. With my eyewitness testimony. They'll want a few days to check it out, but I can have it at a major Spanish paper tomorrow morning. The wire services will have it across the Atlantic in a heartbeat. The CIA could have prevented the KLM bombing in 88 but didn't because they didn't want to jeopardize one of those cowboy operations that got old Reagan in trouble? The CIA's man on the spot actually handled the suitcase that held the bomb? And that guy is in line for a top job in a new administration? See what that does to your candidate's campaign this summer.'

Pascual waits him out, ear plugged against the hollow roar of the busy echoing concourse, and it takes no more than five seconds. 'What do you mean, you want the killers?'

'I mean you give them to me. You tell me where and how to find them. The boss, anyway. I'll want the boss, the man who hired them. I'm sure you didn't do it directly. You just dropped a hint in someone's ear. That's the guy I'll want.'

'You're living in a fantasy world.'

'I'm living in a city where a lot of people have died suddenly, and I was there for most of it. Don't tell me where I'm living. And you can drop the denials. The fact that you're on this line means you know exactly what I'm talking about. We are two rational adults making a deal here, Mr McDuff, and my proposal is this: you finger the contractor for me, and in return I'll go on just like I was before Morris Weiss found me – blissfully ignorant. I don't give a shit about you and never did, and the proof of that is the last twelve years. I have to say, it's damn generous of me to make you this offer instead of helping a politically inspired Spanish judge carry out a vendetta against you. Especially after you made this personal by putting me on your hit list.'

'I didn't do any such thing.' Perhaps sensing that Pascual is drawing a lungful of air for a laugh, McDuff adds, 'It's possible my intentions were misinterpreted.'

'Fine, I'll buy that. But you've got to admit you owe me one.'

'I'm not admitting a fucking thing. I get crank calls all the time.'

Pascual gives it a leisurely count of three. He says, 'So long, Mr McDuff. See you on the evening news.'

'Hang on. Hang on, for Christ's sake.' McDuff has not raised his voice, but the note has changed, just a bit. 'I have a feeling we need to talk at greater length about this and maybe face to face.'

'I agree. How fast can you get to Barcelona?'

A whiffing noise comes over the line. 'I can't possibly get away.'

'You'll have to. I can't afford a plane ticket. And this is where the action is.'

'I'm in the middle of a political campaign.'

'Which is going to take a big hit in a week or so if my memory suddenly clears up. Take a personal day, have a medical crisis, have a nervous breakdown. Discover urgent financial matters or family problems. Sneak away with a mistress. But get over here. Or else the story hits the papers in the morning.'

Pascual watches pretty Catalan girls go by in flocks while on another continent a man exercises his crisis management skills. After a long pause McDuff says, 'How would I find you?'

Sticking his hand through the rip in the side of the musty straw-packed mattress, Pascual extracts the little .25 automatic from its nest. He removes the clip. It is, as he expected, empty, but when he pulls back the slide the round that was in the chamber pops out on to the floor. He picks it up and stares at it for a few seconds before rechambering it. His life now possibly dependent on a single round, he pockets the little gun and leaves the cellar.

There have been no messages at his *pensión*. His life is in ruins and the one person who could help salvage it has gone missing and silent. Pascual finds he is beginning to lose interest in CIA intrigues and contract killers. All he wants is Sara.

He walks all the way to the Ribera, under a sky that has gone grey and menacing. The rumbling city looks sullen and chaotic to him, three million unconnected souls in Brownian motion. He makes token efforts to watch his back, but he finds that a strange recklessness has taken hold of him.

When he enters the Tavern del Born, Enric is behind the bar, smoking and turning over the leaves of a newspaper. Custom is light in this drowsy afternoon lull; old Creixell in his *boina* is brooding on things past at the bar and a pair of adolescents, presumably of differing sexes, are hard at work mixing saliva at a corner table. Enric watches Pascual walk the length of the bar like a peasant watching a cobra come through the rice. 'Are you quite sure it's a good idea for you to be here?' he says.

'I'm almost certain it's not,' Pascual says, settling on to a stool that allows him to watch the door. 'Where's Sara?'

'How should I know? She asked for time off until the police have caught these people who are after you.'

'She left no message, no way to reach her?'

Enric shakes his head. 'It seems you've put us all in danger.'

'My profoundest apologies. Give me a coffee, will you?'

He can see Enric giving serious thought to tossing him out, but eventually Enric moves, with a deliberateness that is almost insulting, to set the machine brewing and place a cup beneath the spout. 'What do the police have to tell you?' says Enric, glowering at the trickle of black liquid.

'*Suerte*,' says Pascual. 'Best of luck. That seems to be the official line at this point.'

Pascual sits and watches the street as the coffee cools on the marble countertop. He does not know precisely what he is waiting for, but he has no better strategy for regaining control of his destiny. He has taken one sip of lukewarm coffee when Fernando darkens the doorway. The gypsy betrays no surprise at seeing him; without breaking stride he gives Pascual a nod, just perceptible, and takes a stool two metres away. '*Tabernero*, pull me a *caña*,' he calls to Enric.

'What's happened to all you lads?' growls Enric, delivering the beer. 'Am I suddenly off-limits?'

Fernando grins. 'There's been a strong smell of *pestañí* about the place recently. When that fades a bit, you'll see the boys back in here.'

'I'll have to sell out before that happens, at the rate we're going. They'll come back and find some Yanqui hamburger chain here.'

When Enric has gone back to his paper, Fernando lights a cigarette and looks squarely at Pascual. 'What are you doing here? Putting your head in the lion's mouth?'

'Where's Sara?' Pascual says.

'Don't worry, she's safe. Pilar too.'

'With you?'

Fernando nods. 'With me.'

'And Lola?'

'Lola's dead.'

Pascual shakes his head slowly. 'I have to see Sara.'

Fernando smokes, studying Pascual. 'She doesn't want to see you. Not yet.'

Fleetingly Pascual thinks that the single round in his weapon would do nicely for Fernando, but he makes an effort to channel his thoughts in a more productive direction. 'She's appointed you her spokesman, has she?'

'For the moment, yes.'

'And when am I to be allowed to approach her?'

'She'll let you know.'

Pascual has a notion to knock the gypsy off his stool, but knows that in his current physical state the mere effort of throwing a punch would leave him doubled over in pain. 'What the hell's going on?' he says.

Fernando squints at him through a cloud of smoke. 'What's going on is, somebody's trying to kill you. You stay alive a little longer, Sara will be ready to see you. *Vale?*'

Pascual goes through a dozen scenarios in half as many seconds and says, '*Vale.*'

The taxi driver gives Pascual a long sceptical look and then a snort of laughter. '*Collons*, not again.'

'What, you're going to tell me this happens all the time?' Pascual settles on to the back seat with a grimace.

'More than you'd think. Too many movies, that's what it is. "Follow that car," people say and they've no idea how hard it is to do that.' The *taxista* sets the meter running and puts the car in gear.

'If you can't follow that museum piece, you should turn in your licence.'

'I never said I couldn't.' The taxi peels away from the kerb with a mild keening of tyres. 'What is it? Drugs? Spies? Your wife cheating on you? The last fellow who wanted me to follow someone claimed it was Anna Kournikova travelling incognito and he had to have her autograph. We followed her to Hospitalet, where she got out at a podiatrist's, looking about as much like Anna Kournikova as my wife does. The bastard didn't want to pay me.'

Pascual tosses money on to the front seat. 'There's a down payment. Just keep that Chevrolet in sight.'

The Chevrolet stands out of the crowd even three hundred metres ahead, weaving from lane to lane on the Passeig de Colom, the greasy waters of the port lying leaden and unquiet on the left. 'Friend of yours?' says the driver.

'So I thought.' This puts an abrupt end to the conversation and for long minutes the pursuit goes on in silence, the taxi closing and falling back again with the vicissitudes of traffic. By the time they are labouring up the slopes of Montjuïc, Pascual is fairly certain of their destination. 'You can let him pull ahead. I know where he's going.'

When they come to the Plaça de l'Armada, Pascual tells the driver to keep going. Fernando is just getting out of the Chevrolet, parked at the edge of the plaza in much the same place where he brought Pascual a few days ago. Pascual has the driver go on around the bend and drop him. 'I wish you better luck with your friend than I had with *la Kournikova*,' says the driver, pocketing his money. Pascual slams the door.

Before hiking back he removes his leather jacket and slings it over his shoulder, first extracting his sunglasses from the pocket and donning them, just enough of a change he hopes to ensure that Fernando will not spot him with a stray glance. He keeps to the opposite side of the road, shielded by parked cars and idling tourist coaches, and works his way back. Fernando has had enough beer today, apparently; rather than going up the steps on to the restaurant terrace he has chosen to stand at the low parapet next to the coin-operated telescope, looking out over the city and smoking. Pascual finds a stone bench with a view of the spot and waits.

The newcomer takes him by surprise; Pascual has been gazing

into the haze over the city and looks back to see Fernando offering a cigarette to a man who has just joined him. Pascual rises from the bench and walks closer, observing the body language of two men engaged in close consultation on a matter of importance. Fernando is the smaller of the two, but he has a way of staking a claim to territory like a bigger man, chin jutting and shoulders thrown back, challenging his interlocutor. His earring glints in the sun as he turns his head to avoid blowing smoke in the other man's face. There is nobody within earshot of the two, but they stand close together, intent, the bigger man leaning so close at times that the brim of his panama hat nearly touches the gypsy's forehead.

The heat must be easing, Pascual thinks, if Torres feels free to pull out the hats again. He watches until Torres stalks away and gets into a BMW parked on the other side of the road. Fernando grinds out his cigarette with a heel and stands for a moment looking out to sea before getting back in the Chevrolet and departing.

Pascual begins the long walk down the mountain, heavy of tread and heavy of heart.

20

Pascual is beginning to enjoy taking chances, whether because the little pistol with its single round has emboldened him or because death has ceased to seem the worst option, he could not say. In any event it is with only cursory attention to the environs that he makes his way into the Tavern del Born.

An alto saxophone is meandering through a melodic minefield on the CD player. No one appears to object. Custom is starting to pick up again, evidently, though Pascual sees few familiar faces. The clientele is changing, perhaps, a new element drawn by the notoriety. Enric is behind the bar tonight, and with him is someone Pascual does not know, a young woman with abundant chestnut hair and sparkling eyes who in normal times would distract him from whatever purpose brought him in; under the circumstances he barely notes her. 'Taking chances again?' says Enric when Pascual leans on the bar. 'I shouldn't think it's quite safe yet.' He is visibly displeased and Pascual has a feeling that a process of severance has begun. Enric beckons to the new girl. 'Look, this is Marisa. I've had to take her on in your absence. I'm starting to think neither you nor Sara is ever coming back.'

Pascual nods in response to a pretty smile. 'I can't answer for Sara. Or me, for that matter. Look, I've got a favour to ask.'

'I can't loan you any money. I'd love to help you out, but . . .'

'I don't want money. All I want you to do is take a message. A man's going to phone for me tomorrow and I need you to take a number where I can reach him. He's American and I don't know if he has any Castilian. I'd have had him ring my *pensión*, but old

Prat and his wife have even less English than you do. Can you manage that much?'

Enric glowers. 'Do me a favour. Don't get me involved in any more messes.'

'He's not even going to know where you are. All he has is the number here. You ask him where he can be reached and you write it down. I'll phone you at intervals until I get the message. Can you do that?'

Enric is drinking on duty tonight; he takes a slug of the best Scotch without taking his eyes off Pascual. 'I can do that.'

'Thanks.' Pascual exchanges the barest of glances with the new girl. He catches Enric's wrist. 'Can I ask you a question?'

'What?'

'Where does Fernando get his money?'

The saxophone expires, giving way to a somnolent plodding bass, as Enric gives him a long blank look. 'What do you mean?'

'I mean how does he make a living? How does he afford nice clothes and expensive gifts? Where does the money come from?'

Enric's eyes narrow. 'How would I know?'

'You're the one who's best pals with Tío José. I thought they were all your friends.'

Enric stalls, shifting his glass on the bar. 'You don't ask a gypsy that. It can be a sensitive topic.'

'I can imagine. What was he in the Modelo for?'

'I'm not sure.' Enric sips whisky. 'Why the interrogation?'

'I'm just curious. I'm just now starting to get curious. Maybe too late.'

'What the hell are you talking about?'

Pascual takes a long brooding look around the room where he has been so happy. He pushes away from the bar. 'Nothing,' he says. 'I suppose I'm just jealous. I'll ring you tomorrow.'

With the single bulb extinguished the darkness is utter and complete in old Ferrer's underground cell, a total and oppressive absence of light. Noises come through the foundations to Pascual on his mattress, distant Metro trains rumbling beneath the earth, water rushing through pipes, doors slamming remotely several storeys overhead.

It is the perfect metaphor for his life, Pascual reflects, buried alive in the heart of the place he most loves, self-exiled to a home he can never regain, imprisoned in darkness in the only place where he can remember light. He shut himself in this cellar for ever on that day when, still dazed by shocks cultural and otherwise, he stepped timidly across the threshold of the PFLP offices in Damascus bearing a letter from a smooth and persuasive veteran of *mai soixante-huit* back in Paris who had sold him on the armed struggle. His mother had died three weeks before under the wheels of a bus and Pascual had refused to cry. He has frequently wondered if a few tears at her funeral might have changed his life.

He has lived with the consequences for eighteen years; Pascual has never blamed anyone but himself for his decision to enter the service of death. Seldom, however, has he felt as bitterly as tonight the true dimensions of what he has lost. To have clawed his way to a kind of happiness only to find that his past has the power to corrupt all he touches is an almost fatal blow. The one thing he clings to here in the dark is the thought that there may be a few accounts he can settle.

If, that is, he has figured it right. He goes over it all again, pieces falling in place.

From the window of Father Costa's room Pascual dominates one end of the park. The bench in question is some way to his left, but that is less important than his view of the environs. He can see the length of the park and half a block down Provença. Everett McDuff has been sitting on the bench, showing signs of anxiety and high alertness, for twenty minutes. A park is made for idlers, so there is no easy way to scan for watchers, but Pascual believes he is clear. None of the idlers he can see displays the veiled intentness that a veteran target of surveillance learns to recognize. Nor is there a likely vehicle; on a busy street a car that disrupts the flow of traffic would stand out and he has seen no suspects.

Pascual turns from the window and paces to the bed. 'I must go, Father. I thank you for listening.'

Father Costa is a shrunken, desiccated shell of the man whom Pascual has come to love, but in his eyes burns the fervour of a man who will relinquish his grip on life only when it is ripped from his grasp. His brows contract and his mouth works in silence as he summons the energy to speak. 'He can dispel darkness,' he whispers. 'I have faith if you don't.'

Pascual nods, troubled. 'The truth, Father. Has your faith given you happiness?'

Father Costa closes his eyes. Pascual waits; after a time the priest opens them, frowning, and says, 'Happiness is not a commodity, something you obtain. Happiness is something you do. It is a course of action.'

'I don't understand you.'

'I cannot put it more simply. To follow the path of right-eousness is to be happy.'

'By definition, I suppose.'

'It is not a logical exercise. There is no more profound source of peace than right conduct.'

Pascual nods slowly, listening to voices echoing down a long corridor. The priest has closed his eyes again, exhausted by the exchange. 'I will come again tomorrow,' says Pascual.

A tremor passes over Father Costa's features and he manages a final whisper. 'I may not last until tomorrow.'

Pascual presses the old man's hand, thin and yielding on the sheet. Once again, in spite of himself, the freeze is setting in; he knows he should mourn, break into sobs, bury his head in the old man's breast, but a strange paralysis suffuses him. With an effort he leans close to the dying man's ear and whispers, 'You should have been my father. Not the other one.' All the response he gets is the slightest tightening of the priest's frail grip.

Pascual walks slowly down the corridor to the stairs and descends. He pauses just inside the main entrance, jostled by white-coated internists and bewildered familiars of the sick and hurt, looking out into the sunshine.

McDuff gives him one look as he approaches but does not fix on him; the forecourt of a hospital is a perfectly natural place for a man with a bruised and swollen face to be. Pascual shambles to the opposite end of the bench and sits with an unfeigned grimace, pulling the newspaper from under his arm. He gets it open and flails at pages flapping in the breeze for a minute before he subdues it and says, 'Hello, Mr McDuff.'

'That's a pretty good make-up job,' says McDuff.

'But you spotted me anyway, huh?'

'Process of elimination. I wouldn't have recognized you.'

Pascual looks up from the paper. McDuff is a metre away from him, in green windbreaker and trainers, a camera on his lap, the picture of a tourist who has strayed off the beaten track. He is a middle-aged bald man with a paunch and a natty little beard and in living colour he looks about as satanic as the greengrocer next door. Pascual says, 'And I wouldn't have recognized you, either. That's what's so stupid about this whole thing. If they'd left me alone I wouldn't have had the slightest idea who you are.'

McDuff gives him a long look and Pascual can see the professional at work behind the narrowed blue eyes. 'Can we talk about this objectively?'

'That's a good one. Yes, I suppose we can. I'm perfectly capable of being objective about a man who ordered my murder.'

'I didn't order your murder.'

'What, somebody exceeded his instructions, is that it?'

McDuff's eyes are restless, lighting on Pascual only at intervals. 'I had a problem of information control. I told somebody to manage it. There are a lot of ways to handle a problem like that, and killing somebody is just about always the messiest and riskiest, not to mention the most expensive solution. I certainly never intended it and the decisions that were made after I handed off the problem were out of my hands.'

'That's a pretty good formula for deniability. I imagine you've had a lot of practice.'

'I was an intelligence officer, not a hit man. There's an awful lot of bullshit that gets thrown around about the intelligence profession.'

Pascual folds his paper carefully and lodges it under his arm. 'I'm not going to argue with you. Let's take a walk, shall we?'

He can see McDuff thinking tactics, the professional at work, weighing relative difficulty of moving versus stationary surveillance, likelihood of swindles, traps, the double-cross. 'All right,' he says.

They rise and Pascual leads him down Via Casanova, past the Ninot market, where housewives are jostling at the booths lining the pavement and smells of produce and freshly killed flesh waft from inside the cavernous echoing structure. The weather has turned fine again and the leaves are out on the plane trees and

Pascual is heavy-hearted, feeling everything he loves slip away. 'The question is, how are we going to work out our deal?' he says.

McDuff walks like a man on point in bandit country, looking for trouble. 'Why don't you tell me exactly what you want?'

Pascual smiles. 'So it's on the tape? To compromise me if I'm wearing a wire?'

'You're not wearing a radio transmitter, but you could have a recorder on you. Unless you're going to let me search you, you're going to compromise yourself before I say anything.'

'That's impressive. You must have some kind of silent detector. What does it do: vibrate if it detects a transmitter?'

Eyes lighting on Pascual for an instant, McDuff says, 'Why don't you tell me what you want?'

Pascual draws a deep breath. 'All right, I want to know who's running the killers. I want you to give him to me.'

They pause at a stoplight, traffic tearing past. McDuff has to lean close to make himself heard. 'I'm not going to finger anybody for you. That's not going to happen.'

In McDuff's ear Pascual says, 'I'm not talking about having him arrested. I shot a man the other night, Mr McDuff. That's what I'm talking about. Is that frank enough for you?'

They cross with the light and amble slowly down the gently sloping street. At length McDuff says, 'It's pretty frank. I don't know that it's believable.'

'Will you believe it if you see it? You set him up, you watch me do it. Is that good enough for you?'

McDuff has the look of a man who has looked for a long time and finally found something that shocks him. 'What the hell makes you think I would help you kill someone?'

In the heart of the Eixample they weave slowly through crowds of young girls with armfuls of books, workmen in blue coveralls, men in suits with mobile phones pressed to their ears. Pascual could be a man explaining the latest family dust up to his uncle. 'Because however deniable you think you are, whoever you talked to is going to give you up the instant the pressure comes down on him. That's how the police work this type of thing – they get one man and they work back, cutting deals at each stage to get the next person up the chain of command. You know two of these shooters have been killed already, right? The Spanish cops are not that bad, and before too long they're going to trace these guys to whoever hired them. And then the heat's going to come down on you. Unless that guy's dead. Presto, end of chain. That's your final layer of insulation.'

There is a long silence. 'You'd still be around.'

'Yeah. But you know I'm not going to give you up. If I was ever going to give you up I'd have done it the other day. I've got no incentive to give you up. What could I possibly gain? As for blackmail, this is it. I'm blackmailing you to give me something that will make us both safer. Your interests and mine converge here. We both want everyone to forget all about what happened in the eighties. You've got an election to win, and I just want to go back to doing what I was doing before Weiss showed up. Which brings me to another reason you should help me.'

'What's that?'

They have reached another busy intersection, traffic shearing off Aragó on to Roma, and again Pascual has to lean close to make himself heard. He looks McDuff square in the face, seeing the faintest sheen of sweat high on his forehead, the tension in the contracted brows above the blue eyes. 'You owe me. I've spent the last twelve years of my life doing nothing but trying to forget. I refused to talk to Weiss, did you know that? I refused to acknowledge who I was. I wasn't bothering anybody. And you sent people to kill me.'

McDuff does not flinch under Pascual's gaze. Pascual waits for another denial, but it never comes. The light changes and they cross the broad street in silence. As the noise of traffic abates McDuff says, 'Well, look at it from my point of view. I thought I'd put all that behind me, too. We've all got things we'd like to forget. Intelligence is a pretty dirty game sometimes. You think I'm proud of everything I did in those years? I think about those three hundred dead people every day of my life. Backing Ilmeddin was the worst mistake I ever made. But mistakes happen in a war, and by God that's what it was. We had a fucking war to win, and we won it, and the world's better off for it, whether these damn European socialists want to admit it or not.'

'I'm not arguing with you. Why do you think I crossed over? As for regrets, I bet yours are nothing compared to mine.'

The silence lasts another block or so. Pascual is beginning to hurt from the mild exertion and he proposes a halt. 'Fine, if you let me choose the place,' says McDuff, ever the professional. He passes up the first bar and steers them across the street and into another a block down, in sight of the Gran Via. Inside they perch on stools at the end of the bar near the door, heads close together over their beer, to the casual eye two Yanquis murmuring about whatever Yanquis concern themselves with in their blissful ignorance of their surroundings.

'So it was a real change of heart, was it?' says McDuff with a sceptical look. 'The consensus when you came over was that your time had run out on the other side.'

Pascual nods. 'It had. The truth is, I don't know that I had much of a heart to change in those days. I'd like to think I've grown one since then, though. What do you think I've been working on for the last twelve years?'

McDuff's expression softens just a little as he reaches for his beer. 'It was a dirty fucking business, wasn't it?'

'That it was.'

McDuff drinks and then sets down his beer with a thump. 'I want you to understand this. Here I am, trying to move beyond all that, all the dirty work, trying to make a contribution, make sure our victory means something, and then out of the woodwork crawls Ilmeddin. Everything I'd worked for for thirty years was in danger because of a mistake in judgement I made in the field. And Ilmeddin was a very low form of life. That much I knew.' He reaches for the beer again, but halts it half-way to his mouth, looking at Pascual over the rim. 'And to be very brutally frank, it wasn't much of a stretch to put you in the same category. I'm not sure how far your defection goes in excusing what you did for all those years.'

Pascual nods slowly, sadly. 'So you said what the hell, take 'em both out.'

McDuff drinks again and replaces the glass very gently on the bar this time. 'Like I say, my instructions may have been exceeded. You want an apology?'

'Mrs Weiss might appreciate one.'

McDuff freezes, and then he begins to laugh. In a tone of disgust he says, 'That's pretty fucking rich. They saw you, you know.'

'Who? Who saw what?'

McDuff leans towards him with the air of a man who has just pulled the ace of trumps out of his sleeve. 'They saw you kill Weiss, asshole.'

So far Pascual has felt that he is in adequate control of the proceedings, but this is a stunner. Assuring himself that he has heard McDuff correctly, he gropes for something to hang on to. 'Who saw me?'

McDuff peers at him and then smiles. 'Oh, no you don't. I'm not making it that easy. That's just something for you to think about. If they get hauled into a courtroom, so will you. But I think that's an eventuality we all want to avoid, right?'

'There's a misunderstanding here somewhere. I didn't kill Weiss.'

'Fine, you didn't kill him. I don't give a shit.'

Pascual gives it another few seconds' thought. 'Somebody's been lying to you. Maybe Weiss was an overreach or a mis-interpretation, too, and they had to make it easier to take by telling you I did it. They seem to be a pretty enthusiastic bunch. But in any event, if somebody reported back to you, there goes your deniability. As far as I'm concerned, anyway.'

McDuff leans back on his stool with the air of a man who has regained the upper hand. 'Why don't you just tell me what you want me to do?'

'I want the man you told to manage the problem. I'm betting it's Hampton.'

McDuff is too good to flinch, but Pascual has years of experience reading faces and the things they betray. 'Who the hell is Hampton?' says McDuff.

'Your old pal from your terrorist-hunting days. The one who told you Ilmeddin was a great prospect. It's all in Weiss's notes. There's an *H* in there that's got to be Hampton. MI6 was involved in setting up BCCI and that could have been how Hampton hooked up with Ilmeddin before he sold you on him. And I'm betting he's even more compromised than you are or he wouldn't be helping you. He must have blotted his copybook in a big way to be worried about this now because he's a private citizen with no political capital to lose. Am I right?'

'How in the hell do you come up with this stuff?'

'Just tracing things back. The hit team found out somehow that they'd got the wrong guy, and they also learned the name of a reporter who was working on the story. I gave away both those things when I talked to Hampton. You don't have to be a genius.'

McDuff's blank expression is fighting a losing battle and Pascual can tell he is starting to realize it. 'Well, you guessed wrong there, partner.'

'OK, you're not going to give up Hampton. Fair enough. You're old comrades, came through the war together, shared a foxhole, the whole thing. Fine. There will be a local link, the subcontractor, the paymaster, the recruiter. The guy Hampton put in charge, the foreman. He's here in town, leaning on one of Hampton's clients for resources and running the killers. I want him. Just him – I'll let the cops roll up the triggermen. That'll make me feel better and it'll make you safe. The cops are going to trace the dead men to him sooner or later and then you and Hampton are at risk. I'm offering to cut out that link.'

McDuff is not buying any of this, not yet, Pascual can see. 'And why would you do that for me?'

'So we can both get on with our lives. I don't hold anything against you. We were both in a dirty game and you won, like you said, and I've got no complaints, not even about how you dealt with Ilmeddin. I understand exactly why you acted as you did and I've got no hard feelings. But you have to give me the guy who ran the killers because he went after my friends, too. You give me him and we're even.'

McDuff stares at him long and hard. 'That would be hard to do. I can't just give you a name and fly home.'

'I know that. All you need to do is just what you did before. You call Hampton and tell him you have a problem. This time the problem is simple blackmail. I've eluded his hit teams, I'm beyond their reach and I'm going to make you pay. I'm asking a hundred thousand dollars, in cash, or the story hits the papers tomorrow. You can afford the money better than the notoriety, and you've decided to pay, even though you know it's just a temporary solution. You can't risk any trouble until after the election. You tell him to take care of the payoff.'

McDuff is shaking his head, a wondering look on his face. 'How would it work?'

'How about this? His man has a contact number and we set up a meet. When he shows up, I eliminate him. You don't even have to put up real money. You can tell him to stall, negotiate, fill a bag with newsprint, whatever. I don't want your money. The important thing is, the guy who shows up had better be the right guy. I don't want any mistakes. Tell Hampton that. I want the team leader. When he's down, it'll all be over. You go get your man elected, Hampton goes on making money and I go back to keeping my head down.'

McDuff lets out a long breath and shakes his head. 'You're a fucking madman.'

'I'm just reading the logic of the situation. We'll both be safer this way.'

McDuff's gaze wanders away out of the door into the tumult of a Barcelona afternoon. 'I'll need a day or two,' he says.

21

Pascual is smoking his last precious Ducado down to finger-singeing length when Fernando appears, striding out of the Carrer Montcada into the Passeig del Born. The old church that towers over one end of the avenue stands somnolent and dignified in the late afternoon. Pascual tosses the fag into the gutter and moves.

Fernando has just turned the ignition key when Pascual raps on the passenger side window. Fernando leans across to pop the lock and Pascual gets in. '*Primo*,' says Fernando. 'What a surprise. What are you doing here?'

'I'm not your cousin,' says Pascual.

His tone of voice freezes Fernando. 'We call everybody cousin,' he says finally, coolly. 'Friends, anyway.'

'We need to talk,' says Pascual. 'Don't let me hold you up. You can drive if you want.'

Fernando switches off the engine. 'What's the matter with you?'

Pascual holds up his maimed left hand, pretending to examine it. 'I'm upset today about losing my fingers. Rubbing elbows with you *gitanillos* has made me want to learn to play the guitar.'

Fernando is giving him a puzzled scowl. 'It's a little early to get drunk, isn't it?'

Pascual's hand drops to his lap. 'Look here. That American reporter who came looking for me, the one who started the whole thing, he knew I had two fingers missing.'

'So?'

'Who told him? It seems he'd been tipped to my whereabouts

by that Arab who got himself killed on the boat. But the Arab hadn't seen me for twelve years, and I got my fingers chopped off in Paris only a couple of summers ago. He could only have found out where I am from somebody who knows me, here and now. And I saw you the other day talking to a man who worked for the Arab, up on Montjuïc. Yes, that was me in the taxi. Now, I'm giving you a chance to explain what's going on and it better be good. All right, *primo*?'

Fernando's look has gone very grave. He takes cigarettes from his jacket pocket and offers them to Pascual, who waves them off with a flick of the hand. Fernando takes his time lighting one. 'That was just business,' he says. 'My business, nothing to do with you at all.'

'Your business? And just what is your business? I know what Torres's business is. You're in the same line of work, are you?'

'That doesn't concern you.'

'Ah, no? You're in business with my enemies and it doesn't concern me? That's the man that kidnapped Lola. I'm supposed to believe you've got business with him that doesn't have anything to do with this catastrophe? Do you take me for an idiot?'

'Not at all. But I didn't give you away, and not everything Torres does has to do with you.'

Pascual resists the urge to grab a handful of Fernando's jacket. 'Where's Lola? And don't tell me she's dead. I've seen her.'

Fernando gives him a long blank look, the look of a man who has learned to control his expression in a very harsh school. 'She's with Sara and Pilar.'

'Then take me to see them. Now.'

'I can't do that. Not yet.'

'I'm tired of hearing that. I'm sick and tired, Fernando, believe me. I've had enough. Take me to Sara.'

Fernando sizes up the little .25 that has appeared in Pascual's hand and apparently decides that at close range even a toy like this will do more damage than he is willing to risk. He exhales, flicks ash out the window and says, 'You want to be careful with that thing.' He sticks the cigarette in the corner of his mouth and reaches for the ignition.

'Where are we going?'

'Where do you think?' Fernando eases away from the kerb. 'We're going to La Mina.'

La Mina lies at the ragged northern edge of Barcelona near the feeble and ill-used Besós river, effectively fenced off from nicer neighbourhoods and the nearby sea by motorways and industrial wastelands. La Mina is the badlands, the outlaw territory every great city spawns out of its need for vice and tales to frighten children. La Mina is a gigantic housing estate thrown up to warehouse people chased out of their shanties by their enlightened betters. La Mina is a textbook in social pathology, a chronic headache for bureaucrats and social workers and policemen and a zoological garden of street life. It is a scandal of inhumane architecture and a failure of social engineering. La Mina is a good place to buy a dose of heroin or lose your wallet, a good place to look down on from a car speeding north to the Costa Brava beaches. Ask a *Barcelonés* to name a gypsy *barrio* and La Mina is the first name that comes to mind.

Fernando steers the old Chevy past ranks of identically bleak brick row houses, barracks for the army of the poor. Graffiti cover every accessible surface, names of people who will never have anything other than this stretch of wall to prove they exist, proclamations of love, obscure talismans: *Mari la Chula*, *Paco Gordito*, *Jabier y Isabel*, *Monopoly*, *Love*. They are approaching the heart of the quarter, the twin monolithic white blocks, ten storeys high and two hundred and fifty metres long, that stand facing each other fifty metres apart, forming a long plaza between them. Across a deserted street from this monstrosity stretches a row of low brick buildings given over to struggling industrial concerns. Fernando pulls up beneath a sign reading *Talleres Hernández* and honks twice. The door goes up and a dark moustachioed man in greasy coveralls waves him inside. Fernando parks in a far corner of the garage and takes two minutes to banter with the man and a boy who could be his son, who is elbow deep in the engine of a vintage Peugeot.

'I pay Rafael to store the car there and he keeps it running like a dream,' Fernando says, leading Pascual across the street. 'He's a cousin, a real one.'

Pascual gawks like a tourist as the blocks tower above him.

They have named the plaza after poor dead Camarón, the Passeig José Monge Cruz according to the plaque on the corner of the nearest building. Rows of balconies rise to the sky like boxes in an enormous opera house and Pascual feels he is stepping on to a stage. Somebody had the good sense at least to designate the ground floor for commerce, and the mix of shabby bars, newsagents and various and sundry shops creates a hum of life around the rim of this architectural dead zone. There are a dozen dramas going on in the vast open space, gypsy women with long hair and long skirts crossing paths with anomic youths in tracksuits looking for trouble or diversion, a man on a bench feeding a dog something in a paper wrapper. Above, laundry flaps gently in the breeze as far as the eye can see and there is no shortage of satellite dishes affixed to the railings; somebody is doing well out of something. On a second-floor balcony an old gypsy woman is clapping and singing something Pascual cannot make out.

Fernando greets half a dozen friends as they cross the plaza. Pascual sees no signs of promiscuous drug dealing or imminent attack, only the same cheerful defiance of poverty he has seen in slums from Damascus to Brooklyn. Fernando leads him into a dark reeking passage, pulling out a key. They climb stairs past the shaft of a lift that Fernando says has not worked since dinosaurs stalked the earth and four floors up they go through a door into a long echoing hallway with doors on either side.

Fernando unlocks one of them and Pascual follows him through a small foyer into the main room of the flat. Someone has made the best of concrete as an element of interior decoration; there is a lot of bright colour, from the yellow of the walls to the riotous tropical hues of the tablecloth he can see through a doorway. There is also sombre religious imagery, Christ expiring on a wooden crucifix above the door and a Virgin mourning in a gilt frame above a long sofa. A faint smell of incense contends with a thick fug of stale tobacco.

'Don't let the decoration scare you. The flat belongs to some cousins of mine,' says Fernando, lighting a cigarette. 'They've gone to France.'

Sara comes through the doorway and halts, in shock. '*Hola, guapa*,' Pascual says. Sara's face looks thinner and in her eyes there is no warmth. Perhaps because of the long skirt she wears, she looks more gypsy than ever.

'What are you doing here?' She comes slowly towards him.

'I came to see you.' He reaches for her. She embraces him, but there is no joy in it. 'How are you?' she says.

'Alive. Free. Couldn't be better.'

Fernando waves him towards the sofa. 'Want something to drink?'

Pascual catches Sara's arm. 'I want you to tell me what's going on. I want to see Lola, for starters.'

Something flares for an instant in Sara's eyes and then fades. '*Vale.*' She disengages her arm and trades a long look with Fernando, who manages to convey a shrug with the slightest movement of his head. Sara turns towards the archway into the dining room. 'Lola,' she calls.

Pascual's eyes meet Fernando's as he listens to the scrape of a chair on the tile floor. The gypsy blows smoke and smiles at him. 'You never believed it, did you?' he says.

'Just long enough to cry for her,' says Pascual.

Lola stands in the doorway, thin and pale in jeans and a dark green sweater that sags off her frail shoulders. Her eyes are enormous in her freshly sheared skull. '*Hola*, Pascual,' she says. She comes towards him with arms outstretched. 'I thought they'd killed you.'

'That puts us even then.' Pascual holds Lola in his arms, the fuzz on her head tickling his cheek. 'What a joy to see you.'

Lola pulls away, wiping tears with a finger. 'Forgive me. I know I've made things hard for you.'

Another step sounds and Pascual looks up to see Pilar in the doorway, serene as ever. Pascual nods at her and looks back at Lola. 'Why?'

'I was scared.'

'Have you been here the whole time?'

'More or less.'

'But you came looking for me that night.'

Lola nods. 'Sara convinced me it wasn't right to keep you in the dark.'

Pascual glances at Sara, but she is examining a fingernail. 'And how much longer are you planning to stay dead?'

'I'm through with that.'

'That means talking to the police.'

'I know. I only wanted to talk to you first.'

'Why?'

'To let you know what's going on.'

'We've got a bit of a confession to make,' says Sara. She is looking at him now, warily.

Pascual makes his way to the sofa and sits gingerly, ribs protesting. 'I'm listening.'

Lola sits at the opposite end of the sofa. Pilar and Fernando have disappeared; Sara stands across the room with her arms folded, leaning on the wall. 'What did the fellow in the hat tell you?' says Lola.

'Nothing.'

'Nothing at all?'

'Not a thing. What was he supposed to tell me?'

'I thought he might have told you how he got hold of me.'

'No. I've been wondering about that, though. I have a feeling he didn't just grab you off the street.'

'No.' Lola trains her great guileless eyes at him and says, 'He was waiting for me at Gabriel's place.'

At least five seconds tick off, very slowly. 'What?' Pascual says.

Across the room Sara draws a deep breath and says, 'She did it for me.'

'Did what?'

'Broke into Gabriel's house.'

'Hang on, you've lost me already.'

'In Castelldefels. Lola went down there to try to get my money.'

Pascual's eyes narrow. 'What money?'

'Gabriel owed me money from performances I'd done. Our deal was, he collected for my appearances and took his cut when he passed it on to me. Only he had a habit of financing his other schemes with my money. He generally came across with it sooner or later, but he owed me a fair amount when he got killed. When that happened, Lola saw a chance to get the money. I knew he kept cash at his place in Castelldefels. Lola figured we could get there before the police got around to it. Only I didn't have the courage, so she went there alone.'

Pascual blinks at Lola, stupidly. 'You broke into his place?'

Lola is looking at the floor. 'I had a little experience in those things when I was a kid,' she says. 'There was a balcony shielded from view and a window I could break.'

'And that thug was waiting for you?'

'Waiting for Gabriel, actually. But it turned out it was you he really wanted. As soon as I told him Gabriel was dead he wanted to know all about that and then he asked me about you.'

'But that means . . . *Cago en Déu.*' Scales fall from Pascual's eyes. 'Gabriel was in it from the start,' he says. He shoots a look at Sara. 'That's who betrayed me.'

She nods, looking wretched. 'I think so, yes.'

'Did you know?'

'No, I swear it.' Sara looks like a dog waiting for a beating. 'He asked about you after he saw us together, but I told him nothing about your past. You hadn't even told me about it at that point, remember?'

Pascual nods. 'Did you know he was a crook?'

Sara shrugs. 'I knew he was careless with other people's money.'

'You should have told me. I'd have taken him down an alley and ruined his precious good looks.'

'I know. That's why I didn't tell you. Or Joselito. I think Joselito would have killed him.'

'I'd say that's a good bet.'

'I thought I had a better chance of getting my money and avoiding trouble if I was patient. But Lola was angry about it.'

'He was a shit,' says Lola, aroused. 'I was glad when he died.'

Pascual looks at Sara and says carefully, 'How on earth did you get involved with him?'

Sara paces to a window overlooking the plaza. Distant shouts and laughter float up to the window. Sara stares at whatever she sees and says, 'I never told you the whole story about Gabriel. I'd known him for a lot longer than three months.'

'I did wonder. He seemed to come out of nowhere.'

'Out of prison, to be exact.'

'Ah.'

'In France.'

Pascual waits. 'What did he do?'

'He sold drugs. Heroin, principally.'

Pascual nods as if she had said Gabriel sold detergent or cooking oil and says, 'Was he still in the business?'

'I don't know. That was when I left and came back to Barcelona, when they caught him. I hadn't heard anything from or about him in six years.'

Pascual works through implications. A great sadness has taken hold of him. Quietly he says, 'And what kind of hold did he have on you?'

Sara raises her eyes from the floor and he can see the tears just beginning to gleam. 'He had help in Marseilles, see? He got caught but I never did.'

'Ah.'

A few seconds pass. Sara wipes away a tear with her fingertips. 'What would you have done?'

'I don't know.' They sit in silence for a moment. 'How much of this does Serrano know?'

'About Gabriel? Everything. He got it out of me the day after he was killed. He knew there was something fishy about Gabriel because his papers weren't in order. And once he got started asking questions he just broke me down.'

Pascual's lips tighten. 'Did he threaten you with charges?'

Sara shakes her head. 'He said narcotics weren't his section and France was somebody else's headache. He said he had a murder to solve, and if I'd given him a lead he wasn't going to reward me by giving me to the French for things I did years ago.'

'Decent of him.'

'Yes. So I even told him where Gabriel lived, even though I hadn't heard from Lola and for all I knew she was still down there ransacking his house. I caved in completely.'

'Who can blame you?'

Sara's lips are parted, on the verge of speech, but for a long moment she says nothing and finally her head droops. Pascual levers himself painfully off the sofa and goes to join her at the window. He cradles her face in his hands and forces her to look at him. 'You think any of this makes any difference to me?'

Her eyes are opaque; Pascual is searching but cannot find the Sara he knows. 'I was young,' she says. 'My mother was dead, I had left school and I was tired of working in the bar. I ran away. I had a little money saved and I'd dreamed of going to Paris since I was a child. I never made it that far, of course. My money ran out fast and I was almost desperate enough to beg from my mother's relatives, which I'd sworn I wouldn't do. Gabriel bought me a meal in Narbonne and told me he could find work for me in Marseilles. And that was that.'

The big question hangs in the air. Sara's eyes meet his and she says, 'Yes, we were lovers. For a time.'

Pascual essays a shrug. 'It doesn't matter.'

'He was the type of man who got tired of women quickly. But then by the time he moved on to someone else I needed the money. There was good money for anyone willing to take a few risks. It's not something I remember with pride.'

'I don't care,' says Pascual, watching her as a tear detaches itself from the corner of her eye and tracks down her cheek. 'I don't care.'

Lola has told it all without losing her composure, until just now. Watching through the glass, Pascual can guess what point in her story she has reached when her shoulders begin to shake. Even Serrano's merciless gaze wanders for a moment as Lola falters. Sitting beside her, Pilar puts a hand on her arm. Sara watches, chewing on a nail. Pascual closes his eyes and rubs his throbbing temples.

He opens them when he hears the door to the interview room open and looks up to see Serrano's partner beckoning him in. He joins Serrano and the women inside while Delgado closes the door and goes to a telephone out in the office.

Serrano is regarding Lola with head tilted very slightly to one side, a thoughtful man considering life's conundrums. 'We might have caught you in the act, you know, if Heredia's papers had been in order. It wasn't until your friend here told us where he lived that we were able to go take a look. She seemed a bit reluctant, and now I can see why.' He watches as Lola shifts uneasily on the chair. 'Don't worry, I'm not sure it's worth our while to charge you with anything. Particularly since the victim's no longer around to complain. I only wish you could cast a little more light on what happened on that boat.'

Wearily Lola says, 'I told you, I was hiding in the closet the whole time. What was I supposed to do, stick my head out and enquire who that was making all the noise?'

'Nobody's reproaching you,' Serrano says, sounding almost sincere. His gaze rests on Lola for a few seconds and then takes in the other three people in the room. 'And you've all known for the past week that she was alive?'

'No,' says Lola. 'Nobody knew.'

'But you told me that your friends here persuaded you to come in.'

'Nobody knew until last night. Then I phoned Sara and she told me about Pilar, and I thought it was better after all to come and talk to you.'

'What precisely were you afraid of?'

Besides the usual gentle treatment, thinks Pascual, watching Lola's face. 'The killers,' she says. 'If they knew they'd left a witness alive they might come back.'

'But you didn't see them.'

'They might not know that.'

'I see.' Serrano taps a finger on his lips a few times and looks at Pascual. 'Anything come back to you? Something you noticed, something you didn't think to tell us before?'

Pascual gives it a few seconds and says, 'I noticed they were all dead. That didn't particularly sharpen my powers of observation.'

Serrano grunts. 'No, I imagine not.' He turns to the women. 'If you'll wait with my colleague out in the office, he'll take care of a few formalities and then you can go. The judge will be wanting to speak with you tomorrow, I imagine.' He keeps Pascual on his chair with a gesture.

When the women have left Serrano says, 'Your friend Campos got the fright of his life yesterday. It's a good thing one of you thought a murder attempt was worthy of a police report.'

Pascual shrugs. 'I knew he'd take care of it.'

'Your attitude is getting more and more cavalier.'

'I brought in Lola, didn't I?'

Serrano nods. 'So you never suspected it was Heredia who betrayed you to Ilmeddin.'

'No. Is that definite?'

'He went to prison in France for his role in a heroin network that was traced back to Ilmeddin. And the flat in Castelldefels

202

turns out to be owned by a company that is part of Ilmeddin's legitimate business empire. I think Heredia was back on the payroll. So I'd say it's a fairly good guess.'

'But how did he know who I was? Who I'd been, I mean? How did he know Ilmeddin would know me? Sara says he was curious about me but swears she refused to answer his questions.'

Serrano muses and says, 'I would imagine you're fairly notorious in certain circles. Ilmeddin would certainly know that your old comrades had put a price on your head. And he might well have spread the word through his networks to be on the lookout for a man of your description and name. They knew your name in Damascus, didn't they?'

'Of course.'

'So it's not that much of a coincidence. Sooner or later somebody was bound to run across your trail. I did tell you you should have changed your first name as well, didn't I?'

'I suppose you knew all along?'

'We never doubted he was involved, somehow. On the first day Delgado and I spent a good deal of time trying to find out a few basic things one likes to know about the victim of a murder, and we came up strangely empty. For a man of business Heredia didn't leave many tracks. He hadn't lived at the address on his DNI for fifteen years.' Serrano pauses, studying his shoes. 'Do you still think Heredia's death was a mistake?'

Pascual has not yet processed all of this and he can only shake his head. 'I heard the shooter call my name. That's all I know.'

'So the wrong man got shot, but the wrong man was in it up to his eyes.'

'So it seems.'

'Curious.'

'Yes.'

Serrano is smiling his grim smile. 'You made me a promise the other day.'

'I haven't forgotten.'

'I'm telling you to forget it. The only thing I want from you is a low profile. I want you alive and well to testify when we haul these bastards in. That's an order. Whatever ideas you had about handling things yourself are to be abandoned. You go hide with your women friends and don't come out until I call you. Is that clear?'

Pascual nods, the picture of contrition. 'Perfectly.'

The women have disappeared from the outer office by the time Serrano releases Pascual. He descends to the side exit, hoping to find them waiting. There is no one there except the old desk sergeant, on friendly nodding terms after all Pascual's comings and goings. '*Mire*,' the sergeant says. 'She left this for you.' He hands Pascual a note, folded over once.

We've gone back to La Mina, it says in Sara's handwriting. *Tomorrow I'll leave a message for you at the bar. All my love, Sara.*

Pascual stands forlorn and resentful in the doorway until the sergeant gently moves him along. Wandering in the narrow lanes of the Gothic Quarter, jostled by cheerful crowds, he screws up the note with one hand and drops it on the cobbles. He can feel Sara slipping away from him. He fights down panic; this is one he was certain he would not lose. He walks and smokes, recklessly, to the Ramblas and down to the end, back to the Plaça Reial and through the arcades, looking for friends and finding only strangers who are laughing, perhaps at him. She is ashamed, he thinks, and needs time for it to fade.

Pascual is familiar with the phenomenon.

22

The only advantage of Pascual's cellar is that there are no tell-tale signs of morning to wake him; no light and little noise penetrates, and when he emerges, fully rested for the first time in days, he finds it is past midday. He begins to walk, through a city that looks splendid and engaging under the sun.

Hygiene is becoming an issue; Pascual came close to spending the night at his *pensión* but decided that a bedtime arrival was a little too predictable. This morning, however, a quick nip upstairs for a shower and a change of clothes seems an acceptable risk.

There are, surprisingly, no messages for him, only the studiously blank look of Senyora Prat, who no doubt puts his irregular habits down to dalliance with women. Clean, shaven and clad in fresh linen, injuries healing, Pascual feels marginally more in control of his fate. He descends to the street.

Light filtered through the plane trees dapples the Ramblas; all these people moving up and down the great promenade seem to know where they are going. Pascual envies them. He finds a telephone and plugs one ear with a finger.

Enric answers the phone at the bar. 'Your American rang again. All he left was a phone number. Ready?'

Pascual takes down the number. 'No other messages?'

'Nothing else. Expecting something better, were you?'

Pascual laughs gently. 'No, I think that's a habit I've finally kicked.'

Pascual punches in the number Enric gave him and does not have to wait long. After two rings a man answers with a simple '*¿Si?*'

'Pascual here. When and where can we meet?'

'As soon as possible.' The voice is smooth and assured, the Castilian fluent but with the faintest trace of accent. 'I'm out at the airport, at the hotel. I suggest you come join me here.'

Pascual thinks for a few seconds and says, 'I think that's a little too private for me. I think I want us to meet in a public place. There's a certain degree of risk for me and I deserve a little insurance, don't you think?'

He waits out a brief silence. The man at the other end of the line says, 'I have to catch a flight out at five this afternoon.'

French, thinks Pascual; a Frenchman who has spent time in Spain. 'It doesn't take long to get into the city. Here's what I suggest. You rent a car and I'll phone back in half an hour and you give me a description of it. I've got a good open place to meet where I can be sure you're not hiding any gunmen under the bed. You park and wait and I'll come and get in the car and we conduct our business. I get out, you drive back to the airport. It'll take about an hour to do the whole thing.'

When he speaks again the Frenchman's voice carries the faintest edge of annoyance. 'Where would this place be? I'm not going to spend my day driving about, I can tell you that.'

Pascual punches in the number of the flat in La Mina, deeply conflicted. He would prefer not to speak to Sara but at the same time wants desperately to hear her voice. When she answers, his heart contracts. 'I have to talk to you,' she says. There is a new note in her voice today, something quiet and calm that was missing before. 'I have a lot of things to tell you.'

Pascual can feel his resolution crumbling by the second. He wants nothing more than to fly to Sara's arms. Slowly he says, 'I've got some business to take care of first.'

Without visual clues he cannot tell if her silence is hurt or merely contemplative. 'When can you be here?' Sara says.

Pascual steels himself. 'Give me a couple of hours. When I see you next, it will all be over.'

'What's going on? What are you doing?'

'I'm going to see some people who can put an end to things.'

'Pascual.' This time the note in her voice goes straight to his heart. 'Don't put yourself in danger.'

'I won't, I promise. Listen, is Fernando there?'

When the gypsy comes on the line he sounds as jaunty as ever. 'What's going on, *primo*?'

'I need your help,' says Pascual.

'Anything I can do, you know that.'

Pascual takes a deep breath. 'I need the gun. Don't let Sara see you take it.' The previous evening Pascual slipped Fernando the little pistol to hide in the flat before taking the women into the Jefatura.

Seconds pass. 'What are you up to?'

'I'll explain it all. Just bring the gun, *vale*?'

In the background Pascual can hear a murmur of female voices. Fernando says, 'When and where?'

The Frenchman sounds like the type of man who, once resigned to new arrangements, undertakes them with dispatch. 'I've got a red Audi. You can't miss it. Have you got a pen? I'll give you the licence number.'

Pascual takes it down. 'How well do you know the city?'

'Pretty well. And I've got a map.'

'All right, you can find Montjuïc then. On the city side of Montjuïc there's a square called Plaça de l'Armada, which overlooks the harbour. There are parking spaces there and there's a restaurant on the roof of the cable-car station in the side of the hill. Park as close as you can to the restaurant and wait. If you can be there in an hour, I'll find you.'

A distant rustling of paper comes over the wire. 'Got it. Yes, that doesn't look too bad. An hour, you say?'

'If you can do it,' says Pascual.

'Why don't we make it . . . let's say three o'clock, just to allow for unexpected hitches.'

'Perfect. We'll be done in time for lunch.'

'You Spaniards and your late hours,' says the Frenchman. 'I think I'll have a bite to eat here at the hotel first.'

'*Estás loco.*' Fernando pronounces the words with complete sincerity and total conviction. He shakes his head and peers out through the windscreen at the trees of the Ciutadella. 'You'll get yourself killed. That's all you'll do.'

'There's a chance of that, yes.'

'They'll have a whole team of professionals waiting for you.'

'There's a limit to how many men they can deploy. They'll have one or two close, that's what counts. And I'm hoping to spot them when I make my pass.'

'One or two. And you've got one round left in that gun.'

'Enough for one man. And then I run.'

'You can't run faster than a bullet.'

'I can make it to the wall and go over. They'll never hit me on the slope. There's plenty of brush for cover.'

'You'll break every bone in your body. Again.'

'It'll hurt for a while, but I'll live.'

For the first time since Pascual has known him, Fernando looks as if he has come across something he cannot simply laugh away. He gives Pascual a pained look and says, 'Walk away from it. Let the police handle it.'

'They'll never catch them. This is the only way to draw the key man into the light.'

'Then let me get some people together. I can get five or six *compañeros* from the Modelo together inside the hour and we'll give those bastards a taste of gypsy steel.'

'They'll have guns.'

'*Primo*, what do you take me for? So will we.'

Pascual shakes his head. 'It's not your fight.'

'You are crazy,' Fernando says again, with something like respect in his voice. He doesn't like it, but in the end he releases a sigh and reaches into his pocket. He slaps the little automatic into Pascual's palm. 'One shot, *coño*. Make it count.'

'I will,' says Pascual. 'And remember one thing.'

'What?'

'There's always at least a chance he's decided to play it straight.'

Serrano is not in the office but Pascual has the number of his mobile phone. '*Dígame*,' growls the old policeman through the ether.

'This is your goat speaking,' says Pascual.

'Don't waste my time. I've got witnesses to intimidate and suspects to beat. What the hell do you want?'

'I want to make sure there's somebody up in the tree when the tiger jumps out of the forest.'

'You've got three seconds to make yourself clear.'

'In about an hour there's going to be an ambush on the Plaça de l'Armada, up on Montjuïc. The men who have been shooting up the city in pursuit of me are going to get one last chance. If you're in place in time, you'll be able to catch them.'

A brief pause is filled with white noise, and then Serrano says, 'I warned you.'

'You told me not to try to handle things myself. I'm following your instructions to the letter. I'm letting you handle them, or more precisely you and a good Special Operations team. You should have plenty of time to mobilize them. At three o'clock I'm going to walk along the road in front of the cable-car station and try to talk to a man sitting in a parked car, but I doubt that they'll let me get too close. I'm hoping you and your people will be good enough to keep me from getting killed. I'm going to run like hell, but I should bring some insects out of the woodwork when I do.'

'You're mad.'

'So I'm told.'

'Why didn't you tell me before, give me some time to prepare?'

'Would you have agreed to something like this?'

Pascual takes Serrano's silence as permission to ring off.

He can see the whole city spread out beneath the turquoise sky, from Tibidabo to the Maremagnum, a chaotic Pollackian canvas of a city crowding the edge of the wine-dark sea, the summit of splendour and a sump of vice and the only place he has ever been happy. From the cable car swinging gently high above the harbour the noises of the vast city are muted and it seems somnolent and benign under the Mediterranean sun, a dream or an abstraction rather than the locus of three million human mysteries. Pascual can make out individual strollers on the Ramblas, tiny and unreal.

He has not ceased to doubt his judgement from the moment he heard Sara's voice on the phone, but matters have advanced too far to reverse course. And besides there is always the need to atone, and that perhaps is the real reason he is going to walk across the Plaça de l'Armada; it will allow him to go to Sara tonight with a conscience washed just a little cleaner. If he survives the next twenty minutes he will take Sara away somewhere.

He has bought a ticket from the Barceloneta all the way to Montjuïc, and he changes cars at the tower on the Mallorca Dock and begins the slow creaking climb to the station nestled in the side of the hill below the Plaça de l'Armada. He can see nothing of the plaza, approaching it from below, but he doubts very much in any event that preliminary surveillance would make a difference. The key is going to be what surprise he can manage, in fast and out fast, and this is the approach which will be hardest for a man in place to observe.

Pascual shares the car with six other people, four French tourists and a Japanese couple. He had hoped for more but will take what cover he can get. The slopes of Montjuïc pass beneath them. Through the vegetation fifty metres beneath his feet Pascual catches glimpses of the winding footpath that leads from the plaza down into the narrow streets at the foot of the mountain, the escape route he hopes to reach alive.

The car slows as it approaches the station, drawing into the shadow of the hill. Looking up at the restaurant overhead, Pascual can see drinkers at the table where he and the gypsies sat a few days before, looking down on the car as it pulls closer. He can see the operator in his glassed-in booth inside the station. He can see the gate in the railing through which they will disembark and the stairs that lead up to the door.

The cable car docks under the concrete roof with a mild jolt and is locked into its berth. In the glassed-in booth the operator is sipping coffee, having brought another craft safely home. The French disembark, laughing. Pascual follows the Japanese on to terra firma. He checks the Rolex Fernando gave him a million years ago and makes for the stairs. His heart has begun to pound. He slips his hand into his jacket pocket to grasp Joselito's pistol, pathetic and inert.

One shot. Pascual does not expect to get close to the Frenchman or whomever is in his place; he hopes to spot any hostile moves in time to take to his heels. He knows that only an expert marksman can hit a moving target more than a couple of metres away with a handgun, and while he would not be surprised to encounter experts, he believes his chances are decent if he sees things happening in time. Once the balloon goes up it will be up to the police. He has no idea what Serrano will have been able to muster but trusts that he will have produced something. Ahead, the French have emerged from the station on to an outdoor landing and are already on the second flight of stairs that leads up the side of the external wall of the station to the level of the street, next to the restaurant terrace. The Japanese have halted on the landing to gape at something. Pascual waits patiently until they move on and steps out on to the landing.

'Here's where you get off,' says Fernando, throwing away a cigarette and putting a hand to Pascual's chest. 'You're not part of this show.' He has risen from his seat on the short flight of steps which leads down from the landing to the left on to a narrow shaded strip of parkland that runs along the hillside at the base of the high wall edging the plaza.

For a moment Pascual is too startled to speak, and then he says, 'What are you doing here?'

'Keeping you out of trouble. You go up those steps, it's all over. *Se acabó la fiesta.*'

'I'm not worried. As soon as I spot anybody I'm making tracks.'

'*Mira.* They've got a man near the top of the steps who's going to wander over to take another look down here any second now, one in the Audi and at least one more in the gardens across the street. They're looking for you and they'll have guns with a lot more range than that thing in your pocket. Now follow me.' Fernando is pulling on Pascual's arm.

Pascual resists. 'But nothing's going to happen if I don't go up there.'

'Who knows? Life is unpredictable. Sometimes you just have to see how the dice come up.'

Pascual fixes the gypsy in the eye. Fernando could be leaning on the bar at the Tavern del Born, nursing a *caña*, for all the tension he is showing. 'What have you done?'

'Me? Nothing. You seem to have made all the necessary arrangements. Now it's time to go home.'

Bewildered, Pascual follows him down the steps and through the narrow glade. They walk in shade over uneven patchy turf for fifty metres and come to a double flight of steps leading up to a mirador, a stone platform built out from the edge of the plaza; at the parapet above them stand tourists, clicking cameras. Further along the glade, beyond the stairs, is the start of the footpath leading down the mountain.

Fernando looks up at the mirador, calculating. 'We're going to walk up there like we haven't a care in the world and go down the road to my car. There are *pestañí* all over the place, and I wouldn't be surprised to find some up there mixed in with the tourists. But they won't know what you look like, will they?'

'I don't know. Serrano will, if he's there.'

'Your inspector friend? The old white-haired bastard? He's in a Renault just around the bend down there with a mobile phone to his ear, trying hard not to look like a cop. He won't see us. Most of the action is going to be right in front of the restaurant.'

Pascual has surrendered the initiative and follows mutely as Fernando mounts the right-hand flight of stairs. 'How long have you been here?'

'Long enough to see what's going on. You picked a great spot, *primo*. With all these tourists it's hard to sort out the villains from the *pestañí*.'

At the top of the stairs a dozen or so tourists are milling, admiring the view; a coach stands rumbling at the kerb. Pascual follows Fernando towards the old Chevrolet parked a stone's throw down the road.

Fernando halts at the edge of the mirador and pulls out cigarettes. 'We're just in time for the show,' he murmurs, handing one to Pascual. 'Turn around but don't look too interested.'

Looking back along the road, Pascual can see the red Audi parked directly across the road from the restaurant terrace. Reflections on the windscreen make it impossible to tell if the car is occupied. Pascual can see nothing that indicates imminent violence, no one but the idlers any such spot attracts. His mind is racing through scenarios at light speed, but he has a feeling he has missed something vital. 'What's happening?' he says.

'That,' says Fernando. Pascual has no idea what he is talking about until he sees the man ambling down the steps from the restaurant terrace, a man without cares on a lovely spring day, idling the afternoon away. He watches the man pause to light a cigarette on the pavement across from the red Audi and he understands nothing.

In his panama hat Torres looks like a tourist who has strayed from the beach. Pascual can just make out the moustache and the hard flat face beneath the brim as Torres looks right and left. Torres is not in a hurry, evidently, as he ambles across the road towards the Audi. 'No,' says Pascual, feeling sick.

Torres has almost reached the driver's side of the Audi when the shots ring out, two sharp cracks separated by a half-second. The first one kicks Torres in the chest, jolting him backwards, and the second knocks the panama hat off his head in a spray of pink. Torres hits the asphalt like a bag of rice falling off the back of a lorry.

Fernando is pulling Pascual away, but Pascual is still trying to process what he has seen and heard. The red Audi peels out of the parking space with a squeal of tyres and comes tearing up the road towards them; men are shouting somewhere nearby and other engines are coming to life. Two men who have been lounging on the parapet not ten metres away have sprouted firearms and are sprinting wildly back towards the restaurant. The other tourists have only just become aware of the commotion and are looking after them in expectant confusion.

'A rifle,' says Pascual, in wonder, looking across the road. 'In the gardens.'

'And that would be you with your head in pieces,' says Fernando. '*Camina.*'

Things are suddenly happening close at hand; the red Audi tears past them but brakes hard to avoid broadsiding the black Peugeot that has slewed across the road out of a parking place not twenty metres away. The screech of tyres gives way to the thump of a mild collision. Doors fly open and all is frantic shouting, adrenaline-charged voices of men who do not wish to be shot and will fire impressive automatic weapons at anything moving before taking the least chance of that happening. In six seconds the Plaça de l'Armada has become an armed camp, a *tableau vivant* with weapons and halted vehicles. 'I think we'll forget the car,' says Fernando. Now he is pushing again, forcing Pascual back towards the stairs leading from the mirador down to the hillside.

'Tell me what just happened,' says Pascual.

Fernando has a firm grip on his arm as they trot down the steps. 'You saw it all. He took a bullet for you. Light a candle for him in Santa María del Mar tonight.'

Pascual has difficulty matching Fernando's brisk pace on the path that winds down the hillside through thick vegetation affording intermittent views of the port close beneath them. The awkward downhill gait jolts his sore ribs and his head has begun to throb. He is beginning to make sense of what he has seen when he becomes aware of the rapid footsteps behind them. Fernando shoots a glance over his shoulder. They have just rounded a bend and whoever is trotting after them is not yet visible. Fernando gives Pascual one keen look and then shoves him without ceremony into the brush at the side of the path. When the man in the blue and maroon FC Barcelona cap comes into view, Fernando is kneeling in the middle of the path, tying his shoe, and Pascual is trying to pull himself to his feet, thrashing at branches.

The man halts in surprise. Pascual has seen this man before; it takes him a long second to place him in the crowd on the mirador. It takes him a somewhat shorter second to recognize the tactic of using distinctive headwear to distract attention from the face, and by then it is nearly too late. He recognizes the South African soldier of fortune Adrian Coetzee just as Coetzee reaches inside his denim jacket for the gun that killed Gabriel Heredia.

Coetzee's attention is split, but by the time the impressive blue steel automatic is clear of the holster he has apparently decided that the wild-haired gypsy kneeling in front of him is a more pressing concern than the flailing Spaniard in the bushes, perhaps because the gypsy is coming out of his crouch at speed.

The handful of dirt Fernando has scooped from the trail catches Coetzee in the face before he can get the gun trained, but Coetzee has the reactions of a professional and he dodges with his eyes shut, avoiding the main force of Fernando's lunge. Pascual has finally fought free of the brush, and is tugging frantically at the little automatic in his pocket, but the wretched object will not come out, the hammer caught fatally on a rip in the lining. Fernando has Coetzee's arm in the crook of his elbow, spinning him around, but Coetzee has seen all the tricks and he lets the arm go limp and jerks it free, winding up with the gun pointing directly at Fernando's head. Pascual saves Fernando's life by putting his shoulder into Coetzee's back. Fernando catches Coetzee by the jacket as he sprawls and the pair of them roll over in the dirt in a tangle of limbs. Pascual stumbles after them to see to his great dismay that Coetzee has wound up on his back on top of Fernando with the gun pointing at Pascual's chest, his brow contracting as he aims. Pascual has managed to pull the automatic free but it is too late; he will never fire in time. He draws breath for a scream that will say everything, goodbye to Sara and goodbye to Father Costa and goodbye to the exquisite turquoise sky, but Coetzee's face changes suddenly, the look of homicidal expertise replaced by one of shock mutating rapidly to distress as the muzzle of the blue steel automatic wanders away to point at nothing. Fernando grunts as he shoves Coetzee off of him, tugging his knife out of its perfect placement just below the left shoulder blade. Blood oozes from the slit in the denim jacket.

Coetzee has not dropped the gun, but he has used it for the last time. He crawls a pace or two on hands and knees, says something in what sounds like Afrikaans in a husky liquid voice and collapses with his face in the dust.

Fernando wipes the knife with two quick swipes on Coetzee's trouser leg, stows it in his boot and seizes Coetzee by the legs. He drags the body off the trail on the downhill side, into the bushes. Climbing back, he says, 'With any luck they won't find him for a few hours. What are you doing with that thing?'

Pascual looks down at Joselito's gun lying bright and inoffensive on his palm, still bearing its single round. Without further thought he flings it into the brush.

Near the bottom, the path levelling out and apartment blocks looming above, there is a channel carrying cool water to spill over a slope into a fountain. Fernando stops to wash his hands with an air of absorption, scrubbing blood from his wrist with a thumb. He says, 'Sara's waiting for you at the flat. Her flat, in Princesa.'

Pascual can only take so many urgent concerns at a time. When Fernando straightens up, shaking water off his hands, Pascual says, 'Explain to me what just happened.'

'There was a cock-up,' says Fernando. 'And you were never here.'

23

Joselito is weeping, a harsh unsettling sound in the echoing stairwell. He is back on the job, dressed in his blue coverall, but the gauze bandage that covers the shaved side of his head and the creakiness of his movements testify to the effects of his injuries. '*Hombre*,' he manages through his tears. 'Forgive me. They left me no choice. It was you or Pilar. They didn't leave me any choice. Forgive me.'

The little man's embrace is constricting Pascual's ribs painfully, but Pascual bears it in silence. 'There's nothing to forgive,' he squeezes out. 'You saved my life. Now get a hold of yourself.'

Joselito blows his nose with an extraordinary blaring noise that echoes up the stairwell. 'She's waiting for you,' he snarls.

Upstairs the breeze is at work again, just as it was a week ago, billowing the curtains and moving air that has grown stale. From the street below come voices and the low rumour of passing cars in a street too narrow for the traffic it bears. Sara and Pascual stand for a long minute in each other's arms. '*Se acabó*,' breathes Pascual into her hair. 'It's all over.'

'I know,' she says. 'Fernando phoned.'

'Where are Lola and Pilar?'

'They've gone out. We've got the place to ourselves.'

Sara's face has a melancholy beauty that takes Pascual's breath away. 'I have many things to tell you,' he says.

Sara places her hand over his mouth. 'Not now.'

Sara's room is just big enough to hold a wardrobe, a chair, a small dressing table and the narrow bed. Pascual sits on the bed and lets Sara remove his shoes; she lays him down on the pillow with great tenderness, kisses him gently. 'I have a lot to tell you, too,' she says. Standing at the foot of the bed, she begins to take off her clothes, unhurried, unaffected, eyes downcast. When she stands naked before him, she finally meets his gaze. He has propped himself up on his elbows to watch, transfixed; in all these months she has never displayed herself so frankly. She stands with legs slightly apart, broad hips framing the perfect triangle of hair that points like an arrow to the heart of her sex, dark nipples crowning her breasts, black hair cascading past her shoulders. 'For you,' she says. 'If you want it.'

For a week and more there has been no room in Pascual's psyche for anything sexual; even now there is something more solemn than seductive in Sara's bearing. Merely as a visual spectacle however, she is stunning. He flails for appropriate words and settles finally for breathing her name.

'For you,' she repeats. 'All of it for you, always, nobody else, ever.'

Pascual's mind is racing. 'Sara, whatever happened with Fernando, forget it. I don't want to know.'

'Nothing happened with Fernando. You don't understand.' She has come up the side of the bed and is stooping to tug at his belt. 'You don't understand anything.' She tugs his trousers off, and parts of him are suddenly recovering rapidly from the stresses of the past week.

She straddles him, moving with great care so as not to hurt him. 'What is it I don't understand?' he says. Again she muzzles him with her moist palm. '*Nada, querido.* Nothing.' She eases him into her, working her hips, gasping as he slips inside. Sara seizes his chin with one hand, supporting herself with the other, and presses her mouth on to his. She is hurting his swollen lips; he can taste the blood. She draws back, letting him breathe. Fiercely, hoarsely, she says, '*Huele mi cuerpo a lumia, como el fraguero a humo.*' This is a song he has heard but cannot place. My body smells of *lumia*, she is saying, a gypsy word he does not know but can guess at, having known all the smells of her body.

'*Te quiero,*' he says. This is all Pascual has ever wanted: quiet for a troubled soul. He is hardly aware of the biological functioning, and there is no question of technique; all that is happening is that he and Sara are holding each other, and as long as she has him

217

inside her like this, her heat radiating slowly up his root to the very heart of him, there is no death, not yet. He bucks at her weight on top of him as he comes.

He awakes some time later. Night is beginning to fall outside. Sounds of domestic alarms and dramas reverberate faintly through the old stone; in the street below traffic rumbles, shaking the windowpanes. He is alone in the bed. He panics for an instant, sitting up with a painful start and calling her name. Soft footsteps sound in the passage and Sara returns, wrapped in her robe, feet bare. She sits on the bed and brushes hair from his forehead. 'Quiet, *cariño*. Everything's all right.'

Pascual's heart slows eventually and he clasps Sara's hand. He could lie here for ever, but there will be an end to all this soon; he remembers Fernando's words and knows that it will be impossible to maintain the fiction that he was never there. 'I have to go,' he says.

'Soon, *querido*. Not yet.'

Pascual traces her lips with a finger. 'What's *lumia*?' he says.

Sara's eyes fill with tears; first one eye brims over and then the other, and Pascual watches appalled as tears run down her cheeks. He hoists himself up on an elbow, grimacing at the pain from his ribs. 'What's wrong?'

'*Lumia*,' she says, rising from the bed. She paces to the window. 'Don't you remember the song? It's one of the bitter ones. Your body reeks of it, he says.'

'I remember. What's *lumia*?'

Her back turned, Sara says, '*Lumia* is the gypsy word for *puta*.'

Pascual fights free of the covers and goes to her. 'What the hell are you talking about?'

She wards off his reaching hands, pushes him away. 'I've lied to you,' she says, 'from the start.'

'What?'

'*Puta*. I'm a whore, Pascual. Understand?'

Pascual understands nothing except that Sara is in pain. 'No, never.'

'You think selling drugs was all I did for Gabriel?'

Pascual is so staggered he has to collapse on the bed. 'No,' he groans.

'*Yes*.' Sara's voice has gone ragged, heavy with tears. 'He broke

218

me, he turned me, he put me on drugs and he put me on the street.'

'*No!*'

'I didn't just sell heroin, I *used* heroin, and I turned tricks for Gabriel. For two years, until they caught him and threw him in jail. I was a whore in Marseilles, you understand? *Puta era*. I must have fucked a thousand men, Pascual. Ten thousand.'

'I don't care.' Pascual rises from the bed and tries again, reaching through Sara's flailing hands to pull her to him. 'I don't care, I don't care. I love you.'

Her voice breaks. 'How can you love a whore?'

It is his turn to seize her face and turn it to him. 'Whore is just a dirty word. It's you I love.'

Her collapse catches him by surprise; he tries to hold her upright but she slides to the floor, eyes squeezed shut and shaking with sobs. He winds up sitting with his back to the wall cradling her head against his bare chest, whispering her name. At length her weeping subsides. Pascual listens to remote laughter and quarrels and the endless tumult of the streets.

Sara stirs, sits up, wipes tears from her face. 'When you need a fix, you'll do anything to get it,' she says. 'There wasn't a day that went by when I didn't resolve to quit, run away, get clean and stay clean. And then the need would come on and I would head for the street, like a robot, shoving what was left of my dignity down deep somewhere. Gabriel had the money and the drugs, and it was too easy to let him run my life. When they put him in jail I did the one smart thing I've done in my life and ran. Another girl had told me about a place near Aix run by some nuns where they would help you get off the drugs. I almost didn't make it. If I'd found a place to score a hit in Aix that night, I'd be a junkie today. But I'd phoned ahead and they sent somebody out to look for me. They grabbed me off the street and saved my life. The first few days were hell, but once I was clean I knew I'd never go back. I came home and found Lola and Pilar and I've never been tempted again. I started to sing again, I started to have an idea of what it is to put together a life. I met you. Then Gabriel showed up.'

'My love. You should have told me.'

'He was reformed, he said. No more drugs, only legitimate business. He was going to make me a star. I said no at first, but he made it clear my past would not be a secret for long if I refused. And then he got me the appearance at the Feria de Abril and it seemed he really could help my career, and if he was going to exploit me this was at least better than prostitution. So I went along.'

'You should have told me. I'd have killed him myself.'

'That was what I was afraid of. That, and losing you.'

Pascual's heart is breaking. '*Vida mía*, the things I've done, how could I reproach you?'

Sara's eyes are enormous, luminous, bottomless. Her hair hangs limply in her face and her nose is red from crying and she has never been more beautiful. 'No more secrets, Pascual. Secrets rot the soul.'

'No more secrets.' He pulls her close, and she begins to cry again, softly. Pascual waits, stroking her hair.

A loud hammering resounds through the flat; someone is pounding on the door. Sara sits up abruptly, wiping her face on the sleeve of the robe. '*Qué putada*,' she says bitterly and without apparent irony. 'Just as I finally win you, I have to lose you.'

Pascual will never get used to these shocks; he has gone cold. 'What are you talking about?'

Sara stands, tightens the belt of her robe, brushes hair from her face. 'I have to go away, Pascual. Maybe for a long time.' The pounding resumes.

'Why?' He struggles to his feet, follows her out of the room. 'Talk to me.'

'That will be the police. You'd better get dressed.'

'The police? How did they know I was here?'

'I called them,' Sara says. 'But they haven't come for you. They've come for me.'

Serrano is finally beginning to look like a man ready for retirement. Beneath the close-cropped white hair the eyes are going hollow and the shoulders are beginning to slump. His voice, however, concedes nothing to age. 'What the hell happened to you?' he barks.

Pascual has to make an effort to bring his mind around to Serrano's concerns; ever since Delgado appeared at Sara's door he has been waiting for someone to explain things to him. 'I ran away when I saw Torres get shot,' he says with an absent wave of the hand. 'I panicked.'

Serrano makes a dismissive noise. 'And I suppose you have no idea how he came to be there.'

'None.' Pascual is grateful to be able to tell the truth, though if pressed he would be able to say who might have an idea. 'I was coming up the steps from the cable car when I saw him. And then the shooting started.'

'I see.' Serrano trades a sour look with his partner. 'Are you aware just how irresponsible your actions were? How many people might have been hurt?'

'I had confidence in you. Did you get them all?' Outside in the main office Sara is sitting at a desk with her head in her hands. Next to her is a dapper little man with a grey beard in a jacket and tie who appeared a few minutes after Delgado brought them in and has not left her side since.

'Who knows if we got them all?' says Serrano. 'We got the Frenchman in the Audi and the Cuban in the gardens. I've got a feeling we missed a few. The South African was spotted, but he disappeared in the confusion.'

'Well, you've got a couple of live ones. You'll be able to get someone to talk.'

'For your sake I hope so. If I have to bring charges of obstruction against you, I will.'

Pascual shrugs. 'I can tell you what I pieced together. The Frenchman will be the key. He's the link between Hampton and the killers. Present him with a stark enough choice and he'll talk.'

'Ah, many thanks for the advice. I think we can handle it. What I need from you is a complete account of your part in it. Espinoza's got a chair reserved for you over at the *juzgados*. We've got a lot to sort out.'

Pascual has lost interest in the whole sordid mess, but he realizes an effort is required. Rather disingenuously he says, 'If you ever find the South African I can finger him for Gabriel. And most likely you'll be able to pin Weiss on him as well. Him and the Cuban.'

Serrano shakes his head, a schoolmaster exasperated by obtuseness. '*Imbécil.* They didn't kill Weiss.'

It takes a couple of seconds for the words to filter through to Pascual's conscious mind. 'They didn't?'

Serrano snorts with laughter. 'Of course not. They *witnessed* Weiss's murder.'

'What?'

Serrano flaps a weary hand. 'Delgado, you explain to him.'

The thin man taps a pencil on the desk, one leg crossed casually over the other. 'A witness finally came forward a few days ago. He was a junkie, and he'd gone out to Avillar Chavorro to score. He'd just shot up and was settling down in the bushes when he saw a car pull up and heard two shots inside. Then a man got out and cut down the slope to another car parked on the road below. He passed within a few metres of our informant, who fortunately was still in condition to observe things, and he was able to give us a good description.'

'Which was?'

Delgado smiles. 'He said the killer was dressed entirely in black.'

Pascual goes slack and gazes at the ceiling for a moment. He remembers Gabriel pushing through the crowd, mobile phone to his ear. 'Incredible,' he says. 'He was gone just long enough to do it.'

'At that time of night you can get from the Born to Avillar Chavorro in under fifteen minutes,' says Serrano. 'He was gone for about half an hour, wasn't he?'

'About that. Incredible.'

'But true. I'm sure our two killers will confirm it. Our junkie friend saw them come creeping up a few minutes later and look into the car with the two bodies in it.'

Pascual's head is beginning to spin. 'They followed Gabriel. From the hotel where he picked up Weiss.'

'Not Gabriel – the other one, Fernández. He picked up Weiss at the hotel, then phoned Gabriel at the bar and came to pick him up. They drove out to Avillar Chavorro and Gabriel shot them both, leaving no witnesses. The dead gypsy had quarrelled with Gabriel over drug receipts, it seems. Probably he was enforcing discipline and covering his tracks at the same time.'

'But how did they get Weiss to come with them?'

'I don't know, but there's an easy guess. They told him they were taking him to meet you.'

Pascual can only gape as light dawns. 'And the other two had tapped Weiss's phone.'

'That's right. And I'm sure you can draw the next conclusion.'

It takes Pascual a moment, but he does not disappoint Serrano. 'They thought they were seeing me. They thought Gabriel was me.'

Serrano smiles at last. 'So you see, the right man got shot after all. They got Pascual and they left town.'

Pascual is trying to deal with overloaded circuits. 'But why? Why would Gabriel kill Weiss? It doesn't make sense. Ilmeddin gave Weiss the story in the first place.'

'That I can only guess at. You're better versed in the political part of it. What was the object of setting Weiss on the story in the first place?'

Pascual works at it for a few seconds. 'McDuff had already had the extradition effort called off. Ilmeddin used Weiss to pressure McDuff, and when the pressure worked, it was time to turn it off. To save it for future use. A story like that can only be used once and it's more valuable in reserve.'

'That's probably about right. Lovely people, eh?'

Pascual shakes his head, feeling ill. 'What a cesspool.'

'To put it mildly. You see it all now, do you?'

'I think so.'

'Then here's one last question for you.'

'What?'

'Who was Gabriel talking to on the telephone when he was shot?'

Pascual gives him a suspicious look. 'How should I know? And what does it matter?'

'Well, who rang him on the bar phone? He had a mobile and presumably anyone who needed to reach him had that number. Who knew he was sitting at the bar at that moment?'

Seconds tick off the clock as Pascual feels his way around it, probing, nudging, seeing if it will bite. 'Any number of people.'

'Yes. But how did it happen that he took the call just at that moment?'

Pascual puts a hand to his throbbing temple, eyes closed. 'They marked him. That's how they marked him. They made sure they had the right man by phoning, asking for him and seeing who took the phone.'

'That's right. And who did they ask for?'

Pascual's eyes come wide open. 'They asked for me.'

'You see it now, don't you?'

'*Is that why she's here?*' Pascual is up off his chair, rigid with anger; Delgado is on him in an instant, an iron grip on his arm. Serrano has not moved. Out in the office Pascual hears chairs scrape on the floor, senses urgent motion. 'She's here because she handed the phone to him instead of me?' Pascual wheels to look out into the office and meets Sara's haunted eyes. 'She saved my life,' he says, shaking off Delgado's hand.

'And sealed Gabriel's fate,' says Serrano.

Pascual sinks back on to his chair. 'He deserved it. He deserved everything he got.'

'Nobody's disputing that.'

Pascual glowers. 'No, I don't believe it. How did she get involved? Surely they didn't just walk in and recruit her to set up their victim.'

'They didn't recruit her. She manipulated them.'

'How?'

Wearily, Serrano says, 'Why don't we bring her in here and let her tell you herself?'

Sara is perfectly calm; whatever storms she has sailed through, now she has complete self-possession. Her lawyer sits and watches her as she speaks, like a parent watching his child perform at a recital, alert for errors.

Eyes locked with Pascual's, in a clear voice Sara says, 'He was French. He didn't have much of an accent but I could tell. He sat at the bar and asked me if I knew you, and you were sitting right there at the table with the gypsies. Remember? We'd gone for a walk and you'd told me all about your past.'

Pascual nods. He can see the man in the fleece-lined jacket, talking to Sara across the bar. 'I thought he was making a pass at you.'

'He said he had to talk to you about last night. *Lo de anoche*, he said. So I could see immediately, first that he didn't know you,

224

and second that he'd confused you with someone else. You'd been by my side the whole evening, so whatever *lo de anoche* was, it didn't concern you. And it wasn't hard to guess who he was talking about. I asked what you looked like and he told me you dressed all in black.'

Pascual swears under his breath. 'And you knew.'

'I didn't know they were going to kill him. But I knew I had to protect you. It would have been simple to say, "Look, you've got the wrong man, it's Gabriel you want, that's Pascual over there." But I knew you were afraid of strangers, and I knew that if I said he had the wrong man he'd only ask me to point out the right one. And I decided that however the confusion had happened, Gabriel must have brought it on himself. So I just went along. He asked if Pascual would be in any time soon, and knowing he meant Gabriel I said yes, probably later that evening.'

Pascual leans forward, intent. 'And when the phone rang and the man asked for me?'

'I recognized his voice, his accent. And I gave the phone to Gabriel.'

Pascual turns to Serrano, bristling. 'How can you possibly charge her with anything on the basis of that?'

There is a silence and the three other men in the room trade what might be embarrassed looks. 'That's not what she's here for,' says Serrano.

Pascual has been here too long, had too many shocks, gone too far on too little food and sleep. 'What the hell is she here for, then?'

It is Sara's lawyer who leans forward to speak, in a pleasant, precise voice. 'She's come in to confess to the murder of Philippe Giometti,' he says.

24

'Philippe Giometti was a *conseiller municipal* in Marseilles,' says Serrano. 'I don't know whether he had any connection with the crime family or not, but he was hardly a model of probity. He was reputed to be the *milieu*'s man in the municipal government, or one of them anyway. He had a bad reputation with the reforming types, but he was a popular man out on the streets. It made quite a stir in the press when he died.'

Pascual is not sure how much more he wants to hear. 'I remember it vaguely.'

'Then you may recall he was found dead in his villa with his throat cut. Some seven years ago, I believe.'

'August 19th, 1993,' says Sara. 'A Friday night.'

An uncomfortable silence follows. 'Shall I continue?' says Serrano gently. Sara nods. 'Giometti had bled to death from a slash in his throat, made apparently by a fragment of a bottle. Somebody had done some hurried cleaning up, but a few fragments of glass were found. He was naked and had been engaged in sexual activity, according to the medicos.'

'Stop.' Pascual is not going to sit here and make Sara go through this. 'I can guess the rest.'

'It was known that Giometti had a taste for . . .' Serrano pauses, delicately.

'For whores,' says Sara.

Serrano shrugs. 'His habits were known and the population in question was thoroughly investigated. But nobody was ever charged.'

'I was a perk,' says Sara, with perfect calm. 'I was part of the system of bribery that kept Gabriel's networks in business. Keep Giometti happy and keep moving the drugs. All of Gabriel's women had to take a turn or two at keeping Giometti happy. That night it was my turn.'

Serrano soldiers on. 'It appeared that a few items had been stolen and robbery was thought to be the motive. But now we know the truth.'

'Why don't you show him the video?' says Sara.

Pascual closes his eyes. Serrano says, 'I see no need for that.'

'The video,' says Pascual bitterly.

Sara's voice goes slightly husky as she says, 'He liked to watch himself, later.'

Pascual opens his eyes to see the tears tracking down her cheeks. 'That's what Lola was looking for, wasn't it? Not money. That's what Torres had. He must have taken it from her.'

Sara shakes her head. 'She never had it. He went back and found it later. He didn't believe the story about the money. He found the whole package.'

'The whole package?'

Serrano says, 'Heredia kept the video and the fragments of the bottle. They had her fingerprints all over them. The two of them constitute as good a case as a prosecutor will ever have.'

'I phoned him,' says Sara. 'In a panic, hysterical. He came and cleaned up and got me out of there. He told me he got rid of everything and I was fool enough to believe him.'

Pascual looks at Serrano. 'How did you get hold of them?'

'Torres handed them over to an UDYCO officer last night. To show his good faith, he said. Hoping for future favours, no doubt.'

'I finally told him he could go to the devil,' says Sara. 'I should have done it long ago, with Gabriel. I'll be freer in prison than I was with that secret ruling my life.'

A silence follows. 'What now?' says Pascual to Serrano.

The old policeman shrugs. 'It's nothing to do with me, thank God. I've notified Marseilles and they're dispatching a couple of officers to question her.'

The dapper little lawyer clears his throat. 'She's making a voluntary confession and there are extenuating circumstances. She has an excellent case for self-defence, in my estimation. Ironically, the video is her best defence.'

Stupidly, Pascual says, 'How?'

The little man turns a matter-of-fact gaze on him. 'Prior to her . . . act of violence, the video shows clearly the outrage perpetrated on her.'

'I took the bottle away from him,' says Sara. 'There are some things even a whore won't do.'

'What the hell am I going to do with you?' says Serrano.

'Whatever you want.' Pascual can barely stay upright on the chair. Sara has departed with her lawyer and he has not yet found a way to keep certain images at bay. 'Put me on the stand. I'll testify to anything you want.'

'Well, we'll want you to identify Coetzee, certainly, presuming we can find him. We'll get him for Gabriel, and we may get the other two for various kidnappings and other depredations if your friends can identify them. And that gives us a basis to start making deals and working our way back up the tree to Hampton and McDuff. We'll see how it goes.'

Pascual very nearly tells Serrano where he can find Coetzee; he is sick unto death of lying and the last thing he wants is another secret to keep. This one, however, is not his to betray. He passes a hand over his face and says, 'What about the killings on the boat? Surely you can connect them with that?'

Serrano shakes his head slowly. 'You really think so?'

'Why not? You said you'd found the boat they used.'

'That boat we found had been stolen by some drunken teenagers, it turns out.'

'So they used something else. They must have left a trail.'

Serrano smiles. 'Those lubbers never went near the sea. They hadn't a clue where Ilmeddin had gone after Marbella.'

Something in Serrano's look tells Pascual that he is about to have his legs chopped from under him again. 'What are you saying?'

Serrano leans closer, intense. 'Tell me what you saw on that boat. Do you remember how the bodies lay?'

Pascual can picture them, each one, but his mind refuses to go further. He begins to shake his head. 'No.'

'Yes. The man on the steps was rushing below decks when he was shot. The man in the passage was heading for the stateroom in the stern. And the man in the stateroom, your old Arab pal, was shot at very close range. With his trousers down.'

'No. I won't believe it.'

'Believe it. There were no boarders. The bodyguards would have been heading up the steps if there had been.'

'Impossible. How could a girl like that get the jump on three armed men?'

'My guess would be that the Arab tried something on her.'

'Oh, Christ. Poor Lola.'

'Yes. That would set her off, wouldn't it? And I'd bet the old bastard had a weapon lying around, or stuck in his belt or something stupid like that. Where sex is concerned men's judgement goes out the window. I'd bet she got a hold of it and shot him, just like that, and then shot the other two as they came running, from ambush, one at a time. You'd be surprised what anger can do to a person.'

'I found her in a closet, scared out of her wits. Why didn't she swim for it?'

'Who knows? She threw the gun overboard and went back down to wait for dark, maybe. I wasn't there, but I'd stake my career on this. She shot them all.'

'Have mercy, Serrano, for God's sake. If it's true, consider what she's been through.'

The old policeman, looking every bit his age, leans even closer and lowers his voice. 'Who says I haven't? If I had any hope of proving it my professional conscience might be tested, but as things stand, this is one I'm willing to let her have. It's not every day a villain gets exactly what he deserves.'

Pascual looks into Serrano's eyes for a long moment, seeing things he has never quite made out before. 'I didn't hear any of this,' he says finally.

'Of course you didn't. Now, we've got your statement, yet again, so I suppose I have to let you go, but there's yet another examining magistrate who will be needing to speak with you. Where can we reach you?'

Pascual considers. 'At Sara's. I'll be with her until . . .'

'Yes. As long as she's at liberty. What a household that must be. I wouldn't make any of those women angry if I were you. And one more thing.'

229

'Yes?'

'I'd still like to know how Torres wound up in your place today.' Serrano shoves away from the desk. 'You've got some rum friends, you have.'

'The best,' says Pascual. 'Nobody could ask for better ones.'

The gypsies are back at the corner table, Antonio and Diego laughing, bantering, calling for drinks, tuning their guitars. Enric and the novice Marisa are hard at work behind the bar, pouring, giving change, straining to hear above the tumult. Night has fallen and the Tavern del Born is full.

'So how the hell did Coetzee's body get all the way around the mountain to Avillar Chavorro?' murmurs Pascual into Fernando's ear. They are leaning side by side on the marble countertop. Pascual is unaccustomed to the view from this side of the bar, but finds he is enjoying letting other people pour the drinks.

'Never you mind,' says Fernando, toying with his *caña*. 'It cost me and a couple of mates a very careful night's work, that's all I'll say. But the *pestañí* don't seem to be questioning it.'

'Serrano had me in for another talk, but his heart wasn't in it. I think he really wanted to believe Coetzee blundered into the place running away from the shootout and got stabbed for his wallet.'

Fernando nods. 'So they're looking for gypsy villains again. It was me that found the junkie who saw the American killed, too. Life's a fucking joke sometimes, isn't it?'

Pascual shakes his head. 'And Torres? Are you ready to tell me how you managed that?'

Fernando's eyes gleam over the rim of his glass. 'I told him a former client of Sara's was willing to give him ten thousand dollars for the video. All he had to do was look for a red Audi. The bastard was so greedy he believed it. He'd made a copy of the video, of course, so he could sell it if the chance came up even after giving it to the police.'

'What a beautiful human being.'

Fernando lets out a whiff of disgust. 'Sara wouldn't let me kill him. I'd have done it in an instant. But she forbade me. Said nobody else was to die on her account. So I didn't. I suppose you could say my interpretation was a little loose.'

'He had it coming.'

'Mind you, I still think I could have got it from him in the end. I offered him money for it, but his price was too high. I couldn't come up with more than half a million pesetas. And after that Sara told me to forget it, she'd go to the police. I tried to talk her out of it, but she'd made up her mind.'

Pascual gapes at him. 'You'd have paid half a million pesetas to get Sara off the hook?'

'*Hombre*, I'd have gotten it all back sooner or later, one way or another. But yes, I was ready to pay. For Sara, anything.'

In unison they turn to look at her, sitting with Lola and Pilar and Joselito at a table along the wall. Sara has one arm around Lola's shoulders and the other stretched across the table, holding Pilar's hand. Joselito is gesturing wildly with a cigarette, sending hot ash flying. Pascual watches Sara laugh and her beauty takes his breath away. 'She looks happy,' he says, in wonder.

'*Ojalá*,' says Fernando. 'If there's one person on this wretched earth that deserves a little happiness, it's Sara. Is she going to sing tonight?'

'Why do you think all these people are here? The word's gone round that this is her last night.'

Fernando shakes his head. 'There is no fucking justice.'

'There's hope,' says Pascual. 'Her lawyer here has lined up somebody to represent her in Marseilles. He says there's a good chance she'll get probation even if she's found guilty, given the circumstances. It's a high-profile case because of who Giometti was, but there's a chance of an acquittal. And if worse comes to worst he says she'll get no more than three years, based on similar cases.'

'You'll let me know, right? Whatever she needs? Money can grease a lot of wheels, even in prison. You only have to ask.'

'For Sara's sake, I'll let you know.' Pascual broods for a moment and says, 'Do you mind my asking where the money comes from? You weren't really in business with Torres, were you?'

The pirate grin spreads across Fernando's dark face. '*Coño*, what do you take me for? No, *hombre*, the money's in rabbits, these days.'

'Rabbits?'

'Well, rabbit skins. I've got a cousin down near Tarragona who raises them. I peddle the skins to the Koreans and they make jackets out of them.'

'The Koreans?'

'Yes. I've been in Seoul twice this year. It's been a good year.'

'You amaze me. So there's nothing actually illegal about what you do?'

Fernando's grin has gone a little sheepish. 'Well, we may play fast and loose with the taxman occasionally. *Joder*, I'm a gypsy. We have our traditions to uphold.' Fernando raises his glass. 'That's a secret now, between you and me, *primo*. I'm trusting you.'

Pascual clinks his glass against Fernando's. 'Till death, *primo*.'

The guitarist is a poor gypsy tough from La Mina who will never headline at a *tablao* or see the inside of a recording studio, and the *soleares* and *bulerías* he is producing have nothing to recommend them except the earnestness with which he plays. The *cantaora* is a woman who might almost be a gypsy herself by the look of her, and if in her jeans and pullover she lacks all the folkloric trappings, her voice removes any doubt about where she comes from and what she has lived. The music itself has a dark power that has transfixed the crowd jammed into the tiny bar, and tonight she is a woman possessed. She is singing her heart out, and at the end she will have nothing left to give.

At the end of the bar, hemmed in by strangers, stands a man with a maimed hand, and more than anyone else in the room he wishes she could go on singing for ever; he knows what must come when she stops.

Time has run out, and it has come down to this, a last embrace on the pavement in front of the Jefatura, with two French policemen waiting by an idling car, and a cluster of Spanish officers and one dapper lawyer shuffling their feet awkwardly nearby. Ten metres down the way stand Joselito and Pilar and Lola, looking as bleak as the end of the world.

This morning Sara is at peace and Pascual thinks on all the wretched earth there cannot be a lovelier woman. 'It's going to be a while, *amor mío*, even in the best case,' Sara says. 'It will be weeks before I even come to trial.'

'I'll be there.'

She shakes her head. 'Pascual. Wait for me here. If we have a life, this is where it will be.'

'My life will be wherever you are. Fernando's lending me some money and I'm coming north.'

'Pascual, I'll be in jail.'

'I don't care. I'll be there in the courtroom. I'll be there outside the prison walls. If they give you twenty years I'll be waiting for you outside the gates when you walk out.'

'What will you do in Marseilles?'

'Whatever I have to do. As long as you're there, I'll be there.'

Now the tears are beginning to come, as Sara's forehead touches his. '*Si el querer que yo te tengo . . .*' She pauses and finds the breath to try again. 'If the love I have for you were made of gold . . .'

Pascual finishes the couplet. 'In all the world there would be none richer than I.' He kisses her and then he wheels and walks away.

'Mr McDuff?'

'Who's this?'

'Pascual. That's right, they missed me.'

'I don't know what you're talking about.'

'All bets are off, Mr McDuff. You double-crossed me.'

'Now wait a minute.'

'I'll be talking to the press soon. The progress of the investigations should carry the story through late summer, at least, I'd say. You might wish to resign now, save your candidate some embarrassment.'

'We need to talk about this.'

'It's way too late for that, Mr McDuff. Goodbye.'

'Campos here.'

'When do we start?'

'Start what?'

'The book. I've got a story to tell.'

'*Hombre.* Are you sure?'

'I'm sure,' says Pascual. 'No more secrets. I made a promise.'